BEHIND THAT DOOR

After his father's death, Gerald Lavering returns to England to sort out the family's estates — Hartford Manor and Nancrannon in Cornwall. The houses bring only heartache to Jerry. His dear mother had died in Cornwall when he was a child and his father had immersed himself in civic affairs, ignoring his son and his homes. When Jerry decides to pay a final visit to Nancrannon, accompanied by his friend George Lashing and George's sister, Tessa, he learns the shocking truth about his mother's death.

*Other books by George Goodchild
in the Linford Mystery Library:*

THE DANGER LINE
McLEAN DISPOSES
THE LAST REDOUBT
NEXT OF KIN
McLEAN INVESTIGATES
SAVAGE ENCOUNTER
FALSE INTRUDER
DEAR CONSPIRATOR
TIGER, TIGER
LADY TAKE CARE
THE BARTON MYSTERY
STOUT CORTEZ
BRAVE INTERLUDE
DOUBLE ACROSTIC
McLEAN SCORES AGAIN

GEORGE GOODCHILD

BEHIND THAT DOOR

Complete and Unabridged

LINFORD
Leicester

First published in Great Britain in 1943

First Linford Edition
published 2005

British Library CIP Data

Goodchild, George, *1888* –
    Behind that door.—Large print ed.—
Linford mystery library
1. Detective and mystery stories
2. Large type books
I. Title
823.9'12 [F]

ISBN 1–84395–572–5

Published by
F. A. Thorpe (Publishing)
Anstey, Leicestershire

Set by Words & Graphics Ltd.
Anstey, Leicestershire
Printed and bound in Great Britain by
T. J. International Ltd., Padstow, Cornwall

This book is printed on acid-free paper

1

Every time Gerald Lavering came down the long staircase at Hartford Manor he had to pass the ancestors. They were all in strictly chronological order, from that first recorded Josiah Lavering, who lost his life at Cressy, to him who had died but a month ago, and was displayed in oils in his mayoral robes, and chain of office. This sternfaced gentleman was Gerald's father, whom Gerald had not seen since that portrait had been presented to him by the citizens of Hartford seven years ago, for when he arrived in England from a small farm in Alberta his father's body had already been in the family vault for over a week.

How potent now were the familiar surroundings to bring to life the scenes and events of long ago! Life in that great house had been pleasant enough while his mother had lived, and while he was young enough to confine his activities to those pursuits dear to the heart of youth, and which the fine old-world garden and park were well able to provide. But on the death of his mother, in Cornwall, and the importation of a housekeeper at Hartford, all that had been joyful and healthy became overlaid with taboos and restrictions. School offered a temporary escape from the torture of a house from which love had vanished, and laughter was rare. His father — a vain and headstrong man — became more and more entangled with civic affairs. He became Chairman of the hospital, Sheriff, Mayor — three times in all — Justice of the Peace, candidate for Parliament, suffering two defeats, which embittered him beyond recovery.

He became harsh to the tenants of his lands — small farmers who were hard put to it to make a living even in the most favourable circumstances. He was harsh, too, on the local bench with transgressors of the law, and he was equally harsh with his own son, even when that son reached the fringe of manhood.

Between Gerald and his father there grew an unsurmountable barrier. Their points of view on every question were opposed. Gerald could see nothing deserving veneration in the careers of the majority of his ancestors. True, several of them had died for their country, but others had been profligate, and some flagrantly dishonest. One Lavering had re-established the depleted family finances by traffic in human flesh and blood, between West Africa and the cotton plantations of the United States. So far as he was able to discover few of them had ever engaged in an honest job of work. As landed gentry they took their immunity from personal toil for granted.

How the family had become possessed of the fruitful Lavering estate, which had always been the mainstay, since rents came in when other ramifications failed, Gerald had never discovered, but he had a very strong suspicion that it had been a free gift by the reigning monarch to some Lavering for services rendered, though what those services were remained a subject for speculation. His mother had come from less privileged stock, and had never been ashamed to admit it, to her husband's ill-concealed annoyance. It caused young Gerald to wonder mightily, for his mother had been a goddess in his eyes, to whom he could lay bare his heart, confide his most cherished secrets, and receive in return her warm sympathy, and unquestioned wisdom. With his father it was different. One could not hope to scale the dizzy heights which led to that pinnacle of moral rectitude and unctious self-satisfaction.

So, in due course, Gerald, at the age of nineteen, worked his passage to Canada, hired himself out for a year or two, as he won his way westward, and finally found anchorage on a small holding, which in five years of unremitting toil he had transformed into a real home. Letters passed between there and Hartford Manor, and numerous invitations for him to come back were declined, until the telegram which informed him that his father was seriously ill, and unlikely to make a recovery.

Now, as he walked over the estate, ghosts popped out from every corner. Not one single person remained whom he had known in the old days. The servants that remained were strangers to him, and they treated him as he knew they must have treated his father, with awesome respect, as the heir to Hartford. In the stables there were four nice hacks, obviously spoiling for exercise. But the horses he had known and loved were gone. The Bailiff was new like the rest. He was a smirking kind of person, keen to keep his job, which seemed to Gerald to be somewhat of a sinecure. The only person who was no stranger was Canting, the solicitor. He didn't look a day older, and he still retained his old habit of pushing his gold-rimmed spectacles up his thin nose with his two fingers.

'You're going to have your hands full,' he said. 'There are a lot of things to be done, which should have been done long ago. I don't know why they weren't done.'

'Don't you?' asked Gerald.

'Well, yes. That was a polite fiction. But your father became completely immersed in civic affairs; he didn't even appear to be conscious of the ravages of time on the property. I have here a lot of estimates — '

Gerald waved the batch of papers aside.

'Not now,' he said. 'You see, I haven't made up my mind about running the place.'

Canting pushed his spectacles up his nose and stared.

'In what way?' he asked.

'I may not stay.'

'But it was your father's wish. Of course, it isn't exactly a condition of the will, but it never occurred to me that you mightn't welcome this marvellous opportunity to make the place live again. I'm sure it never occurred to him either.'

'Didn't it occur to him that I had a place of my own — a place which I made out of nothing? I didn't ask his help, and he never offered it. I'm not sure that I could ever be happy here.'

'You could — given certain conditions.'

'Such as — ?'

'A wife and a family. The income is ample to enable you to maintain the status — .'

'The privileged status of the Laverings.'

Gerald laughed, and drew himself up to

6

his full six feet two inches. He looked magnificent, with his tanned face, twinkling blue eyes, and Greek features.

'Look!' he said, and held out his hands. 'The Laverings have had a cuckoo in the nest. I'm no Lavering. Did any of them ever have hands like these, with callouses all over them, and broken nails? Were they ever hewers of wood and drawers of water? When my father left me all this, and the various other properties elsewhere, it was with the idea that I should perpetuate the Laverings. I'm not so sure that they deserve to be perpetuated. I believe there is a new world about to be born. I believe my father's class has outlived its usefulness. They do not even win wars now, for modern wars call for the brain and brawn of the toiling millions. This great house, with all its outbuildings, gardens, and appurtenances is an anachronism.'

'Anachronism!' gasped Canting. 'It provides work for scores of persons.'

Gerald laughed again. How often he had heard that argument! How often too he had pondered over it, and wondered what was wrong with it, since something was obviously wrong. But now he knew, and because he knew he had no wish to debate the point.

'I've found a new world since I ran around this place,' he said. 'No, Mr. Canting, it isn't as simple as you imagine to accept what my father offered. It might be better to give the land to the farmers who work it, and the house to the National Trust, if they'll accept it. But I need a little time to get my thoughts sorted out. I'm going to take a holiday first.'

'Excellent!' said Canting. 'Have you any particular resort in mind?'

'No, but the sea makes a definite appeal. Until I crossed in the liner I hadn't seen the sea in seven years. What about the holiday house in Cornwall. Have we still got that?'

'Yes. I wanted to talk about that. It's a white elephant, and is falling to pieces. No one has lived there since your mother died. Your father has never even been there. All this time he has paid rates because he wouldn't sell, or store, the furniture. But it's been looked after to some extent by old Poltimore, who used to be butler there, and the garden gets attention at intervals. It's a dead loss, and my advice to you is to put it up for auction, and save the unwarranted expense. At least have the furniture stored without delay.'

'I'll let you know about that.'

In the days that followed, the last Lavering rode the various hacks over the beautiful surrounding country, and visited many spots that were dear to his memory. He still dallied with the idea of taking a holiday but never succeeded in making up his mind just what to do. This transplanting was a curious experience. Not yet was he rooted again in his native country, for those seven years of travel and hard toil had been very potent years, and he had taken it for granted that he had found a permanent anchorage. But the premature death of his father was now presenting him with a problem that was not at all easy to solve.

Then, one morning, while he was still hesitant, he had a pleasant surprise. He was wondering whether to ride or take the car out for a change, when Ratcliffe, the smirking butler, brought in a visiting card. It bore the name George Lashing, and at once Lavering's mind went whirling back over the years.

'What's he like?' he asked, realising there might be two George Lashings in the world.

'Young gentleman, sir, rather stoutly built. Fair complexion.'

'Show him in.'

A minute later George Lashing entered the room. He gave a howl of delight, flung a somewhat battered hat on the couch and rushed at Lavering, to pump his hand vigorously.

'This is marvellous!' he said. 'Jerry, what on earth have you been doing to yourself?'

'In what way?'

'You're about three inches taller, and where did you get all that sunburn?'

'Where did you get all that weight?' retorted Lavering.

'You would mention that,' growled George. 'Fact is I've wasted my young life in a damned bank. No exercise except a bit of tennis now and then. Still play tennis?'

'I haven't touched a tennis racket in seven years.'

'What have you been doing with yourself, and why didn't you write sometimes?'

'I did write, but the letter was returned to me.'

'Yes, I suppose it would be. You see, we left the old house six years ago. My father died, and left us with some problems. Well, it's darn good seeing you again. I wouldn't have known you were here but for John Colbrook. He told me in a letter that he had seen a paragraph in a local newspaper — about your father's death. My logical brain at once told me that the odds were you would cease wandering and come home. Being the owner of what used to be a motor car, and to-day being Sunday, I took a chance.'

'I'm glad you did, George. Think it's too early for a drink?'

'It's never too early.'

Lavering pushed the bell and Ratcliffe

slid into the room.

'Bring us some drinks, Ratcliffe.'

Over the plentiful array of drinks the two men revived a lot of old memories, most of them connected with the school where they had first met.

'Those were good days,' sighed George, over his third sherry. 'How we used to hanker to get through the School 'cert.' and be off on a career of some sort. I didn't think I'd ever finish up in a bank. My idea of a career was a farm, with some rough shooting thrown in, and a good man to do all the worrying. But my father had other ideas, and like a dutiful son I fell in with them. So instead of walking over my broad acres admiring my crops, I spend my life writing figures in books and getting fatter and fatter. If I hadn't got a holiday due to me next week I think I should expire. And that's another example of how the best laid schemes of mice and men gang aft agley. After booking accommodation in what appeared to be as nice a farm as there is on Dartmoor, the farmer wrote me this morning to say he couldn't have me.'

'Why not?'

'His wife has been taken ill, and paying guests are out of the question. Nice thing to do to a chap. I say, this is damned good sherry!'

'My father's taste in wine was always supposed to be excellent. But I can't tell sherry from port. Help yourself.'

George filled his glass again, and stared through the window at the pleasant country scene.

'I suppose you're the Squire now?' he asked.

'If you like to call it that.'

'Lucky devil!'

'You think so?'

'Don't you?'

'I'm not so sure. I can't get myself used to the idea. Out in Canada I've got a small place of my own. I worked like hell to get it and develop it — . But tell me about this prospective holiday of yours. What are you going to do about it?'

'Oh, I expect I shall finish up in a third-rate boarding house at Brighton.'

'George, I've got an idea. Do you like Cornwall?'

'Yes, but it's too late to do anything there. You don't stand a chance so late — .'

'That's what you think. But I happen to own a house down there. My father inherited it from his brother, and he and my mother spent their honeymoon there. After that, when I came into the world, we used to go there every summer. I can just remember it. It's tucked away in a coombe, with a private path down to a little cove, where there was yellow sand, and pools of water left by the tide, in which I used to catch shrimps. The furniture is still in it, and my father seems to have had a sentimental interest in it since he refused to dispose of it, even when he had no further use for it. What about going down there — you and I — and opening up the old place?'

George's eyes seemed to bulge from his head.

'Are you serious, Jerry?' he asked.

'Absolutely. I need a holiday almost as badly as you do. I've a whole lot of problems to solve, and I believe I could solve them down there by the sea.'

'Man! It sounds too good to be true. There's nothing I should like better, but I'm afraid it can't be done.'

'Why not?'

'Well, I've a young sister, who expects to — .'

'Can't she come too?'

'She could, but — .'

'But what?'

'I wouldn't inflict that upon you.'

'Why not? Is she unpresentable?'

'She's pretty awful. I mean she'd put paid to any idea of a peaceful bachelor party. She'd stick an apron round your waist and make you wash up just when you felt like a jaunt to the nearest pub.'

Lavering laughed at George's rueful expression.

'Where's your courage?' he asked. 'We're two to one. I'm willing to take a fair chance.'

'And no recriminations?'

'No recriminations.'

George thrust out his beefy hand and gripped his friend's harder one.

'It's a bet,' he said.

'Good. When can you leave?'

'Next Saturday morning — at any hour you like. What do we do about transport?'

'I've got a car here wasting its young life.'

'That's fine, because my tyres are down to the canvas, and most of the gadgets are tied on with bits of string. I daresay you can see her from the window.'

He went across to the wide casement window and looked away to the left.

'Genuine 1920 model in going order,' he said. 'My God, she looks worse from a distance. That list to starboard is doubtless due to my avoirdupois. I'll have to fix that number plate or I'll get pinched.'

Lavering sauntered across to the window and got a glimpse of the car. It was indeed a fearful-looking vehicle, and he was glad they wouldn't be compelled to attempt the journey in it.

'Did you win it in a raffle?' he asked.

'I swopped a motor cycle, two push bikes, and a ten pound note for it. But you'd be surprised the way it continues to hang together, when by all the known laws of cause and effect it should disintegrate. When I've done with it I shall present it to the Victoria and Albert Museum.'

Later they walked round the well-kept grounds, the stables, and the orchid houses in which Lavering's father had taken so much pride. In a large garage they came upon the car which was to take them into the wilds of Cornwall. George whistled as he ran his envious eye over the lines of the big vehicle.

'Rolls-Bentley,' he said. 'We're in luck. I suppose you'll let me take a turn at the wheel?'

'I think it can be arranged.'

'Wow!' cried George. 'What a time we'll have. Any chance of tennis where we're going?'

'I believe there's a hard-tennis court in the garden.'

'You're not an ordinary man. You're the veritable Shah of Persia. Don't tell me you run to a yacht?'

'No, only an ordinary boat, with an outboard motor — if we can get it going.'

'We'll get it going. Now, what's the exact programme?'

'You'd better drive down here in your own car, and park it here until we return. In the meantime I'll write to the fellow who's been looking after the house, and tell him we're coming. That will give him a chance to uncover the furniture and air the beds. At what time can you get here next Saturday?'

'Any time you like. What about nine o'clock?'

'That will do fine.'

'Good. We'll be here on the dot. I hope you'll like my kid sister,' said George, dubiously.

'I hope she'll like me,' said Lavering, with a laugh.

2

By the following Saturday morning, Lavering was ready for the road, and looking forward to the experience. Ratcliffe, who had driven the big Bentley on occasion, made him acquainted with the controls, and finally Lavering drove it to the front door, and was immediately impressed by the feel of the powerful, but silky engine. The suitcases and various loose articles were put aboard, the oil and petrol levels checked, and a last polish given to the already mirror-like coachwork by Ratcliffe, who seemed a little hurt that he was not invited to accompany the party.

'You may find it a little difficult to get any service down there sir,' he said. 'The house is a little off the map, as one might say.'

'All the better,' said Lavering. 'We'll manage. Poltimore thinks he can lay his hands on a good woman.'

It was half-past nine when Lavering heard a terrific rattle, as if a large number of dustbins were being violently shaken together. It proved to be George's car coming up the long drive. Steam was rising from the radiator cap, and boiling water escaping on to the road. George, clad in grey slacks and a sports coat in large check, pulled up the car with a jerk, and jumped out.

'Cheers!' he said. 'I never thought I'd make it. I ran a big end about ten miles from here, and there was nothing to be done about it. Well, I'm here, and that's all I darn well care. Jove, she is boiling, isn't she?'

'Wouldn't surprise me if she blew up. I thought you were going to bring your sister.'

'I did, but I had to jettison her at the bottom of the hill. Otherwise I'd never have got this box of tricks up that gradient. Of course, she was rude about it. Simply couldn't understand that her extra weight made all the difference. Gosh, Jerry, that car!'

He was standing with his hands on his

wide hips regarding the Bentley with speechless admiration.

'I'll bet she could do a hundred miles an hour,' he said.

'She might, but I assure you she isn't going to,' replied Lavering. 'Look here, don't you think you'd better go and look after your sister?'

'Oh, she's all right. I'll chuck out our stuff, and take this eyesore to the garage.'

'All right,' said Lavering. 'Ratcliffe will give you a hand. I'll go and meet your sister, before she gets a bad impression of me. Hey, Ratcliffe!'

Mr. Ratcliffe regarded George's car with undisguised horror, but he started to transfer the baggage, and Lavering walked down the drive to pick up George's discarded passenger. Then he suddenly remembered that he didn't even know her christian name. By the time he reached the top of the hill on the main road, George's sister was already there. Lavering blinked his eyes, and wondered if he hadn't made a mistake. He had got the impression that George's sister was a fledgling, but he now saw before him a very hot young woman of about nineteen, with amazing eyes, hair and features. She gave him the impression of being dynamic — almost explosive, as she stared into his enquiring eyes.

'You must be Jerry Lavering,' she said.

'Right first time. How did you know?'

'My dirty-dog brother described you. My name's Tessa, in case you don't happen to know.'

'I didn't know. It's rather nice.'

'What is?'

'Tessa.'

'Glad you think so. I always feel I'm missing something, and can't make up my mind whether it's a barrel organ, or a monkey.'

Lavering could not refrain from laughing at this unexpected retort. He was just beginning to understand George's cryptic remarks about his sister. Undoubtedly Tessa was a nice handful of complex femininity. She carried herself with an air of confidence, and was never afraid to meet his analysing gaze.

'Ease up!' she said. 'I've climbed that beastly hill, and you haven't.'

'Sorry.'

He shortened his abnormally long step, and she nodded her satisfaction, and was now able to get her breath back.

'I knew George would bust something,' she said. 'We started late and he tried to make up time. If there's one thing Ethel can't stand it's hustle.'

'Who's Ethel?'

'The car. She's all right up to about forty miles an hour, but after that she heats up and bangs things about.'

'She seems to have banged big ends about.'

'I warned the silly mutt, but you know what George is. 'I'm driving this 'bus,' he said. 'If you've any complaints put them into writing.' With which example of masculine wit something went bang, and went on banging. As we came through the village everyone stared to see who was responsible for the noise. A dog who was asleep in the middle of the road stood up and barked at us.' She broke off from her narrative as they came to the wide entrance to the drive, and she saw in the distance the big house. 'Is this your home?' she asked.

'Yes.'

'My hat! What a mausoleum! George never told me it was like that. Why, it could house the Wallace Collection, and still have a few rooms left over.'

'My father liked space.'

'And now it's all yours?'

'Yes, I suppose it is.'

'Well, is it, or isn't it?'

'Madam, the answer is in the affirmative.'

'Phew!' she said. 'Any ghosts?'

'Quite a lot,' he replied, more seriously. She gave him a long glance, and they walked up the drive in silence. The lovely gardens obviously made an instant appeal to her for Gerald could see her eyes gleam as they took in the lost vistas of floral borders, and flowering shrubs. Then they came upon George.

'So you found her?' said George casually.

'What do you think I am — a lost umbrella?' retorted Tessa. 'Why didn't you wait at the top of the hill for me?'

'I was late, and I hate being late.'

'He hates being late,' she said to Gerald, appealingly. 'He hates being late, and yet he's late for the office every morning.' Then her gaze switched to the Bentley. 'Do we travel in that?' she asked.

'That's the idea,' replied George. 'And not a bad one either.'

'I can't live up to it.'

'Well, it's the only car I have,' explained Gerald.

'You'll get used to it,' said George with a grin. 'Just wait until I get my foot on that pedal.'

'Which pedal?' asked Tessa innocently.

'You'll see,' grunted George, who knew that Tessa was laughing at him, with those expressive violet coloured eyes. 'None of your cheek, my girl. Well, all the stuff's inside, including a nice-looking hamper. What's inside it, Jerry?'

'Cold chicken and salad. Is that road-map there, George?'

'On the front seat. I'll be official map-reader.'

'If you are we'll find ourselves up in Scotland,' said Tessa. 'What are we waiting for?'

'Isn't that like a woman?' pleaded George. 'She pops up here after all the work is done and says, 'What are we waiting for?' Oh, here comes the sun. It's going to be a grand day.'

Lavering nodded as he stared at the blue sky, and the vanishing cloud. Overnight it had rained, and now the air was full of sweetness. Before them stretched that intriguing road into the west, which would end in the wind-swept Cornish cliff, and the little sandy bay where he had spent so many delightful days.

'If we've got everything there's no reason why we shouldn't make a move,' he said.

'I bet you've both forgotten more things than you have brought,' said Tessa.

'There's one thing we haven't forgotten, my child,' said George, with great dignity.

'Beer?' asked Tessa.

'No — our manners.'

'A large spanner is more important. Where do I park myself?'

'In the back,' said George. 'You can put

up your feet and go to sleep if you like. There's tons of room.'

Gerald opened the rear door for her, and she entered and bounced herself up and down on the soft upholstery.

'Steady!' said George. 'There's no need to play marionettes. Gosh, I've forgotten my cigarette case.'

Tessa squealed and produced the case from the pocket of her short light coat. George mumbled his thanks and lighted a cigarette after Lavering had declined one.

'Now we're really ready,' he said.

'Oh no we're not,' said Tessa. 'George, where's your hat?'

'Hat?' asked George.

'Yes, H-A-T — hat. You started with one.'

'Good Lord, I must have left it in my car. Won't keep you a minute, Jerry.'

George came back with his hat in his hand, to find Lavering seated at the driving wheel. He threw the hat into the back of the car, and lowered himself into the very comfortable seat beside his friend.

'Map?' he asked. 'Don't tell me, Tessa. I

know — I'm sitting on it.'

He dragged the map from under him, and gave a little sigh of pleasure as Lavering started the engine. Ratcliffe appeared for a brief moment, and begged to wish them a good journey, and then the lordly car sailed down the long drive, turned to the right on the main road and began to purr like a cat.

'We're off!' said George. 'To hell with the bank! Here's to the open road!'

'Remember, I'm leaving it all to you,' said Lavering. 'Unless you direct me otherwise, I'm going to drive straight on.'

'That's the idea. We do a bit of criss-cross stuff until we reach Basing-stoke, and then the road is pretty straight for a hundred miles.'

'Except for several turns this side of Andover,' said Tessa.

'I know — I know.'

George's map reading wasn't too good, for the simple reason that he was intensely interested in the behaviour of the car. Lavering had no intention of becoming a speed-hog. The country was too glorious to engage in such wild progress. But occasionally the speedo-meter moved to the sixty mark, and George was able to appreciate the reserve of power which lay under that long bonnet.

'Sixty on less than half throttle,' he said. 'And you wouldn't think we were doing forty. Tessa, isn't she marvellous?'

'Who?' asked Tessa.

'The car, of course.'

'Oh yes. I expect it would go quite fast if you wanted it to.'

'Fast!' snorted George. 'Women have no mechanical sense at all. She can't see the difference between this and my sardine tin.'

'Don't be absurd!' said Tessa. 'Your car is much smaller, and it's quite a different colour.'

George became quite inarticulate, and Lavering, in the driving mirror could see those attractive orbs of Tessa filled with quiet mischief. She was, he felt sure, enjoying every minute of the journey, but pretending to be quite unimpressed — even blasé, and he was bound to admit that as a car mascot she left little to be desired.

'Were you able to fix up any domestic help?' asked George.

'Yes, Poltimore's daughter can come in every day, and cook a meal for us, make beds and so forth.'

'Who's Poltimore?'

'He's been keeping an eye on the place. Lives in a cottage about a mile from the house, and manages to make a living out of the sea — and the visitors, not to mention ten shillings a week which my father has been paying him to look after the house, and keep the garden tidy.'

'Is there a village handy?' asked George.

'Yes — two miles away. It's called Trewith, and is the grimmest sort of place, wedged into a little cove up which the tide roars and foams when there's a wind on. Just an inn, a church, a handful of cottages, and a few boats.'

'What's the house called?' asked Tessa.

'A most curious name. It's 'Nancran-non'.'

'Why?' asked Tessa.

'Why what?' asked George.

'Why Nancrannon?'

'Why not?' demanded George 'It's distinctive, and I don't see that it matters two hoots what it's called.'

'But it must mean something.'

George couldn't see why house names had to mean something. Perhaps his exacting sister would prefer 'Ocean View,' or 'The Anchorage,' or 'Blue Gables,' or any other of the damned silly names one could see by the thousand from Margate to Bournemouth.

'Anyway, I like it,' he said, finally.

'That doesn't make it any more sensible,' Tessa pointed out. 'You like strawberries but they produce spots on your face. Oh, just look at that cow, behaving like a lunatic.'

'Where?' asked George.

'Over there in the meadow by the farmhouse.'

George switched his gaze, and shook his head despairingly.

'She wouldn't know,' he said to Lavering.

'Oh yes I would,' retorted Tessa. 'It's Mr. Cow, and not Mrs. The mistake was visual and not biological. Now I'm going to sleep, and don't wake me up with any idiotic remarks. Call me when lunch is in the offing.'

The road unfolded before the fast car, and after passing Andover, George's dream became a reality. He took over a spell of driving, and crooned his delight as the pleasant undulations of the plain sped past. Periodically, Lavering uttered a soft remonstrance, and George got back to a respectable speed, but on one long stretch where there was a good mile of visibility, Lavering remained silent and George put his big foot down, and let the powerful car have full rein. He blew out his cheeks when at last he was compelled to slow down.

'What did we touch?' he asked.

'Ninety,' replied Lavering, 'and that's enough racing for to-day.'

George appeared to be satisfied, but still wanted to go on driving.

'You can take over after lunch,' he said. 'I always like a snooze after a meal, but can never get one except on Sundays. I know a gorgeous place for a picnic. It's soon after we cross the boundary of

Devon — where the road commences to run down into Honiton. Tessa's pretending to be asleep, but she isn't.'

Lavering, denied a view of Tessa through the driving mirror, turned his head, and saw her curled up on the long seat, with her cheek resting on one of her hands.

'I think she is,' he said.

'Not if I know her,' replied George. 'She's thinking up something rude to say. Piling up reserve ammunition against any possible emergency. Isn't that so, fair sister?' he asked.

'Rats!' retorted Tessa, without opening her eyes.

In due course, George reached the spot which he had in mind for lunch, and it was immediately approved by Gerald. An open farm gate permitted the car to be drawn well off the road, and a rug was spread in an open space on a knoll above an undulating field of golden wheat across which the steady wind created ever-changing patterns. From this point the whole country sloped away towards the west, and already the tang of the sea was potent in the breeze.

'A loaf of bread, a cup of wine . . . ' quoted Tessa.

'Beer, to be exact,' interrupted George. 'And a bottle of lemonade for the child. For the love of Mike open that hamper Jerry.'

The long hamper was opened, and a few minutes later the delicious cold chicken and salad were in process of disappearing.

3

Exeter was now in their rear, and the car was running on the western fringe of Dartmoor, where George, who thought he knew Dartmoor very well indeed, gave the wrong names to several distant tors, and engaged in reminiscences, in which remote inns and strange drinks played by no means subordinate parts. Tessa occasionally gave voice to wholehearted appreciation of the incomparable scenery, to remind them that she was still there, although Lavering needed no such reminder, for he could see her for hours together, reflected in the driving mirror.

'Cornwall,' said George at last. 'Goodbye, Devon!'

'How do you know we're in Cornwall?' asked Tessa.

'Because it's here plain — on the map. That bridge is the boundary.'

'We've crossed a dozen of them.'

'D'you think I can't read a map?' asked George.

'How should I know. Lend me the map.'

'Be quiet, my child. Eat your bun.'

Thereafter the map was in constant use, for Trewith was not easy of approach, and most of the signboards on the secondary road gave only the name of the next village. Once they finished up in a farmyard from which there was no outlet, and George's map-reading suffered a heavy blow. But the incident had its compensations, for Tessa seized the opportunity to buy a bowl of Cornish cream, and two pounds of very late strawberries. George gazed at these hungrily.

'Maybe I'll risk a few spots on my complexion,' he said.

'Oh, no,' said Tessa. 'Jerry and I can manage them between us.'

George scowled as Tessa sampled the largest strawberry which she could find, and rolled her lovely eyes.

'A bowl of cream, a pound of fruit, and thou beside me in the wilderness, and wilderness were paradise to boot. Omar Khayyam,' she said.

'Get into the car, or I'll murder you,' threatened George. 'And mind that cream, or you'll spill it. They make it thin in Cornwall.'

'You won't catch me spilling any of it. Well, back we go, brother mine. It's two miles to where you read the map upside down.'

They made their way back through the winding lane, where foxgloves grew in millions on the hedgerows, and then joined another road and took the right fork whose signpost bore an unpronounceable name.

'Not on this map,' said George. 'But there's no doubt this is our road. We can't be more than ten miles from Trewith.'

The road went down at a terrific angle, and after a mile they passed through a hamlet where a creek came in from the sea, and where a few small craft were heeling over on the low tide. It sent Lavering's mind back into the past.

'I remember this,' he said. 'We're not very far from Nancrannon. There's a very steep hill to climb, and then some miles of moorland from which you get a glorious view of the coast. Here's the hill.'

The powerful car climbed the hill as if it had not been there, and swung round a terrible hairpin bend towards the summit, where heavy timber obscured the view in all directions. Then slowly the timber thinned, and finally the road flattened out, and the broken magnificent coastline came to view. Lavering drew in his breath at the incredible colour scheme — the massive cliffs, with their bases wreathed in spindrift, the innumerable sandy coves outlined in brilliant yellow, the deep blue of the all-encompassing sea, and the pearly sky above all.

'There it is again,' he said. 'The best sight in the world.'

'By Jove, you're right,' agreed George. 'Tessa, just look at all that.'

'I am looking,' replied Tessa. 'But I still can't believe it.'

'You will,' laughed George. 'Oh, boy — this air!'

The road meandered across the broad headland, and then again dived into a deep wooded valley. Here, for the first time, there appeared a signpost which gave the name Trewith.

'Only two miles,' said George.

The valley narrowed until it became little more than a rocky gorge, through the open end of which the sea was visible, above the granite wall of a small harbour. On the right of the small inlet a few cob buildings stood out in dazzling white against the brown rock mass. The whole formed a most delightful picture.

'We cross the bridge down there and take the road behind the 'Wreckers' Inn,' said Lavering. 'It used to be a terrible road, but perhaps it has since been improved.'

When at last they reached the said road his hope was proved vain, for the road had been cut out of the rock itself, and its surface was wet with spindrift and treacherous at any speed above a crawl.

'Phew!' whistled George. 'One mistake here and we'd be taking a bathe. Thank God I didn't bring Ethel down here. Oh, that's dreadful.'

He referred to a sharp corner where the

low loose stone wall had been broken away, and at which there was a vertical drop of some three hundred feet. Lavering locked the long car over, and the front bumper missed the gap by a bare foot.

'Any more like that?' asked Tessa.

'No. I think that's the worst spot.'

A few minutes later they were on more solid earth, with the road winding through trees which since their youth had been bent eastward by the prevailing west wind, until the land sloped away into a verdant valley where the whole face of nature was changed. Here there were lush meadows, and many flowers, bees and butterflies, and sluggish rivulets.

'Nancrannon!' said Gerald suddenly.

'Where?'

'Right ahead. You can just see the gable on the western end. In a moment you'll see all of it.'

This was subsequently borne out. An intervening hummock was crossed, and Nancrannon sprang into full view. George had expected a small Cornish cottage, but instead he saw a substantial house built of local stone, and obviously very old. It was enclosed by high stone walls but they were still high enough above it to be able to see over these.

'Why, it's lovely,' said Tessa. 'I thought we were coming to a tiny holiday place.'

'Oh, it isn't so large,' said Gerald. 'I think it has been in our family for about four generations. Why my father preferred to live at Hartford I never could discover, but I think it was because he found social life restricted here. You see, half a century ago this district was prosperous, and there were a number of country houses in the occupation of their owners. Then something happened in the tin industry. The local mines were unable to compete with foreign competition. One by one they became abandoned and flooded. All round here you will find rows of ruined cottages, old mine borings, and rusted machinery. The local population moved to places where they could earn their daily bread. The village, too, felt the effects, for without the mine-workers, and the weekly pay-roll, business could not be carried on at a profit. Yet a number of

41

families refused to leave the sinking ship. They turned again to the sea, and to boarders in the holiday season. They're fine characters, these Cornishmen, but inclined to be stand-offish until they get to know you. Of course this is all secondhand information, for I was only a youngster when we last came here. But the happiest days of my life were spent here, and I'm quite sure I shall never be so happy again.'

While he was speaking the car was descending the steep road, and now a sudden bend brought the entrance gates into full view. The car passed through, and Gerald's eyes scanned the grounds. Everything was changed — and not for the best. The overgrowth of trees and shrubs was prodigious. The long herbaceous borders had got completely out of hand. It was clear that some attempt had been made to save the garden from utter ruin, but everywhere Nature had triumphed. The deep rich soil of the valley had laughed at the puny efforts to check its fecundity, and in places the riot was almost awe-inspiring. As the car pulled up in front of a very unusual portico, a man emerged from the interior. He was about fifty years of age, and was clad in breeches, gaiters and a blue jerkin. His face was the colour of mahogany, and he had the complexion of a Spaniard. He welcomed the party with a slow movement of his hand, and then looked from Lavering to George.

'Hullo, Poltimore, don't you know me?' asked Lavering.

'Be you Mr. Gerald, zur?'

'I be,' said Gerald. 'You haven't changed a bit, but I suppose I must have done so.'

'Aye. It's good to see you, Mr. Gerald. When I got the bad news I wondered whether you would be comin' home.'

'This is my friend, Mr. Lashing, and this is Miss Lashing.'

Poltimore took them both in as he bowed somewhat awkwardly.

'I've done what I could to make the house habitable,' he said. 'But you'll understand that I haven't had much time. That gal o' mine has been working like a slave to make the lounge shipshape, and

43

the main bedrooms. 'Zillah!' ' he called.

The girl appeared in the hall. She was about nineteen years of age, and had her father's swarthy complexion. Her eyes were as bright as those of a bird, and when she smiled she displayed a set of small pearly teeth. She looked a mischievous creature, and her interest in the visitors was intense and undisguised. Her strict parent was obviously aware of this, and was quick to admonish her.

'Don't stand there staring, gal,' he said. 'Take hold of that bag and show Miss Lashing her bedroom.'

'Which one?' asked Zillah, in a rich Cornish accent.

'The pink room. I've told you that already.'

'No, you didn't!' retorted Zillah. 'I be neither deaf nor mazed.'

'Well, I meant to,' replied her exasperated father. 'Come, take the bag.'

Zillah put a hand to the large suitcase which Tessa had brought, but she quickly put it down again.

'Too heavy for me,' she said. 'You'm better take that. I'll carry this one.'

She picked up the smallest of the suitcases, and smiled bewitchingly at George, until she met her father's disapproving gaze, when she pranced off, beckoning Tessa to follow her.

'Zillah's a bit rough in her ways,' said her father. 'But she isn't a bad worker — most times.'

The three men handled the rest of the baggage between them, and Lavering and George were shown the bedrooms which had been prepared. They both faced the little sandy cove, which was approachable from the lower side of the garden, and where a stone jetty was built out from the foreshore. Not far from this was a neat boathouse.

'Jove, what a spot!' ejaculated George. 'Is that where you keep the boat?'

'Yes, but it can't have been used for years. What state is she in, Poltimore?'

'Pretty good. I've been looking after her. When I heard from you I gave the outboard motor a clean up. I'll get the boat in the water to-morrow. Her seams should close up in twenty-four hours. I hoped to do it before you got

45

here, but I've been busy.'

'Of course you have,' said Lavering. 'You've certainly got the house looking nice.'

'Glad you think so, sir. I had trouble with the batteries. A lot of new plates had to be put in. I'm afraid you'll be getting a tidy bill for the job. They're well up now, but will want a charge every day. I could come along — .'

'We can manage,' said Lavering. 'We shall enjoy messing about with an engine.'

'Do you generate your own electricity?' asked George.

'Yes. There's no electric light main for miles. Even the village uses oil lamps, unless things have changed a lot.'

'No zur,' said Poltimore. 'There's a movement afoot to bring the main to Trewith, but it won't get any further than talk. The cost would be terrible. Now I'll hustle up the tea. I expect you would be glad of a cup?'

'We certainly would,' replied Lavering.

He went off and the two men immediately changed, and settled themselves into their respective rooms. Lavering donned an old pair of grey trousers, and a pull-over, but George went one better and finally appeared in shorts and a cardigan, plus white shoes and no socks.

'I'm going to like this,' he said, as he burst into Lavering's room. 'Can't take my eyes off that view. Where's the tennis court?'

'Back of the garage. But if you think I'm going to play tennis this evening you're mistaken.'

'Well the sooner I start getting rid of some of this surplus avoirdupois the better. I say, old Poltimore's daughter is a bit of a lass, isn't she?'

'I think she has her eye on you, George. Take care.'

A rap came on the door.

'It's only me,' said Tessa's voice. 'Can I come in?'

'Can she?' asked George.

But Tessa was already in, and the drastic change in her appearance caused her brother to blink. She had got into a kind of Hawaiian costume, which had the effect of making even George look overdressed.

'Great Scott!' he ejaculated. 'What's this?'

'I told you I was making a sunbathing suit.'

'Suit! It's a sarong. I say, old girl, you can't walk about looking like Dorothy Lamour.'

'What about you — displaying those bulging legs?' retorted Tessa. 'At least my legs are brown, and not like — like great chunks of putty. What's wrong with me, anyway?'

She addressed this question chiefly to Lavering, who had already made up his mind that she looked ravishing.

'Tell her, Jerry,' pleaded George. 'Tell her this is a respectable house, and not a blessed nudists' camp. That's not sunburn either. It's stuff she rubs on.'

'Like to bet me,' said Tessa.

'Oh come,' put in Lavering. 'I don't see that it matters what any of us wears, or doesn't wear. You look very nice Tessa, and if you made that outfit yourself you certainly have missed your vocation. What did you do with that cream and the strawberries?'

'Zillah took them. She's going to lay them for tea. I say, she's a tartar.'

'Has she been getting fresh with you?' asked Lavering.

'Oh, no. But she's quite mad, the way she talks about her father. She swears she'll knock him cold one of these days, and I'm half ready to believe it. Oh yes, and something else.'

'What else?' asked George. 'Will she put arsenic in our tea?'

'Not yours anyway,' said Tessa. 'She thinks you're wonderful, and that's without having seen your noble calves. No, she says that the house is haunted.'

'What!' gasped Lavering.

'Tripe!' said George. 'Who haunts it?'

'She hadn't time to tell me because her father came and hustled her downstairs. Probably I'll get the second instalment at a later date. Oh, let's go and hunt up that tea.'

Tea was served on the western terrace, where they were invaded by many subtle odours from the masses of flowers in the garden. Tessa and Lavering made inroads on the strawberries and cream, but

George, conscious of his limitations in that respect, balanced matters by eating half the home-made scones, with abundant farm butter, which tasted of buttercups. Zillah looked very neat in her white apron and cap, as she waited on them, but she spoilt it all when a very insistent wasp settled on her nose, upon which she dumped the extra plate of scones, seized a knife, and made wild cuts at the creature as it was shaken off her proboscis.

'Blast yu!' she screamed. 'I'll give yu what for!'

Poltimore, who always seemed to be in the offing, came out and crooked a finger at her.

'All right — all right,' she said. 'But I hate the dirty swine.'

'Yes, she's certainly a little rough in her ways,' said Lavering. 'To quote her disgusted parent. Perhaps our refining influence will bring results.'

Tessa giggled at this, and finished up the last of the strawberries. A little later they explored the garden and its precincts. George was intrigued by the engine house, and its equipment, which consisted of a petrol engine, and a battery of glass accumulators. He wasn't satisfied until he had found the starting handle and got the engine working.

'All right,' said Lavering. 'The job's yours. If the lights fail you're going to hear from us. Let's get on.'

There were many corners in the wild garden which called forth admiration from Tessa and George — stone statues half hidden in foliage, a pond overgrown with lilies, and alive with goldfish, a lovely avenue of enormous beech trees whose branches interlocked overhead, a cascade which sprang out of a rock and splashed into a mass of ferns. The hard tennis court showed the ravages of time, but the moss had been scraped off, and the permanent lines painted. A new net was stretched across the posts.

'Poltimore has done well,' said George. 'Lucky devil you are, Jerry.'

'Think so?'

'Well, aren't you? If you liked you could dig yourself into this place for life, and let the world go by. Wouldn't I like the chance.'

Lavering smiled and then grew grave again. It was impossible to forget the past, when as a small boy he had wandered in this place, and dreamed dreams. Until he came here again he could but vaguely recall his mother, but now he was in process of bringing her back. He remembered that he had believed her to be the most beautiful woman in the world, and the most talented. Here, on this spot where he now stood, he had reclined on the grass and watched his young mother performing miracles on a canvas, with a paintbrush and paint. Then the little cove, with its curving fringe of rich yellow sand, had been visible from that viewpoint through a leafy vista, and he could vividly recall a shaggy Dartmoor pony which had been grazing at the end of that green corridor, and into the picture had come the pony. He had watched his mother paint it in with confident deft strokes, and he had squealed his delight.

But now there was no outlook on to the

cove. The trees had grown prodigiously into a complete obscuring belt, and between them were many bushes. There, at least, Mr. Poltimore had not been particularly efficient. He sighed, and Tessa looked at him querulously.

'Just ghosts,' he said.

'First Zillah and then you.'

'I was thinking of my mother. She died here.'

'Oh, I'm sorry.'

'That's all right. It's so long ago that I can take a detached view now. We used to be able to get to the cove that way, but we'd better go through the sunk garden. I'd like to look at the boat. Of course I shall need the key of the boathouse.'

Poltimore provided him with this, and then the three passed through the sunk garden, which like the rest of the place sadly needed attention. From there a path through a topiary avenue led to land which sloped down to the wooded foreshore. The tide was coming in and washing along the stone pier, and the water was so clear that the sea bed could be seen in detail at a depth of twelve feet.

Lavering opened up the boathouse, and revealed a well-built boat which had recently been caulked and painted. Close by was a four horse-power outboard motor, and a fifty gallon drum of petrol. Elsewhere were some lobster pots, fish-lines and prawning nets, all of which caused George's eyes to sparkle.

'What a life!' he said. 'I'm going to enjoy it. What about getting this craft afloat?'

'Better to wait for the high tide,' replied Gerald. 'She's heavy to drag all the way across the beach. We'll get her into the water to-morrow morning. After that we can moor her alongside the jetty. Are you a good sailor, George?'

George didn't know, but he hoped so. It looked as if he would need to be, because although there was calm inside the little sheltered cove, the sea outside had a heavy swell which was portentous of rough going in a small boat.

'I'm always sick,' said Tessa. 'But I don't mind being sick.'

'But we do,' objected George. 'Jerry, what about groceries, and so forth?'

'I told Poltimore to lay in all the things we should be likely to need. I expect he's done that. What I didn't include was drink.'

'Good Lord! What an omission. I vote you and I run down to the pub in the car, and lay in a stock.'

'Why only you and Jerry?' asked Tessa. 'What have I done?'

'You don't want to mess about in a pub,' said George.

'But that's just what I do want to do.'

'Not until we find out what sort of a place it is. It may be the roughest sort of show,' argued George. 'You go to the house and check up the groceries. Zillah will probably need some help too. If we work that girl too hard she'll probably run out on us, and then we'll be in a mess. Be nice to her and tell her we'll give her a nice fat tip if she behaves herself.'

'Tell her yourself,' retorted Tessa.

Just before Lavering and George left, Lavering changed the plan slightly. He suggested walking over the cliff, and taking a haversack in which to transport the liquid refreshment.

'The car's a bit too plutocratic,' he explained. 'It will look too much like a blatant advertisement of wealth. I'd feel a bit uncomfortable.'

George looked at him in astonishment.

'Quaint ideas you get, Jerry,' he said. 'I'm with you regarding the advantages of a walk, but I'm blessed if I'll encourage your socialist ideas. What's wrong with wealth?'

'A great deal when you fling it in the teeth of hardworking poorly paid men.'

'But most of the people here will know by this time that you are — well what you are.'

'The heir to so much which owes nothing to my personal efforts. Anyway, let's go.'

He led the way up the steep side of the cliff, disturbing larks and rabbits in the progress. From the summit the lovely coastline was unfolded to their view. The breathless beauty of the thing was only broken by three or four old mine shafts, around which was considerable debris. The largest of these had bits of rusty machinery scattered beside it.

'Tin?' asked George.

'Yes. It used to be guarded when I was a small kid, but the wire's all down, and I presume someone has sneaked the timber for winter fuel. I remember my mother used to give me a little homily every day — 'don't go near the mine, Jerry'.'

'Is it deep?' asked George.

'I've never been interested enough to find out.'

'Then here goes,' said George, and picked up a piece of smelted rock. 'Now what did old Isaac Newton say about gravitation?'

'I thought he was out of date.'

'Not in respect of falling bodies. All material bodies fall at the same rate — .'

'In a vacuum.'

'How many feet per second?'

'I don't know, and I don't care.'

'Funny I can't remember even a simple thing like that. What's the good of having an expensive education if you can't remember anything afterwards? Jove, this is slippery!'

He was climbing up the steep side of the cone of debris, with the missile clutched in his hand. When he was near the summit, Lavering called a warning.

'What's wrong, old man?' asked George.

'Chuck your rock and come down — .'

'I want to see how far I can see down it.'

'And I want to take you home alive. Don't be an ass.'

George tossed the piece of rock into the boring, but he forgot to count until it was too late to make a start. There was a very long silence before a deep splash was heard.

'Must be a couple of hundred feet,' said George. 'And water at the bottom. What a ghastly place.'

'There are dozens of similar open borings in this neighbourhood. But let's get on!'

It was the pleasantest walk imaginable in that invigorating air, and with every few hundred yards revealing new and unexpected folds in the coastal bastion, and at last they reached a kind of goat-track which wound down to Trewith, and came out close to the inn. Through a window Gerald could see a group of men playing darts in the common bar. They all appeared to be 'locals,' and their garb was as varied as anything could be. The saloon bar was next door, and here the furnishings and the patrons were less near to Nature, and the atmosphere less murky from tobacco smoke. Lavering and George entered this room, and made known their requirements. The huge man behind the counter regarded the two newcomers with unconcealed interest, and Lavering smiled as he recalled the big leather-coloured face.

'You don't remember me, Mr. Fouracres?' he asked.

Fouracres scratched his stubbly chin with two fingers.

'I was wondering where I had seen you before,' he replied. 'Just can't think where and when.'

'It was a long time ago, and I have changed a bit.'

'Aye, we all change a lot. Was it in Truro?'

'No, here in Trewith. We were living at Nancrannon.'

Fouracres opened his intensely blue

eyes very wide, and his neck swelled up in his excitement.

'You're not — you can't be — young Lavering that was? The little chap I used to take sailing?'

'None other.'

'Well — well!' Fouracres sized him up from head to foot. 'I never thought you'd grow to be so big. In them days you were just a slip of a boy — a bit pale, and with little hands. Of course, I should have guessed, because Poltimore told me he was going to open up the old house. Glad to see you sir.'

'I'm also glad to be here. This is a friend of mine.'

Fouracres nodded at George, who was a little embarrassed because a holiday-making girl in green corduroy shorts was so evidently amused at his very white large calves, and seemed on the verge of poking them with a walking stick to make sure they were real.

'What about something to take away?' asked George.

'For sure,' replied Fouracres. 'What would you like?'

George began to enumerate the items, which were considerable, and most varied, and for some minutes Fouracres was busy digging out the bottles from various corners.

'I doubt the capacity of the haversack,' said Lavering.

'Oh, we'll manage,' replied George. 'Marvellous beer this.'

Gerald wasn't listening. His sharp ears had caught the name 'Nancrannon' from the public bar. A man with a very thick voice was talking.

'I wouldn't live in that thur house fur anything,' he was saying. 'Must be twenny yeer since anyone went inside 'cept Poltimore. Folks do say she walks thur o' nights.'

'Who walks?' asked a voice.

'Her who used to live there, and were drowned in the sea.'

Lavering's face had gone tense, and Fouracres, realising the cause, turned fiercely to the speaker.

'Shut up, Ned,' he said. 'You've had too much to drink.'

'Me!' retorted the invisible Ned. 'Since

61

when were three pints too much fur me.
Here, whar did I lay them darts. Yer bust
Dixie — clean bust.'

Fouracres began to pack the bottles in
the haversack which Gerald tendered.

'I'm sorry, Mr. Lavering,' he said. 'Ned
Cotter was always loud mouthed. He
don't mean anything.'

Lavering just smiled and paid the bill.
With a rather curt 'good-night,' he and
George left the bar, and were soon
trudging up the steep path. George was
surprised at his friend's sudden change.

'Let me carry that load,' he said, after a
long silence.

Lavering handed over the heavy haversack, and then stopped to gaze at the
darkening sea.

'He must have been referring to my
mother,' he said.

'It was very unfortunate, but of course
he didn't know you were in the next bar.'

'Oh, I'm not annoyed with him. He
meant no harm by what he said, but you
see, I didn't know.'

'Didn't know what?'

'That — that my mother was drowned

here. My father never told me. No one ever told me.'

'Does it make — any difference?'

'No. I suppose not. Death is death in whatever guise it comes. Strange that it should have been the sea, for she loved it intensely. She used to sketch the sea in all its moods, even when it was blowing a full gale, and she was compelled to wear a sou'wester to prevent getting drenched by the spindrift. It seems an ungrateful act on the part of the sea. I wonder what really happened.'

George was tactful enough to maintain silence, and a little later Gerald's mind was out of that particular rut. They met Tessa along the cliff, with the wind playing havoc with her hair.

'Is that all booze?' she asked, indicating the haversack.

'Nectar,' replied George.

'I'll bet you didn't remember to bring any ginger ale for me.'

'You didn't ask for any.'

'Then I'll have to drink beer.'

'What's the matter with the water?' asked George.

'Ask yourself,' she retorted. 'Zillah told me to impress upon you that supper — she calls it supper — will be spoiled unless you hurry. Also, she wants to go home.'

'What has she got for us?' asked George.

'I don't know, but it smells all right. She wouldn't let me help her. Said she didn't want anyone mucking about in her kitchen. She called it just that — mucking about.'

When they reached Nancrannon, Zillah was waiting, with an angry expression on her gipsy face.

'About time, too!' she remarked. 'Sit yu all down, and I'll serve it. I don't like this place after dark.'

She bounced off, and there was a terrific clatter of plates from the direction of the kitchen.

'That young woman is going to be told the truth about herself one of these days,' said Tessa.

4

Zillah had cleared up after the excellent meal which she had cooked and served, and had left the house on a ramshackle push-cycle which she rode with great recklessness down the steep track which wound down to the cove, and then went into the blue. The party breathed a sigh of relief at her departure, for she was like a brooding storm in the house.

'She certainly is a queer character,' said Lavering. 'I'm sorry for Poltimore. Now we can have a look at the house. Tessa, press that switch behind you, and see if the lights work.'

Tessa did this and the several lights came on, and threw a warm glow over the comfortable lounge. Lavering wandered round, looking at things long-forgotten until now. He picked up a bottle containing a beautifully made ship, with perfect rigging.

'We bought this in Falmouth,' he said.

'I remember I made myself a bit of a nuisance, and cried bitterly when my father refused to buy it. My mother was less hard-hearted, and gave way, which of course she shouldn't have done. Shows what an appalling child I was.'

Tessa ran her hands over the keys of the grand piano, and screamed with laughter at the result.

'One thing your precious Poltimore overlooked,' she said. 'It's terrible. Listen to this chord.'

'You wouldn't sound so sweet if you hadn't uttered a sound for twenty years,' commented George. 'Give it a rest.'

Tessa closed the lid, and then picked up a framed picture which was facing the wall by the side of the enormous piano leg.

'What's this?' she asked.

It was the portrait of a young woman done in oils. The eyes were full of laughter, and the lips were slightly parted. She wore a broad brimmed straw hat of the pre-Great War period, and a lilac coloured silk blouse with a low neck. In the background was a suggestion of the present room, with the lighting reduced to give contrast to the bright colour scheme of the portrait itself. It was a striking piece of work, and across the bottom were the initials M.L.

'Lovely,' said Tessa.

Lavering had come across the room and was staring over Tessa's shoulder. She heard him catch his breath, and turned her head to see that he was tremendously moved.

'My mother,' he said. 'It used to hang over the piano. She painted it herself — in a mirror. To think that I had even forgotten that. It's her living image — that quiet smile, and the way she used to hold her right hand, with the index finger up, as if she were admonishing someone. I wonder why my father left it here.'

'Why did he leave everything here?' asked George. 'It's a shame to let all this gorgeous stuff gather mildew. Look at that Buckingham table — nearly ruined. Didn't he ever come back after he left?'

'I don't know. There's so much I don't know,' replied Lavering. 'He and I never got on together. He was an iceberg. You couldn't get near to the heart of him. But come and see the library. I think it's down the long passage, on the left.'

The long passage ran from the hall, at right-angles to the staircase. It was broad and void of furniture. At either end was a suit of armour. Midway was a door leading to the library. It was locked but the key was present. Gerald turned it, and then fumbled for the electric light switch. When the light came on it revealed a long room, three sides of which were equipped with shelves, all loaded down with books. Above the book-case the plain washed walls were decorated with many water-colours.

'There they are,' said Gerald. 'I knew they were here — somewhere.'

'Your mother's work?' asked George.

'Yes. Look, you can see how beautiful the garden was in those days. That's my old pony, and that ghastly object in the blue knickers is me. Oh, and here's a dog we used to have. What did we call him? Gyp. Yes, I'm sure it was Gyp. He was run over shortly before my mother died. I thought the world had come to an end. Later I knew it had.'

Tessa gave him a quick glance. There was something immensely moving in this experience. Here was Jerry recapturing the past with quite bewildering speed, leaping backwards into a world where nothing had changed in twenty years. Every single item had some rich memory for him. He picked up small objects, smiled, and laid them down again. In the bottom of one of the bookcases he turned out a drawing book. This contained his first attempts at drawing. He laughed as he turned the grubby pages.

'That was my idea of a pony's legs,' he said. 'Those firmer lines were drawn in by my mother — but perhaps you guessed that?'

'Yes, Jerry,' she said. 'You loved her, didn't you?'

'I've never quite got over it,' he replied quietly. 'She left a ghastly hole inside me, which nobody attempted to fill. It would be impossible to make you understand.'

'I think I do understand — a little.'

'I say, old man,' said George. 'Some of

these books have suffered. Ought to have had more fires in here. Look, a lovely set of Kipling, in green calf, and rotting with mildew.'

'They're better over here, by the fireplace,' said Tessa. 'Oh, here's a book I've been wanting to read for years, and never could get it. 'The Wallypug of Why'.'

'That's a kid's book,' said George.

'Don't kid yourself,' retorted Tessa. 'You'd call 'Alice in Wonderland' a kid's book.'

'Well, isn't it?'

'Don't be a silly goof. May I borrow this, Jerry?'

'Of course. Borrow anything you like.'

From the library they passed into other rooms, some of which were still shrouded with dust-cloths, and all of them succeeded in reflecting the general atmosphere of the whole house — a strange, brooding atmosphere, tinged with extreme sadness. On an easel in the morning room was a small canvas, depicting an unfinished flower study in oil. Near it was a palette, some brushes, and a paint-box. Even the artist's stool was there. Lavering appeared to be deeply affected.

'There were flowers in that vase,' he said. 'She must have been painting them —. It would have been a fine piece of work.'

Tessa was glad when they left that room. It was just a trifle too reminiscent.

'No wonder Zillah said this place is haunted,' she said to George later. 'It is.'

'Tripe!' retorted George. 'It's entirely due to the way things have been left. Not a thing touched since the tragedy happened. Perhaps Mr. Lavering always intended to come back, and wanted to engage in a game of make-believe. I think Jerry should have sold all this stuff, and saved the rates on the house. That's what I should have done.'

'But you're not Jerry,' said Tessa. 'And you haven't much imagination, or you'd realise one thing.'

'What thing?'

'You'll see,' replied Tessa, mysteriously.

The house was silent when Zillah arrived on her crazy bicycle at eight o'clock the next morning, after which there was a stirring of humanity, for she made enough noise to waken the dead. George tumbled out of bed at last, and grinned to realise that he hadn't to catch the eight-twenty. Staggering to the window he put out his head and blinked at the bright sunshine. Then he surveyed himself in the mirror, and shook his head. Something had to be done about that bulge around his solar plexus. He felt shamefully conscious of it, especially with Jerry in the offing, for Jerry was built on the lines of a statue by Praxiteles. With a grimace he stripped off his pyjama jacket, and got down to serious business.

Lying on a comfortable rug he did certain weird things with his legs and arms, at the same time muttering 'In,' 'Out,' 'Up,' 'Down,' until shortage of breath prevented him doing both things at once, so he concentrated on the movements, and abandoned the vocal accompaniment. It was when he was in his most grotesque position, with his head somehow looking through his legs that he realised he was no longer alone. Standing in the doorway was Zillah, with a small tray in her hands.

'Oh, Mr. Lashing,' she said. 'You du look funny.'

'So would you,' retorted George. 'If you stood on the back of your neck.'

'No I wouldn't,' she replied. 'I can do that easily. Here, you take the tray and I'll show yu.'

George regained the perpendicular, and declined the proffered tray.

'I think you'd better not,' he said with great emphasis. Then, anxious to change the subject. 'Thank you for the tea, but who told you to bring it?'

'My old man. Don't you want it?'

'Of course I do.'

'You don't think I can stand on my head?'

'Yes I do. I believe you can hang by your toes on a clothes-line.'

'So I can. My, haven't you got a hairy chest.'

George, speechless with surprise, grabbed his pyjama coat and put it on — backwards. Zillah put the tray on the small table and screamed with wild laughter. George shooed her out, and closed the door after her.

'My God!' he muttered. 'What a girl.'

There was a rap on the door and Lavering entered, to find George gleaming with perspiration, and gulping down his tea.

'You look hot, George,' he said.

'Hot!' George put down his cup. 'Jerry, that girl's dippy, scatty, bats.'

'What girl?'

'Zillah — not Tessa, her dementia takes a different form. Did she bring you a cup of tea?'

'Yes.'

'Did she want to stand on her head?'

'If she did she never mentioned the fact,' replied Lavering, with a smile.

'She caught me in the act — physical jerks, and wanted to show me how she could do it. Seriously, old man, you'll have to do something about it.'

'Well, I can tell Poltimore we don't want her any more. The trouble is I don't think we shall be able to get any other domestic help. Of course we can try.'

'Bit of a problem,' said George. 'She scares me stiff.'

'I'll talk to her.'

'That's the idea. She'd take notice of you — far more notice than she would of her father, whom she irreverently calls her 'old man.' But for heaven's sake don't let her get the notion that I — well, you know what I mean.'

'You miserable coward,' said Lavering, with a laugh. 'Are you going to bag the solitary bathroom, or shall I?'

'Toss you.'

George tossed a coin, and won.

5

In the hot sunny days which followed the party crowded action and happiness into every passing minute. The boat was got into service, the tennis-court echoed with the banging of balls, and bathing became a twice-daily routine. George's outrageous white calves changed to pink and then to brown. Every morning he weighed himself on the bathroom scales, and the result was most encouraging.

'Don't get a weight complex,' begged Lavering.

'Complex be damned. I've wrestled with this tummy for six years — in vain. Look at me now — almost slim.'

'Almost,' said Lavering. 'Look at what the scale reveals — thirteen and a half stone. You'll have to trim off twenty pounds before you begin to look even respectable.'

'Fat into muscle — that's what I'm after.'

'Man into savage. You've got sand and seaweed in your hair. Get into some clothes, and we'll have a shot for some mackerel. Poltimore has rigged up some lines, and he says there are mackerel about.'

'Grand idea. What about Tessa?'

'She can come with us.'

George stared through the window at the intensely blue sea. It looked calm enough, but by this time he had come to know it was a snare and a delusion. That appealing flatness was only apparent. Out there but a few hundred yards from the cove the sea was running in an endless series of rolling waves.

'She won't like it,' he said.

'Well, we can but ask her.'

Tessa was ready to try anything once. She came as she was — hatless and shoeless, and so destitute of upper garments that Lavering thought he was justified in getting rid of his shirt. Poltimore had left two lines in the boat, equipped with spinners.

'Shan't we want some bait?' asked George.

'No,' replied Lavering. 'Those bright spinners are sufficient. When we get our first fish we can cut it up and use it as bait, if the going is slow. Start the engine, George.'

George gave a sharp tug on the cord which started the engine, and the outboard motor began to revolve. He then dumped his thirteen and a half stone beside the steering arm, opened the throttle a little and made out of the small cove.

'Which way?' he asked.

'Towards Black Rock, but you must keep her well out. Tessa get hold of that line. I'll tell you when to drop it overboard. Let her have it, George.'

George opened the throttle wider, and the healthy engine boomed a higher note. Once clear of the headland they began to meet the deeper troughs, and the small, sturdy boat smacked into them and climbed the opposing watery walls. Tessa gulped as the movement increased, and Lavering saw her hand close tight on the gunwale of the boat.

'She's going to be sick,' said George

disgustedly. 'Before we are really started.'

'I like being sick,' retorted Tessa.

'Well get it over,' said George. 'Because we've come fishing.'

'Go to hell,' said Tessa. 'You're not looking so well yourself.'

'Me!' retorted George. 'Why this is grand.'

'Overboard with that line, Tessa,' said Lavering. 'Like this.'

He flung out his own heavily-weighted line, and Tessa, after watching him, did the same.

'Good!' he said. 'George, keep her head north of the rock. That's better. But ease off the engine a bit. You've got her flat out.'

George did as he was told. For a time there was nothing doing, and Lavering was beginning to regret he hadn't brought some bait with him, when Tessa suddenly gave a start.

'Here it comes,' groaned George.

'I — I've got a fish on my line,' she gasped.

'Then haul it in,' replied Lavering. 'Go on — hand over hand.'

Tessa gave a squeal of intense delight as finally the fish came to view. It was a full-size mackerel, with its lovely colouring enhanced by the bright sunshine. Lavering released the hook, and dropped the fish in the bottom of the boat. A minute later he, too, had a fish.

'We're amongst them now,' he said.

Tessa threw in her line again, and within two minutes she had another. Lavering looked into her excited eyes. Undoubtedly she had felt far from well, but now the green pallor had left her cheeks, and she looked fit and eager. After that it was more slaughter than fishing. George, not to be outdone, gave the motor over to Tessa, and took over her line. It was Tessa's first experience at the helm, and her reaction was obvious. In about two minutes she had the throttle wide open, and her teeth were flashing through the cloud of spindrift which settled on her face.

'Hey, steady!' shouted George.

'Steady yourself!' she retorted. 'Why didn't I do this before? Here we go, boys!'

'Steady!'

'Let her enjoy herself!' said Lavering. 'There's a big fish on your line.'

'By Jove there is!' said George, as he felt the line. 'Feels like a whale. Come inside, lovely!'

As the line came in George became more and more excited, and from his efforts Lavering suspected something bigger than a mackerel. Finally the struggling fish came to view. George bellowed his joy, for the fish was by far the biggest thing he had ever caught on a hook. Lavering grabbed it as it came aboard, gleaming like a piece of polished silver.

'You're a miracle worker,' he said. 'A man who can catch a salmon bass on a mackerel spinner is a magician. If anyone had told me I should have called him a liar. Five pounds if he's an ounce.'

'This is the life,' chanted George. 'Are there really silly idiots sitting in offices writing figures in books? When all this is over I'm going to buy me a boat, build a hut somewhere close to the sea and establish a fishing business. Tessa can fry the chips.'

After that there was a lull, and Lavering gave it as his opinion that they had run through the mackerel shoal.

'Then let's go back and start all over again,' said George.

'Hog! We've more fish than can be kept fresh. Steady, Tessa — here comes that nasty ninth roller again. Keep her head well into it.'

Tessa gulped as she saw the careering green ocean, and George clung tightly to the seat. The curling top of the wave broke as the bows of the small boat split it in twain, and about ten gallons of water came aboard. Tessa howled with delight when they were in calmer water. Her hair was hanging like wet seaweed down her brown face, and she looked like a nymph from some submarine hide-out.

'How did I do, Skipper?' she asked.

'Passed with honours,' replied Lavering. 'We'll make a seaman of you yet. Let's give the fish a respite. There's a marvellous place beyond that old rock, with a shell beach, caves and magnificent rocks. The tide is just about right to make a landing. I'll take over, Tessa.'

'Oh,' pleaded Tessa. 'Just when I was getting the hang of the thing.'

'Let the child play,' said George, as he reclined lazily in the bows of the boat. 'Gosh, I feel like a million.'

'A million what?' asked Lavering.

'Anything. It's a lot anyway. Where is this famous beach?'

Tessa took her instructions from Lavering, and carried them out to perfection. After passing the soaring isolated rock, up which the sea was clawing at roosting gulls, the boat headed for a small shelving beach which gleamed white in the sunshine, and beyond which were fantastic rocks, forming caverns and arches. As they drew nearer the wild beauty of the place became more detailed and impressive.

'Steady here,' Lavering called to Tessa. 'Throttle her right down. That's better.'

The boat crept in between jagged submerged rocks. With a boathook in his hand Lavering indicated the course, and finally the dangerous reef was passed, leaving a safe course to the beach, over which the waves crawled in wide arcs of foam. Then the keel touched down, and Tessa switched off the engine.

'We shan't be able to stay long,' said Lavering. 'The tide is romping in. Overboard you go. Take that anchor with you, George.'

The boat was hauled as far as possible up the slope, and the anchor fixed at the extremity of the long length of rope. Lavering waved his hand to indicate the incredible formation of rock on the left. It was like a cathedral and into its vast mass time and tide had driven a tunnel, the entrance to which was shaped like a colossal Norman arch. Through this the sea was running in both directions, but every few seconds the outflow of the last wave was opposed by the next intruder, with results that were magnificent to watch.

'It goes in a long way,' said Lavering. 'But I doubt if we can get in very far at this state of the tide. I remember there were crevices in the roof which let in the light — a weird and wonderful light which looked unearthly. At the extreme end there are workings of the old abandoned tinmine. Come on. There's no time to lose.'

They entered the weird place, and scrambled over rocks to avoid deep pools. The light diminished as they progressed, and the passage narrowed, leaving little but water. But Lavering was keen that they should see the interior cavern, and made his way upwards to a kind of platform.

'Here it is,' he called. 'Won't be safe to go in, but you can see from here. Careful how you step.'

Tessa came up the rocks like a young chamois, and finally, with her breath coming in gasps, she came close to Lavering's side. Immediately she saw a sight that was incomparable in its sheer beauty. It was a cavern of great size, with tunnels running off in two directions. The whole of the floor space was now covered with water, which was swirling and surging in all directions, under the dominating force of the incoming tide. Far up, in the domed roof were three narrow slits and through these came shafts of light, which were reflected back by the water, and which filled the whole place with changing colour.

'Marvellous, isn't it?' asked Lavering.

'Oh, Jerry!' she said. 'When did you discover this?'

'I didn't. Poltimore brought me here when I was a small boy. It's good to see it again. Unreal, isn't it?'

'Overwhelming.'

George lumbered up and added his appreciation.

'S — sh!' said Tessa suddenly. 'What is that?'

'That deep sighing sound?' asked Lavering.

'I can't hear any sighing,' complained George.

'There — now,' said Tessa.

'I heard a boom — like a big wave breaking. Here it comes too, surging along the tunnel.'

'Your hearing is rotten,' said Tessa. 'I heard it, and so did Jerry.'

'Oh yes, it's real enough,' said Lavering. 'I think it has something to do with the air which is displaced every time a large amount of water enters. Poltimore used to say it was Father Neptune sleeping. Somewhere my mother made a sketch of this, I wish I could find it.'

They stayed for a few minutes longer, watching the everchanging colour-patterns on the water, and then made their way back over the rocks to the little beach, up which the tide had advanced appreciably during their absence. After the subdued lighting of the cavern the sunshine now seemed to be blinding in its intensity.

'Like coming out of a trance,' said Tessa.

'Ever been in one?' asked George.

'No.'

'Then you've no right to talk about it.'

'Oh, throw a brick at him,' said Tessa. 'He's always bad-tempered when he's hungry.'

'Who says I'm hungry?' demanded George.

'I do. You are, aren't you?'

'Yes, I am,' said George stoutly. 'I could eat one of those raw fish.'

Lavering laughed as he hauled on the anchor rope, and slowly brought the boat closer. Already he had come to realise that this constant feud between George and his sister was as superficial as anything could be. At heart they were as close as the leaves of a book, and George's sneaking regard for his sister's innumerable qualities was never quite concealed.

'Of course she needs restraining,' he grumbled. 'If once I let go the traces she'd be bossing me all over the place.'

'Do you good,' said Lavering. 'Get in the boat.'

The journey home was done with wind and tide in their favour, and Tessa, still clinging tenaciously to the tiller, smiled her complete contentment when at last, without any instructions whatsoever, she brought the boat to rest close to the stone steps of the jetty.

'Good for you, Tessa,' said Lavering. 'There's just one thing you've forgotten.'

'What?' she asked, anxiously.

'You forgot to be sick.'

She laughed as she seized his arm, and was helped to the steps.

'Oh, Jerry,' she said. 'Thanks for a lovely trip. If George wasn't here I think I should kiss you. I think I'll kiss George instead.'

'You jolly well won't,' grunted George. 'Come and lend a hand with these fish, and don't stand there talking tripe. Jerry, is that a half-hitch or isn't it?'

Lavering looked at George's insecure knot, and then put it right for him.

'Funny I can never remember,' complained George. 'Do you think that girl's got lunch ready?'

At that moment the loud banging of a gong was heard from the direction of the house.

'There's the answer,' said Lavering. 'We're half-an-hour late, and Miss Zillah will be out for blood.'

'Did you speak to her about — the other morning?' asked George.

'No. If she threw in her hand we should probably have to do all the chores ourselves. She's an independent young person.'

'What's all this mystery?' asked Tessa.

'Oh nothing,' replied George. 'Come on, or she may put poison in the soup.'

On reaching the house they found

Zillah looking most militant. Her nice lunch was ruined, she alleged. One o'clock was one o'clock and not half past. If they couldn't come in punctual to meals they could jolly well find someone else to cook for them. Maybe Miss Tessa would have a go at it.

'Why not?' asked Tessa sweetly. 'I couldn't make a worse mess of the vegetables than you do.'

Zillah gave her one long look, and then pranced out of the room.

'Now you've torn it,' said George.

'About time, too,' replied Tessa. 'You're both afraid of her, and she knows it. What are you paying her, Jerry?'

'I don't know. I left that to Poltimore.'

'Well, you're a fine business man. I'll bet they've soaked you pretty well already. Are you the boss here, or aren't you?'

'I'm not sure,' replied Lavering seriously.

'Well, you'd better make up your mind.'

Time passed and neither Zillah nor the food put in an appearance, and then George uttered an exclamation and pointed through the window. There was Zillah, astride her crazy machine, racing madly down the steep track, as if the Devil himself were after her.

'Walked out on us,' said George.

'Rode out, to be exact,' corrected Tessa. 'I suppose she thinks she is indispensable. Well, we'll see.'

A few minutes later they were eating the overdone meal, but there was such an edge on their appetites that no one complained.

6

It was evening and all three had spent half-an-hour in the kitchen dealing with the accumulated dirty dishes and cooking utensils. Lavering had expected Poltimore to come and enquire about the circumstances which had sent his fire-eating daughter home in such haste, but he did not turn up. George was reading a book from the library, and Tessa was tinkering about with the piano. Lavering was simply lying back, and reflecting. At last George got tired of the monotonous noises from the instrument.

'What on earth are you doing?' he asked Tessa.

'Tuning it, you idiot. What do you think I'm doing?'

'You can't tune a piano with a pair of nut-crackers.'

'They aren't nutcrackers. I got them from the car. Listen to that for middle C — perfect.'

'You'll ruin it. Jerry, why don't you stop her?'

Lavering looked across at Tessa, who played the octave for his benefit.

'I think she's doing quite well,' he yawned.

'Well, it's your piano — not mine.'

As time passed, Lavering became interested in Tessa's labour. He had a keen ear for tone, and he realised that there was method in her madness. One chord after another was rescued from cacophony, and rippling arpeggios were evolved from unmelodious jingles, while Tessa, in her own words, 'sweated blood.'

'Haven't you finished yet, Torquemada?' asked George.

'No, I haven't,' retorted Tessa, brandishing her pair of grips. 'This B flat is —.'

'B flat,' said George. 'Isn't anyone going to laugh?'

Tessa groaned, and then gritted her teeth as she got a fresh grip on a stubborn terminal.

'No good,' she gasped, and swore under her breath.

Lavering rose to his feet and walked across to the piano.

'Let me have a go,' he said. 'Which one is it?'

'That little devil, with the scratches on it. It has to go clockwise, but only a bit at a time. For the love of Mike be careful, or you'll break the string.'

Lavering turned the offending terminal with ease, and brought a cry from Tessa, who depressed the corresponding key.

'Too much. Back a little until I shout.'

The pitch of the note fell as Tessa tapped the key, and Lavering slackened off the wire.

'Stop!' cried Tessa. 'Oh, that's lovely. Listen.'

Her supple fingers moved over the keyboard, and the instrument awoke to new life. Lavering stood there transfixed. A hundred times that melody had passed through his mind, and he had never discovered what it was. All he knew was that it formed part of the background of his youth, and it now had the power to fill in certain gaps in his memory. Then, when he was transported completely to those sunny fields of infantile delight, the music stopped. He shortened his gaze, and met Tessa's warm excited eyes.

'Don't stop, please,' he begged. 'I didn't know you could play like that.'

'Oh, I'm terrible,' she said.

'She's not,' said George. 'It's about the only thing she can do decently.'

Tessa got off the stool and did a perfect curtsey. Then she struck an attitude.

'Ladies and gents. In response to your kind appreciation I will now play you the first movement of Beethoven's Pianoforte Sonata, commonly called the 'Moonlight.' Sit still and hold tight.'

Seating herself she played over again the part which Lavering had already heard, and then went on. Lavering stole across to the settee and sat staring at her. But it was not she whom he really saw, but another woman, and again there came surging up all the ever-living past with all its unfulfilled promises, its tears and laughter. He did not know that the music had finished until Tessa came and sat down beside him.

'Oh!' he ejaculated. 'Thanks, Tessa. You

did that beautifully. We — we must have some more. Clever of you to make that instrument tolerable. Amazing how music can work miracles. I think I'll go to bed, if you two don't mind.'

'Not at all,' said George, stretching his arms. 'I'm feeling that way too. But I'm determined to finish this ghastly book.'

'Well, I'll say good-night!'

'Good-night, old man. Shan't be long.'

When Lavering had gone, George made no attempt to finish his book.

'He's curious at times,' he said.

Tessa gave a short laugh.

'Don't do that,' remonstrated her brother. 'I'm concerned about Jerry. He's a grand chap, but I can't quite get to the bottom of him. You'd think he'd be up in the clouds on account of his marvellous good fortune, and yet he isn't. He doesn't seem to realise just what it means to have more money than you can hope to spend, a place like this, that other huge house, and the power — .'

'Power! Jerry doesn't want power. He doesn't want anything that he hasn't won for himself.'

'Oh, don't start that Socialistic stuff.'

'Well, I know something about Jerry!'

'My dear child — .'

'Don't dear child me. Jerry's in love.'

'What! Oh, don't make me laugh.'

'Jerry's in love,' she repeated, with greater emphasis.

'Go on, I'll buy it,' said George. 'Who's the lucky girl?'

'His mother.'

George's scoffing expression changed. He looked at his sister as if she had handed him a live snake.

'You're as queer as he is,' he said.

'And you're as blind as a bat, and as dense as a piece of granite. Haven't you noticed that Jerry has been gathering together all the very personal things associated with his mother. The drawings that were in the library are now in his bedroom, and he's always searching for anything which brings her more alive. When he mentions the past it is inevitably bound up with what his mother was doing at the time.'

'But that's natural enough, isn't it?'

'Yes, up to a point. But Jerry goes

beyond that. She died when he was very young, in mysterious circumstances — .'

'Why mysterious?'

'Well, for twenty years Jerry believed she had died from an illness, and nobody told him any different. Then when he comes back here he hears that she was drowned.'

'I can't see anything mysterious in anyone getting drowned in a place like this. One could get drowned while bathing, or be capsized in a boat, or fall over the cliff, or — .'

'Don't be so stubborn. You know there's some mystery here. You can smell it everywhere. Look at this house, with everything frozen. Not a thing touched in twenty years. Why didn't Jerry's father come back here in all that time? Why did Zillah talk about ghosts?'

'Oh, she's half mad. I'll go so far as to admit that Jerry is greatly moved by this place, and all the memories it revives. Don't we all pine to bring back our nursery days again? And you've got to remember that for years Jerry has been an exile — that his father was always aloof, and not the real pal he should have been. But all these things are perfectly natural, and you have no grounds for giving Jerry an Œdipus complex.'

'I know nothing about Œdipus. All I know is that Jerry had his mother torn from him at a time when he worshipped her — that here he is devoting every minute of his life to bringing her alive. Didn't you notice the effect of that Beethoven Sonata upon him? That was no coincidence. I knew she must have played it a thousand times, because I found the pages terribly dog-eared in the volume which contains it. She had written across the top 'My darling's birthday motif'.'

'Oh that was too bad,' protested George.

'Why?'

'Well, first you pretend that Jerry is obsessed by an unhealthy kind of passion, and then you set out to feed that emotion.'

'Only to prove I am right.'

'It's a rotten thing to do all the same.'

'Ah, so you are beginning to under-stand.'

'No, I'm not. You leave Jerry alone.'

'Perhaps I will. Perhaps I won't,' said Tessa.

'Just what are you driving at.'

'You'll see. To change the subject, do you realise that if our said lady-of-all-work persists in indulging in a stay-out strike we shall have to get our own breakfasts to-morrow, and lunch, and dinner, and then wash up mountains of crockery?'

'My God, yes,' said George. 'Pity you insulted her.'

'Somebody had to do it, and you two men lacked the courage. It's only because she has an imp-like prettiness. If she were as ugly as her thoughts you'd act differently. She's got you both dithery by exposing her finer animal points, and you gaze at her curves and become speechless. I think I know what her other name is.'

'Then don't tell me because I'm certain it's improper,' retorted George.

'Correct,' replied Tessa. 'Now my big bouncing baby-brother, I suggest we go to bed.'

Lavering found it difficult to get to

sleep, despite the tiring activities of the day. Seeing the cavern again had been a sheer delight, for he had so often brought it to memory since his last visit to the place. From his small farm in Western Canada it had seemed to be far away, in another world — a world made up of childish imagination, overlaid with romance. Yet here it was, in no wise changed, except that it failed to measure up with the vast proportion of his fancy. But this no longer surprised him, because he had experienced the same diminishing propensity with all the things of the past. The house was smaller. The garden, which in his youth, had impressed him as being well-nigh endless in magnitude, had lost this attribute of infinity. The long corridor, with its suits of armour, had always filled him with awe. Now he saw it as an ordinary passage, quite bereft of anything sinister. The child mind had indeed vanished in the intervening years — gone into the bosom of time, leaving but the deep impressions which it had engraved. In retrospect he saw that vanished child running about the place, marvelling greatly at the astonishing world, admonished betimes, kissed and cuddled at others. The house, the garden, the music — every item which he saw and touched recreated the past, which some called 'dead.' The 'Moonlight' Sonata. It had never expressed moonlight to him, but something far more complex and interfused. That stern father, strutting the house, with his shoulders thrust back. That parent, unapproachable in his vast and ridiculous dignity. The soft voice of her on whom all these vivid memories were really hinged — who had made this place a Paradise, and peopled it with fairies. There came to his mind some lines which he had read after she was gone from his world for ever.

'That garden sweet, that lady fair,
And all sweet shapes and odours
     there,
In truth have never passed away:
'Tis we, 'tis ours, are changed; not
     they.'

And again:

'For love, and beauty, and delight,
There is no death nor change: their
   might
Exceeds our organs, which endure
No light, being themselves obscure.'

Wide awake now, he got out of bed, and went across to the open window. There was no moon but several bright stars were reflected in the calm waters of the little cove. Between him and it the large dark trees, heavy with foliage, were silhouetted against the lighter hue of the night-sky. From somewhere in the garden, on the other side of the house, there came a hideous sound. He recalled it was the nightjar, which he had not heard in twenty years. It spoiled the perfect harmony of the scene, and it would not be quiet.

Then suddenly something happened which caused him to catch his breath. A picture fell from the wall with a crash, and the floor under his feet seemed to heave. He gripped the back of a chair and waited for something more violent to happen, but all was still again, and the nightjar repeated its hateful cry. A few seconds passed and then someone came to the door.

'Jerry!'

'Come in,' he called, recognising George's voice.

George entered and Lavering switched on the light.

'What was it?' gasped George.

Lavering was staring down at the picture which had fallen. It was the self portrait of his mother, which he had removed from downstairs. He picked it up.

'Frame's damaged,' he said.

'Yes, but it was more than just that. Nearly flung me out of bed. Was it an earthquake?'

'Never heard of an earthquake in Cornwall.'

'But you felt it, didn't you?'

'Yes. I think it may be the result of a big wave in that old cave. Actually we are not very far from it, as the crow flies.'

'But the sea is dead calm. I had a look at it just now.'

'Then it's your turn to guess,' replied

Lavering, with a smile. 'What's that? Ah, Tessa, come to join the party.'

Tessa, clad in an awe-inspiring silk sleeping suit, and with her radiant hair done in two plaits, slithered through the open door. She had not even troubled to put anything on her feet, and she looked at Lavering for the answer to her unspoken question.

'So you heard it too?' asked Lavering.

'I thought the house was coming down. Jerry, do the mine workings run under here?'

'They can't be far away.'

'Wouldn't it be funny if the house collapsed into them?'

'Pleasant ideas of fun you have,' grunted George. 'Why don't you put something on your feet?'

'You've got nothing on yours,' Tessa pointed out. 'Except two bunions.'

'Bunions my hat!'

'Bunions your foot, you mean. Now, Jerry, unfold this mystery, I am all ears.'

She sat on Lavering's bed and bounced herself up and down gently, until George stopped her.

'This isn't a fun fair,' he remonstrated. 'About the quake — Jerry doesn't know any more than I do, and we're all keeping each other up. Tessa, will you come off that bed.'

'I'll have to swop you mattresses, Jerry,' said Tessa, giving herself an extra bounce. 'This one is lovely. Mine has got bricks in it.'

George pulled her off the bed, and led her to the door.

'Bed,' he said. 'We're going to have a hard day tomorrow, unless we eat off newspapers. Good-night, Jerry!'

7

Lavering woke early the following morning, with the intention of stealing a march on his two guests, and preparing breakfast. Zillah's unexpected departure produced all sorts of problems, and threatened to spoil their holiday unless he could replace her without undue delay. This he proposed to do, even if it meant offering fantastic wages.

Creeping down to the kitchen he investigated the cooking-stove and the culinary utensils. In the larder were eggs, bacon, some sausages, and cold potatoes, not to mention pyramids of canned stuff. Any man who couldn't produce a breakfast in such circumstances would be a nitwit. Behind the door was an overall of small dimensions. He put it on, and got down to business. The stove had been damped down, and was still alight. All that was needed was the manipulation of the regulator, and more fuel. He was engaged in dirtying his hands and face when he heard the excited barking of a dog, which grew louder and louder. Then suddenly into his purview came no less a person than Zillah. She was riding her cycle with her usual ferocity, and just behind her raced a long-legged young dog. Zillah turned her head and waved the dog back, but with no visible result. Arriving at the enclosure outside the backdoor, she let the cycle fall on the ground, and seized the pup by the scruff of his neck, cuffing him violently with her free hand and using language which made even Lavering blush. The animal finally wriggled free and ran through the back door, to take shelter between Lavering's legs. Then came Zillah, breathing fire and fury. She stopped dead as she came upon Lavering, with a frying pan in his hand.

'My apron an' all!' she ejaculated.

'Yes, your apron and all,' replied Lavering. 'What's the meaning of all this?'

'It wur 'im,' she said, shaking her fist at the puppy. 'He got loose and raced after me. Fair little swine 'e be.'

'Never mind about him. What about you?'

'Oh me! I've come back. But I wouldn't if it hadn't been for the old man. He socked me terrible.'

'Socked you?'

'Beat me with a strap. Said he'd learn me to dirty 'is good name. Fair mad 'e wur.' She peered into Lavering's smutty face, and then produced a handkerchief which she wetted with her lips, with the ostensible purpose of removing his blemishes. He warded her off, and removed the overall.

'Now listen, my girl,' he said. 'If you're going to stay here you must change your ways. Understand?'

'No, I don't.'

'Well, in the first place you've got to learn a little discipline.'

'What's that?'

'Doing as you're told, and being respectful.'

'I be respectable,' she retorted. 'And don't yu dare say I ain't.'

'Respectful. Doing your job without so much backchat. I've got two guests, and

109

it's up to me to see that they have a good time.'

'How long are they staying?' she asked.

'That's not exactly your business.'

'It be if I'm to cook for them and make their beds. Mr. Lashing's nice. I like 'im, but Miss Tessa's a fault-finder, and I can't abear fault-finders.'

'Then have no faults to be found.'

'I feel better now,' she said, with a sigh. 'You buzz off and let me get on with the breakfast.'

'Now don't forget,' said Lavering, wagging his finger at her. 'No more nonsense.'

'Not me. I'll be so nice you won't know me.' She turned on the puppy. 'As for yu — I'll learn you to foller me when I tell yu to stay home. I'd give you away but nobody wants you.'

But the puppy had already got quite different ideas. He was looking up at Lavering with his warm brown, irresistible eyes, and wagging his tail.

'What's his name?' asked Lavering.

'Boozer. I gives 'im beer sometimes, an' he likes it.'

Lavering winced, and leaned down and stroked the dog, who displayed extreme pleasure.

'Cunning and wicked he is too,' said Zillah. 'I'd sell him for five shillun, I would.'

Lavering thrust his hand into his pocket and handed Zillah two half-crowns.

'He's mine,' he said.

Zillah spat on the two coins and slipped them into the pocket of her overall. Boozer, as if aware of the change of owner, followed Lavering along the hall.

'Hey, Jerry!'

It was George, leaning over the banisters, with his face smothered in shaving cream. He made eloquent gestures towards the kitchen with the shaving brush.

'Yes, she's come back,' replied Lavering.

'Oh cheers! Whose dog is that?'

'Mine. He cost me five shillings and his name is Boozer.'

'What breed do you call that?'

'How should I know?'

'Bit of greyhound in those hind legs I should say.'

'Bit of sheepdog in his coat.'

'But look at his ears — spaniel.'

'No more,' begged Lavering. 'I can't bear it.'

'I think four bob should have been the top price. You've been done for a bob.'

When breakfast was served everyone was very good, Tessa looked as if she would like to make some unfavourable comment on the toast, but she refrained. With the hideous spectre of domestic chores removed for the nonce, the party was free to explore the vicinity, and to take trips in the car to Trebarwith, Tintagel, Lands End, Bedruthen, and a dozen less-known but no less delightful places. George's indecent white legs were now as brown as the legs of the mahogany table, and he swore positively he was miles slimmer, although it was noticeable that he showed no eagerness to prove the point by weighing himself in public.

Boozer by now had fully accepted his new owner. All three had contributed to his improvement. Lavering had washed him thoroughly, Tessa had trimmed off some of his superfluous coat, and George boasted that he had 'defleaed' him to the last pestiferous parasite.

'Actual casualties eighty-seven fleas, and four sheep ticks,' he said. 'Now he is fit to lie in the lounge.'

Boozer did, and obviously liked it. He embarrassed George by scratching himself at intervals, but George considered this was force of habit, and had nothing to do with any uninvited guests. When Boozer caught George's remonstrating glance he stopped scratching and shivered.

'I expect he dreams about his ghastly unhygienic past,' said George.

Much as Boozer loved his life of ease on the lounge carpet, it was still one step short of Paradise. That final step was taken when Lavering took him out for runs over the cliff, where he chased real and imaginary enemies until finally he staggered back home, to show Lavering the whites of his eyes as if to say, 'That was fun — that was.'

It was on one of these evening

excursions that Boozer outdid himself. It was always easy to turn out a bird, but on this occasion he turned out a young hare. Lavering and Jerry were some fifty yards in his rear when they heard his scream of excitement, and saw the long-legged hare executing weird turns, with Boozer in hot pursuit.

'By jove, he's got something this time!' said George. 'Bit of the hound in him after all.'

Boozer was faster than the hare in a straight run, but the hare had no intentions of competing in that silly sort of game. Every time Boozer got close to him he went off at an incredible angle, causing Boozer to put on all brakes and do a skidding turn which gave the hare time to make up lost distance.

'Ought to use his head more,' commented George. 'Jove, that was a near thing. Good on you, Boozer! Stick it!'

Boozer was sticking it most nobly, and so was the hare. Unfortunately for the latter there was scant cover. Boozer had successfully headed him off from a patch of undergrowth where he might have outwitted the dog. Executing another lightning turn he went straight for the old mine shaft. Here Boozer got him at bay. The hare dived behind the broken-down winding gear, and did a sharp turn to the right, but on this occasion Boozer anticipated him. The hare, within a foot of Boozer's open jaws, did a somersault and raced up the sloping steep side. Boozer gave a howl and went after him.

'Boozer!' yelled Lavering. 'Heel, boy!'

A moment later the hare appeared again, and went on a zig-zag course away to a flank.

'Why, where's Boozer?' asked George.

Lavering ran past him to the unguarded pit. Scrambling to the brink of it he saw what had happened. Boozer, in his mad rush, had overrun the safety limit. From the dark depths came the sound of splashing and the pitiful cries of an animal in distress. George came up, gasping for breath.

'My — goodness! He's down below!'

'Yes,' muttered Lavering. 'Poor little devil!'

'Can't we — do anything?'

Lavering had already turned his gaze to the gear that was lying about. There was the old rusty winding drum, the twisted cable, the battered bucket. While he looked, Boozer's incessant cries came up from the pit.

'It's a question of time,' he said. 'George, run to the house, and get some tools. A heavy hammer, a spade, a hacksaw, and an oil can. Make it snappy, or we'll be too late. All right, Boozer,' he shouted, down the hole. 'Stick it, old boy.'

George went off like a shot from a gun, and Lavering began feverishly to man-handle the winding gear. It was all heavy and stiff. The winding handle could only be turned with an effort, and the steel cable was frayed in several places. At intervals he stopped his furious work to listen, and ever the cries came up, and the sound of splashing. Then he saw George in the distance, with Tessa running beside him. Both were laden with tools, and gasping for breath.

'Is he still keeping his end up?' asked George.

'Yes, but heaven only knows how long

116

he can last. Give me that spade. Tessa, smother that winding gear with oil, and get that handle working.'

Tessa nodded and then looked at him.

'You — you aren't going down there?' she gasped.

'That's the idea, if we can get this gear into position — and in time.'

He began using the spade, to excavate a seating, and George wrestled with the rusty cable.

'Frayed in places old man,' said George.

'I think it will hold. Lend me a hand with this.'

Little by little the crazy gear was erected. The oil had worked wonders with the rusty cogs, and after a few turns of the handle, Lavering nodded his head with satisfaction. The opening was spanned, and the bucket attached to the end of the cable. It was then that Tessa got into a panic. She reeled away from the pit and seized Lavering by the arm.

'Don't go,' she begged. 'It's madness. The cable won't hold. It's already half-broken. Jerry, I won't let you go.

George, why don't you stop him?'

George's mouth twitched. Now that they had reached the actual moment of operations he, too, began to feel a sinking in the pit of his stomach. But it was Boozer who succeeded in scattering these doubts and hesitations. His plaintive wail came up from the pit. Lavering removed Tessa's grip.

'Steady!' he said. 'Don't dramatise it. The cable would hold twice my weight. Help George to hold that handle firm. Go on. There's no time to spare.'

'Yes,' said Tessa meekly.

She went to her brother, stood opposite him, and gripped the long iron handle. Lavering, supporting himself by clutching the drum, got his legs into the large bucket.

'See if you can take the weight all right,' he said. 'Ready?'

'Yes,' replied George.

'Now!'

'That's all right,' said George 'No trouble at all.'

'Good! Now lower me a few feet, and see if you can bring me up again.'

This was done to the accompaniment of many squeaks.

'Then we're all set,' said Lavering.

'Oh wait!' begged George. 'Isn't there likely to be gas down there?'

'If Boozer can stand it so can I. Oh, just hark at him! Wait until I try this torch. Yes, that's all right. Go ahead!'

George gulped and began to unreel the rusty cable. Slowly Lavering's head disappeared from view.

'Stop when I shout,' he called, in a hollow voice.

'You'd better shout loud.'

'I will.'

George now watched the coiled cable on the drum, as it grew less and less. Then he met Tessa's wild eyes.

'Will it reach?' she whispered hoarsely.

'Let's hope so.'

'George!'

'For God's sake don't chatter,' he replied. 'Or we shan't hear Jerry.

In the meantime Lavering was getting lower and lower, and the light was fading out. He switched on the electric torch, and saw the damp walls of the unboarded shaft within a few feet of him. Boozer was still using his panic-stricken voice, but it was now mingled with the squeaking of the machinery. He shone the torch downwards, and saw below him a wooden platform extending from a narrow gallery, with a handrail attached vertically to it. This obviously was the place where the tin-miners had got off to start their arduous toil in the days when the mine was working. Some twenty feet below was the surface of the flood water, and swimming feebly in it was Boozer. The light was reflected back by two green eyes, and Lavering saw from the animal's movements that it was at its last gasp.

'Boozer!' he called. 'Coming, old boy. Cheer up!'

He was about three feet above the surface of the water when the bucket stopped.

'Hey, George!' he yelled, as loudly as he could.

George's muffled voice came back. What he said was not very clear, but he was obviously indicating that there was no more cable left on the drum. Lavering groaned his bitter disappointment, for try as he might, he could not reach the exhausted puppy with his hands. Meanwhile Boozer, realising what was happening, was beating his way to a spot immediately underneath the bucket.

'No time to go back,' muttered Lavering. 'But you're not going to drown, old chap. Hang on!'

He managed to get his two calves intertwined with the cable where it was attached to the bucket in two places, and then, leaning backwards, he began to reach down with his two hands. One strand of the wire slipped and gave him a fright, but his hands were now groping only a few inches above the dog's neck. Boozer tried to raise his forward parts out of the water, and Lavering took the opportunity to let everything go in an all-out final effort. The fingers of his right hand touched Boozer's collar. The next moment two fingers were under it, and Boozer, half drowned, and half-strangled, was hoisted from the water. Lavering did an inelegant upward bend, bumped his head against the wall, but finally managed to regain an upright position with Boozer safely in his arms.

'Phew!' he ejaculated.

Boozer was laving his face with his long tongue in an attempt to express his gratitude.

'That's not where it hurts,' said Lavering, as he rubbed the back of his scalp. 'Get down into the bucket and stay quiet. We're going up to terra firma. Hey, George! George!'

'Got him, Jerry?'

George's voice was clearer this time, and looking up, Lavering saw why. Outlined against the dark sky close to the edge of the round hole was a human head. George had evidently crawled over the edge of the pit and was clinging to the cross-bar of the machinery.

'Haul away!' shouted Lavering.

There was a slight pause, and then the bucket commenced to ascend. It went very slowly, turning in half-circles all the time. As it reached the old wooden platform, Lavering saw something about a foot from the end of the structure. He reached out and picked it up. To his surprise it was a half-smoked cigarette!

8

George, with beads of perspiration standing out on his forehead, gave a lusty cheer as Lavering's head came to view, followed by the battered bucket, from which Boozer's wet muzzle projected.

'You — you've got him!' cried Tessa excitedly. 'Oh, how marvellous!'

'Marvellous or not, continue to hang on to that handle until I climb out of this contraption,' said Lavering. 'Steady!'

Getting out with his shivering encumbrance was not an easy matter, but at last he and Boozer were safely ashore, and George hooked up the empty bucket with a sigh of enormous relief.

'Jove, you gave us a fright,' he said. 'My knees are still trembling. Boozer, you scoundrel, it was all your fault.'

Boozer gave himself a terrific shake, and sprayed water all over Tessa, who showed her instant forgiveness by hugging him.

'It wasn't your fault, Boozer,' she crooned. 'It was the fault of stupid people who leave bottomless holes in their gardens for anyone to fall into. It might have been me.'

'Yes,' said George. 'You chase enough hares. I thought you said the cable wasn't long enough, Jerry?'

'It wasn't. I had to do a circus act. That reminds me.'

He rolled up his right trouser leg, and displayed a tremendous abrasion of the skin on the inside.

'Oh!' ejaculated Tessa. 'You poor thing. It must hurt terribly.'

'Oh no. I'll do something about it presently. Also I mean to get a fence round that ghastly pit.'

'About time, too,' said Tessa. 'It must have been awful down there.'

'Interesting. Near the bottom there's a place to get off, and a gallery running into the mine proper. Oh yes, that reminds me. I found a curious thing on the platform which runs into the gallery. This.'

He took the half-smoked cigarette from

his pocket, and showed it to George.

'Why curious?' asked George. 'Anyone could have thrown it into the shaft.'

'But in the position where I found it it couldn't have been thrown in from the top.'

'Why not?'

'It was well inside the entrance to the gallery. I had to reach out to retrieve it.'

'But how else could it have got there?'

'I don't know. That is what puzzles me. Look at it. The paper is clean and dry. It can't have been there longer than a few days.'

'Is this land yours?' asked George.

'Yes. The Nancrannon boundary runs right up to the stone walls in this direction.'

'H'm! It is a bit queer,' agreed George. 'I suppose we have to hump all these tools back?'

'We have.'

The two men carried the tools between them, and when they were near the house, Zillah was seen beckoning them from the terrace.

'What a girl!' said George. 'Better leave

that pit open, Jerry. I might want to push her down it one dirty night.'

Lavering approached the gesticulating girl.

'What is it?' he asked shortly.

'Parson be 'era,' she said. 'What's 'e want?'

'Why didn't you ask him?' replied Lavering, sweetly.

'Oh I did, but he only smiled, so I comed to see where yu was. Don' 'e ask him to lunch. Us be more'n enough already.'

Lavering sighed as he laid down the tools he was carrying. Clearly nothing could be done with Zillah, unless one had recourse to the whipping-block or the village stocks.

'I'll come,' he said. 'Zillah, your face is awful.'

'What be wrong with my face?' she demanded.

'There's soot all over it.'

'Oh that,' she replied, and wiped her face on her apron. 'Lookee — if Parson says anything about me he's a liar.'

With this she pranced off.

'Social call?' asked George.

'I expect so. Would you like to meet him?'

'I don't think so,' replied George. 'I'm covered with grease, and had better get these back. Tessa certainly can't face him in her half-naked state.'

'Half naked yourself!' retorted Tessa. 'Anyhow, I could change into my crinoline. But no, I'll wash Boozer instead. Tell him we're Plymouth Brethren, and then he won't expect us to go to church.'

Lavering passed into the house, and found his visitor sitting in the hall. He was a man of about sixty years of age, with a pair of remarkably blue eyes, and an amazing crop of curly grey hair. Up to that moment, Lavering had failed to recall him, but as the Rector rose to greet him he remembered that very fine face — even the amused smile which lighted up the features.

'Remember me, Mr. Lavering?' he asked.

'Yes, but only at this moment. I find that with so many things here. Seeing them again unlocks another door. But I'm afraid I'm not so good when it comes to names.'

'Mine is Carmichael.'

'That strikes no chord of memory.'

'Why should it?' laughed the Rector. 'So you are the little boy who used to ride the pony so well?'

'Did I? Nobody else ever told me that. But do come into the lounge, and excuse my appearance. I've been doing a job of work, and wasn't prepared for visitors.'

On entering the lounge, the Rector cast a quick glance round the room, before he sat down in the high-backed needlework chair.

'Remarkable,' he said. 'Not a thing changed in twenty years. It was always an exceptionally pleasant room. When your parents were in residence it was my pleasure to call every Wednesday and have tea with them. You should remember that.'

'I am beginning to remember.'

'Your dear mother used to play the piano afterwards — at my request. She played Bach most beautifully. Other works, too, but Bach has always been my consuming passion. How the latter part of one's life scurries on. In youth a year seems an eternity, but in old age it is like the turning of a page — a rather dull page. But first of all I should offer you my condolences.'

'Thank you, sir,' said Lavering.

'Your father was a staunch friend of the church. It was with the deepest regret that I heard of his passing. Then I heard that you were here again, and I resolved to present myself.'

'I'm very pleased to see you. Perhaps you don't know that until recently I have been in western Canada for over seven years?'

'No. But I often wondered why you and your father never visited the place. It seemed such a waste of a lovely old house. Is it your intention to live here?'

Lavering shook his head slowly.

'A pity. I had rather hoped you would. So many Laverings were born here. Your father, even after he had gone to live at Hartford, spent every summer here, until — .'

'Until my mother died?'

'Yes. After that he never came back. I always thought that was a mistake.'

'In what way?'

'He had suffered a terrible blow. His one idea was to get away from the scene of the tragedy. But he always meant to come back one day, and for that reason he refused to move a single article of furniture, or to consider offers to purchase the place. He wrote me a few letters — all in the same vein. He had let an unreasoning fear undo his resolution. What he feared was a vivid mental reconstruction of the tragedy which had shaken him to his foundations. He thought he would see her again exactly as she had been, in the surroundings which she had loved so much. He believed that it was more than he could stand — that escapism was preferable. I think he was wrong.'

'I know so little about it,' said Lavering. 'All I can recall is a dreadful awakening to a world in which my mother moved no more. I was told she had gone away — a long distance, and then hustled off to Hartford. In time I realised that my mother would never come back from that 'long journey.' But my father was silent about it all, and the servants were no more communicative. I believed that she had died and been buried here, but recently I overheard something which I have had no opportunity to check. It was that my mother had been drowned.'

The Rector nodded his head slowly.

'Was she buried here?'

'No. Her body was never recovered. The circumstances were inexpressibly tragic. Your father had been called back to Hartford on a matter of business. He left by car early in the morning, and his intention was to spend the night at Hartford and to return here the following day. That evening, after you had been put to bed, your mother took out the motor boat. Poltimore saw her leave, and was very anxious because it was clear to him that a storm was brewing. She never returned, but on the following day the empty boat was found washed up on Hangman's Beach.'

'I — I suppose there was some sort of inquiry?'

'Oh yes. It was assumed that your mother had been washed overboard by a big wave.'

'But why did she take out the boat alone, when a storm was brewing?'

'Perhaps she didn't know. Perhaps she over-rated her ability to deal with the conditions.'

Lavering was silent for a few moments, as he let his mind dwell on these new facts. He could not help feeling that there was much which needed explaining. Why had his mother taken out the boat late in the evening? Where had she been going? Why had her body never been found? Why had the boat remained afloat afterwards?

'Curious that I should have been kept in ignorance of these things, when so many other people know about them,' he ruminated. 'I suppose Zillah has built her ghost-story on that tragedy?'

'Zillah's always seeing pixies,' laughed the Rector. 'I hope she is attending to your comfort.'

'She's better than no one at all, but we have to put up with a great deal. One rebuke and she'd start throwing the crockery about. She's already walked out once, but came back again after her father had reprimanded her. I can remember Poltimore vaguely, but I can't recall Mrs. Poltimore.'

'Poltimore was married after you left here. His wife ran away a year afterwards, leaving him with the baby on his hands. The girl takes after her mother, who was the wildest creature I have ever known. Don't you remember the Zaffery family?'

'Zaffery! Wait a moment.'

'There were two boys slightly older than you, and a witch of a girl older still. She was Zillah the first, and she caused enough trouble round here. Old Zaffery had earrings and was as swarthy as a Spaniard. He bought wild ponies and broke them in. Some went to the mines, others he sold as riding ponies. Your own pony was bought from him, and I remember that he got a ridiculous price from your father.'

'Yes, of course. The two sons had biblical names — Seth and — .'

'Ezra,' put in the Rector with an amused smile.

'I used to be fascinated by their brown skins. They used to come here selling things.'

'And stealing things. They've done that ever since. I've never known either of them do an honest day's work. They still live at Swanpool — the two sons I mean. Their father was lost at sea — about the same time as your mother. Two months ago their mother died, and they gave her an astonishing funeral. They gathered up a whole crowd of gipsies from Bodmin, and there was a procession comprising carts, caravans, men on ponies — such a collection as beggars the imagination. When it was all over there was much eating and drinking, and various people in the neighbourhood noticed a strange diminution in their live-stock.'

Lavering laughed at the innuendo.

'Did Zillah attend the celebrations?' he asked.

'No. Poltimore locked her in the house.

He's rather ashamed of his gipsy connections, and I'm not surprised after the way his wife behaved. How he ever came to get mixed up with them passes my comprehension, for Poltimore has always been an honest hard-working fellow. Well, I must get on my way. It's nice to see you here again.'

'It was good of you to look in. Are you sure you won't stay for lunch?'

The Rector seemed to hesitate for a moment, and Lavering feared he was going to accept, in which case he foresaw a spot of bother with Zillah, but finally he shook his head, and added that his appointments prevented it. So Lavering saw him off the premises, and then went to see where George and Tessa were hiding. They were sunning themselves in an alcove behind the summerhouse.

'Has he gone?' asked George.

'Yes. He's really extremely nice. You'd like him.'

'Socially, but not professionally,' replied George.

'Have you a grudge against religion?'

'Oh, Jerry, don't start him on that,'

pleaded Tessa. 'He's got a terrible bee in his bonnet.'

'I'm not irreligious,' growled George. 'But I can't just stand the Church's interpretation of Christianity. It just drives me mad, and when I go to church I come away feeling a worse sort of fellow than when I went in.'

'Who's fault is that?' demanded Tessa.

'Don't interrupt,' said George. 'What was I saying?'

'You were trying to start an argument,' said Tessa. 'It's far too hot to argue, even about something on which you are qualified to argue. Jerry, darling, is it nearly lunch time?'

9

Poltimore paid Lavering a visit that evening. He brought with him two magnificent lobsters straight out of the sea, and apparently the chief object of his visit was to know how his incredible daughter was behaving.

'She's doing quite well at the moment,' replied Lavering. 'But she's rather like a volcano. You never know when she'll go off with a bang and a lot of smoke.'

'Aye, she's like her mother,' muttered Poltimore.

'Temperamentally?'

'In looks as well. But the bad blood is on the Zaffery side. They're Spaniards — the whole lot of 'em. Maybe their forbears came over with the Armada, and got stranded here when Drake set light to their ships, and saved old England.'

'Zaffery doesn't sound Spanish.'

'As for that, I don't know, but I do know a tarbrush when I see it. Zillah's been a great trial to me. It's a hard thing to say, but if some young fellow came and took her off my hands, I'd be grateful to him. She's more'n I can manage.'

'You seemed to manage her very well the other night — when she ran away from us.'

'So the slut told you? I might have known she would. Yes, I leathered her a bit, but it hurt me more than it did her, and that's the sober truth. The names she called me! I don't mind a bit of foul language when it comes from working men. They don't mean anything by it. But Zillah's different. That tongue of hers can wound a man. She knows the soft spots, and she jabs at them until a man sees red. What would you do with a daughter like that, Mr. Lavering?'

'Probably the same as you did.'

'Ah, but it doesn't do any good,' sighed Poltimore. 'She likes being strapped. She howls and swears, but she likes it. Truly I think she's got the Devil in her.'

'Is her mother still alive?'

'Aye — somewhere,' Poltimore's mouth grew hard. 'She went off with one of her own kind, soon after Zillah was born, and left the child on my hands as if it was no more'n a bit of useless baggage. Shows how a man who takes a pride in his commonsense can make a fool of himself when it comes to a pretty face.'

'Does Zillah know all about that?' asked Lavering.

'Know!' Poltimore laughed bitterly. 'There's nothing she doesn't know when it comes to dirt and beastliness. It pleases her to believe that she's not my daughter at all. That used to hurt a lot, but not so much now. She's made me a hard man, Mr. Lavering.'

'I don't think so,' replied Lavering, with a smile. 'Oh, Poltimore, you remember my mother, don't you?'

'As well as I remember my own, zur.'

'Do you remember — the night when she went off in the boat?'

Poltimore nodded his head gravely.

'Did you see her leave?'

'Aye. I spoke to her.'

'To warn her about the weather?'

'Surely. It was growing dark, and there was a lot of wind. I knowd we was in for dirty weather.'

'What — what did she say?'

'She just smiled confidently and said she wasn't scared of a bit of wind and sea. I said it wasn't just a 'bit' of weather that was coming up, but half a gale. She said she didn't intend to be out long.'

'Nothing else?'

Poltimore hesitated for a moment.

'Well?' asked Lavering.

'She said something I didn't rightly understand, zur.'

'What was it?'

'She said something about satisfying her curiosity. Then she laughed and was gone before I could ask her if she would like me to come and handle the boat for her.'

'Which way did she go?'

'Towards Trewith. I watched her until she had passed round the headland. Afterwards I grew afraid, and I hurried to my place and got out my boat. But it was no use. I had no motor in those days and the wind was wrong for my sails. I got home drenched to the skin, and the next day — .'

'I know,' said Lavering. 'But I didn't know until quite recently. Did the police question you?'

'They questioned everyone. They even tried to question you, but your father objected. They tried to make out that — .'

'That what?' asked Lavering, sharply.

'That it wasn't an accident.'

'You mean that she — she never meant to come back?'

'That's how I read it zur, and I wasn't the only one. The whole place was a stinking pit of gossip.'

'Go on,' pleaded Lavering. 'It can do no harm now. What was all this gossip about?'

'I'd make myself as dirty as some others to repeat it.'

'Not to me. I want to know the truth, because all my life — since then — I've known there was much that was being withheld. What did they say against my mother?'

'It was to do with a young gentleman named Sutherland who was staying at the inn at Trewith.'

'What about him?'

'He painted pictures — always of the sea. Your mother — God rest her soul — became interested in him. That was natural enough because she was an artist, too.'

'Yes — yes.'

'It was said that Sutherland got into debt, and that your mother gave him money so that he could stay and go on painting.'

'I can believe that.'

'The servants were asked cruel questions.'

'About my father's reaction?'

'Aye. There was talk of a quarrel between your father and your mother — on the very day he left for Hartford. You see, Mr. Lavering, what it was they were hinting at?'

'Yes, I see — now.'

'Your father denied there was any quarrel. He said that he had spoken to your mother about Sutherland in a kindly way, advising her not to give him any more money because he knew that the young man wasn't using it to pay his bills, but to buy drink. The weeks went by and it all ended in smoke. Your father shut up the house. I thought he would come down again the next summer, but he never came. Nothing was touched — not a single alteration in twenty long year. There have been offers to buy it, but he wouldn't consider them. The garden got out of hand. My one day a week couldn't keep pace with the weeds and over-growth.'

'Of course not. You've done very well, Poltimore.'

'Thank 'ee zur.'

Here Zillah barged into the room, with a tray in her hands, full of polished silver. She gave a swift glance at her father, and then at Lavering.

'Talking about me, I bet,' she said.

'Mind your manners,' said her father, sternly.

'If everyone knew their manners as well as me there wouldn't be no ructions,' she retorted.

'Don't bang that silver down like that,' remonstrated her father. 'It's valuable.'

'Some people have silver, and some have gold, and some have diamonds,' she muttered. 'Others only have china — cheap cracked china. One of these days I'm going to have silver and gold — you'll see.'

'Hold your tongue,' snapped Poltimore.

'Yes, and diamonds!' she shouted. 'Uncle Seth said he'd give me a diamond if — .'

'If what?' growled Poltimore.

'Ah, that's telling.'

She pranced past her irate father, and stuck out her sharp little tongue as she reached the door, which she slammed behind her.

'I'm sorry, Mr. Lavering,' said Poltimore. 'Maybe I shouldn't have sent her here.'

'Oh, we're getting used to her. At times she can be quite amusing.'

'I don't find her very amusing. I told her I'd skin her if she didn't keep away from the Zafferys, but from what she said it's mighty clear she has been there. I don't like it, because they'll only add to her load of mischief. Well, I'm keeping you, zur. I'll be getting back to my place. Nothing you want me to do?'

'No thanks, Poltimore.'

Lavering was much exercised in his mind by what he had heard from Poltimore. He could imagine that situation quite well — his proud, overbearing father being compelled to answer questions that concerned his private life. The suggestion of suicide following a violent quarrel, in which jealousy and mistrust reared their ugly heads. To a stiff-necked aristocrat like his father the situation must have been intolerable. No wonder he had steadfastly declined to talk about the past with his only son. Perhaps, in his heart, he knew the innuendos were not mere malicious gossip. Perhaps — . But Lavering himself found a marked reluctance to continue along this line of speculation. It was as if someone had suddenly hurled a pot of black paint at an entrancing and beloved portrait.

George and Tessa came back from a walk along the cliff to find their host curiously self-centred. His monosyllabic replies to their enthusiastic comments were not in keeping with his usual manner, and Tessa gave her brother a sharp glance. When the meal was served up in most indecent haste by Zillah, who was in a frantic hurry to get home, Lavering took scarcely anything.

'What's all this?' asked Tessa. 'Off your oats?'

'A little. We had tea rather late. But don't worry about me.'

Boozer slunk into the room, and sprawled out at the feet of his master. Lavering did not notice him until his foot touched the obstruction.

'Why Boozer!' he said. 'You certainly have had a spring clean. Good work, Tessa!'

'He needed it,' replied Tessa. 'No dog ever had such an aptitude for picking up dirt. He oughtn't to come in here. He's still damp.'

Lavering reached down and fondled Boozer's neck.

'Oh no, he's quite dry,' he said. 'What do you want, you old scoundrel — a walk?'

Boozer cocked his ears.

'If he doesn't know his own name he knows what walk means,' said Lavering. 'I think I'll give him a run. You two carry on.'

'Oh, but Jerry — !' expostulated George.

'You dare not leave that big jelly untouched, or Zillah will imagine we suspect arsenic. A walk will do me good. Come on, Boozer. We'll give that mine shaft a wide berth.'

Tessa looked at her brother as Lavering went out, with Boozer scampering ahead of him, and raising his voice.

'What's wrong?' she asked.

'Nothing. Why should anything be wrong?'

'Pass the jelly and pull your wits together. Jerry's all upset about something.'

'Easy!' said George. 'You'll burst if you eat all that.'

'I'm not likely to do anything so unpleasant. Help yourself, or that idiot girl will come and clear it away. Poor Jerry!'

'Poor Jerry my foot! I'd give something to be in his place. He must be worth hundreds of thousands of quids. That family has always had tons of money, and here's old Jerry — the last of the Laverings — owning the whole works. Good Lord, it doesn't seem long ago that he used to borrow half-crowns from me, while he told a usually unsuccessful tale of woe to old man Lavering. He was terribly tight.'

'Who was tight?'

'Tight with money, I mean.'

'That wasn't the only thing he was tight with. Don't sit like a sentry over that jelly, or — .'

Her worst fears were realised as Zillah came into the room like a cyclone, with a large tray in her hands.

'Finished?' she asked.

'No!' said Tessa. 'Emphatically no. Why don't you wait until we ring the bell?'

'I hate bells. I've got to clear the table.'

'Oh no you haven't. You'll just wait until we're ready.'

'I won't wait for nobody. It's already after my time for going home.'

Zillah suddenly seized the jelly and whisked it off the table. This was too much for Tessa, who stood up and seized the other side of the dish on which the truncated jelly was doing a rumba.

'Let go,' she said.

Zillah tugged and then let go suddenly with most unfortunate results. The jelly slid off the dish and finished up in George's ample lap. Zillah's anger vanished in a twinkling. She put her hands on her hips and burst into uncontrollable laughter. But the next moment the laugh was stilled on her lips, for Tessa dealt her a stinging blow on the cheek, and showed every intention of following it up.

'Tessa!' cried George, as he spilled the jelly on to the carpet.

'You shut up!' said Tessa. 'I'll deal with this slut!'

Zillah, with her hand to her red cheek, took two steps backward, and then turned and ran for it.

'My God!' moaned George, 'You've done it again.'

10

Lavering's 'stroll' with Boozer had developed into a major exercise. With no objective in view he had rounded the cove and climbed by the cliff path to the big western spur of gaunt rock which rose to some nine hundred feet above the sea, and then descended in gentle slopes to another cove which he remembered as being the place where Poltimore lived. In the gloaming he could see Poltimore's queer cottage wedged between two stark rocks on the western side of the inlet, and the zig-zag path which gave access to a little sandy beach immediately below. He struck across the rear of the inlet, and mounted the opposing slope. Two miles further on was Swanpool, the home of the Zafferys. It lay on the side of a freshwater pool, formed by a small rivulet, and was an amazing place. Half of it was of local rock, cut in irregular blocks, and cemented together. The other half was timber, and did not conform in any way with the main architectural design. The stone-built portion was slated, but the wooden structure had a colossal covering of rough thatch. On the landward side there were sundry outbuildings — all leaning at artistic angles, and propped against the sea winds. There were a couple of meadows, enclosed by walls built of low rock, and in these Lavering could see a number of ponies grazing.

The pool itself was as still as a mirror, and made a striking contrast to the heavy movement of the sea. It was about two acres in area, and part of it was covered with high rushes, topped by brown and black velvety plumes. Seen in the soft evening light the whole setting was impressive and romantic. As he stood and watched, Lavering saw a pair of swans emerge from the rushes, followed by six cygnets whose dull grey plumage enhanced the virgin whiteness of the parent birds. His mother had painted that scene, too.

Beyond Swanpool the firm line of the cliff became broken. Tremendous erosion had driven deep alleys into the rocky bastion, and up these the sea water foamed and boiled. It was giant's country, and Lavering rested here and let his thoughts reach out, while Boozer, apparently indefatigable, went scouting for anything that smelt.

The few red embers in the western sky began to die. Over the whole marvellous scene there came creeping the shadows of night. To Lavering it was all expressed not in colour but in music. Somewhere, deep within him he could resolve all those chromatic chords. Here he had been born. Here he was finding kinship with everything he saw. Here the wind, and sea, and rocks held a meaning for him, as no other place ever had — not even that little place in western Canada into which so much toil and so many hopes had been invested. But now he was aware of disturbances in the even flow of his emotions — a dissonance in the music. What had been revealed to him was ugly — ugly and painful. One could argue that the past was dead and buried — that man must move on with time to the new world. But what was time? It required but a few notes on a piano, a glimpse of a few deft strokes with a paintbrush on canvas to bring back all that was called 'dead' in the objective world, and to relive every experience in the subjective. Everything was here and now, unchanged and unchangeable.

In this mood he retraced his footsteps in the starlight, with Boozer, tired at last, panting at his heels. Overhead the vast arc of the Milky Way scattered its star-dust across the illimitable void, and slowly the moon pushed up through a low-lying curtain of mist, and swam clear in the sky. He stood for some moments watching the play of the sea in that long yellow beam from the eastern horizon.

'Jerry!'

The sudden cry startled him out of his dreams, and he swung round to see Tessa.

'You were so long gone,' she said. 'I thought I'd come out to make sure no one had kidnapped you.'

'How did you find me?'

'I did a bit of logic. What lover of nature could turn his back on a gorgeous sunset? Said I to myself, 'Jerry will go west.''

'You mean westward,' said Lavering with a laugh.

'Oh, Boozer,' she said, looking down at the puppy, who was panting like a steam engine. 'He's walked you to death — the brute!'

'He's had the time of his life. What's George doing?'

'He's found a book on tennis by Tilden, and is busy learning all the tricks of the game. Gosh, isn't the air good?'

'All ours, too.'

'Yes, miles of it. Oh yes, and here's a bit of bad news for you. Can you take it?'

'That depends. What is it?'

'Zillah has bunked again. There was a domestic crisis, and I — well I ceased to be a lady.'

'What did you do?'

'I slapped her face — good and hard.'

'Tessa!'

'I knew I should do it sooner or later. Don't ask me for the sordid details. She went off without washing up. George and I had to do it, to the accompaniment of

George's moans. How that man hates sticking his hands into anything but a till. Oh that's a good one!'

'I wonder if she will come back this time.'

'I don't think so.'

'Perhaps it's as well!'

'Aren't you saying that just to be nice?'

'Not at all. I really mean it. But let's get on, before George gets it into his head that we are now both lost.'

They were still two miles from Nancrannon, and for quite half that distance Lavering maintained almost complete silence, until Tessa grew tired of her vain attempt to make conversation.

'This is where I close down,' she said. 'Tell me if my hard breathing disturbs your thoughts.'

'I'm sorry, Tessa. But my thoughts to-night aren't very profitable.'

'Is that why you abandoned us?'

'Yes.'

'What's wrong, Jerry?' she asked earnestly.

'Poltimore pulled a skeleton out of the cupboard. It didn't look very nice.'

'Something you would rather not talk about?'

'Yes.'

'Then I can't help?'

'I'm afraid not, unless you have the power to undo the past.'

'You couldn't undo the past without undoing the whole universe. That sounds profound, but I didn't mean it to be. Isn't there something in that phrase of Browning's — 'God's in his heaven. All's well with the world!'?'

'Yes, but whose world? Hasn't each of us got his own little world? We start to build it the moment we draw breath. True, we may knock it into a new shape as we gain experience, but it still remains our personal world, full of the things which we ourselves create. I said I wouldn't talk about it, but I will. Tessa, I wonder if you can possibly realise just what my mother meant to me?'

'I had a mother, too, you know, Jerry.'

'But you were different. You didn't lose her as I lost mine — at a time when you were tied so closely to her that it seemed like one life rather than two. My closeness to her — my veneration of her — was increased a hundredfold by my father's strange coldness. It wasn't a cruel deliberate coldness, but something he couldn't help. I believe he loved her in his own fashion, but it was the love which one might have for a beautiful soulless possession. I believe he gave her nothing but a sense of the dignity of her position as a Lavering — the mother of his son — another damned Lavering.'

'Jerry!'

'We've been a damned lot, Tessa. I've been looking up records. Between the whole crowd of us I think we have broken most of the commandments. All that wealth which came down to me is tainted. The solicitor sent me some figures yesterday. He expected me to be pleased, for the estate is in even better condition than he expected. But instead of rows of figures I saw slave ships, shady company flotation, rows of terrible hovels in a London slum. That's my inheritance — the blood and sweat and sin of human beings. But I had another inheritance, too. It lay in the memory of my mother

— a memory so untainted by anything ugly or 'earthy,' that it became a living poem. It was like a suit of armour which I put on when things were not going too well, and I looked like getting hurt. Does all this sound nonsense to you?'

'No. I think I understand.'

'I knew there was something strange about my mother's death. It was so sudden, and in all the years that have passed my father made no reference to it. Then, only a little while ago, I learned that she had been drowned.'

'Yes, I know that. George told me.'

'There's something else. The Rector's reticence about the whole matter aroused my suspicion. Then Poltimore added a bit more to the drab story. There was a quarrel between my mother and my father. It concerned her friendship with a young man — a painter who was staying at the inn. That night she went off in the boat, when a storm was brewing. She went off and never came back. Only the boat was found — empty on a patch of sand. That fact suggested something more than an accident.'

Tessa stopped and stared into his face. 'Oh, Jerry, you don't mean — that she — ?'

'Doesn't it explain everything? Isn't history full of that sort of drama? All the essential ingredients are present in this affair. Secret meetings, suspicion, jealousy, the accusation, and then that way out. Everyone knew it except myself. I was too young to understand — until now.'

Tessa could not miss the note of bitterness in his voice, nor the tense rigidity of his features.

'Are you sure you do understand — even now?' she asked.

'I understand all I want to understand.'

'But Jerry, what can you know of the real inner story. Your mother may have got something from that young painter which no one else could give her. There's a community bond between artists. They understand each other as no one else can understand them. They live in a different sort of world. Mightn't your mother's interest in this man have sprung from the desire to help him carry on with his work? She might have realised he had genius. She might have known that he was deeply discouraged, and on the verge of giving up the battle. If she — if she finally acted as you think, it might have been because someone's trust in her had wavered.'

'Does that make a romance of it?' he asked. 'It's nice of you to try and wipe off the smears. I appreciate the effort.'

'No you don't,' she replied. 'You're not even listening. I thought my brother was easily the most pig-headed man in the world, but I was wrong.'

'Why am I pig-headed?'

'Because ever since we came down here you have lived in the past. All you care about is what happened here twenty years ago. To-day and to-morrow leave you stone cold. You should be happy, but you're not. In short, Jerry, you're just a damned fool.'

Lavering was so astonished by this outburst that he stopped dead. But Tessa strode on faster than ever, and then began to run.

'Tessa!' he called. 'Tessa!'

His cry went unheeded, and very soon Tessa was out of sight.

'Queer girl!' he confided to Boozer. 'Don't ever get mixed up with women, old boy. They're a disturbing element.'

11

With his widowed mother recently dead, Seth Zaffery was now master of the strange house at Swanpool, and this appealed to his enormous vanity, for his mother had been the kind of woman who loved to rule, even if her domain was restricted to a ramshackle house on a few acres of Cornish foreshore. Seth, having inherited the property, half-a-dozen ponies, a weird assortment of furniture, two boats, and a bit of money, had given her what he called a 'slap-up' funeral, which included a procession a hundred yards long, comprised of every conceivable contraption on wheels, and even horsemen, gathered from heaven knows where.

Neither Seth nor his younger brother, Ezra, had ever loved 'Mother Zaffery,' in whose make-up there had been a strong religious streak, and who, after the death of her husband, had endeavoured to inculcate a sense of moral values into them, and their elder sister, with no success at all. Where she had come from they did not know, nor did they greatly care. What was obvious was that she was not of their blood. For them life was a smash and grab business. They respected neither persons nor property, any more than had their father, who could always be relied upon to find a horse when he needed one, or a fowl to shove into the family pot. The boundaries of Swanpool itself had been pushed out almost annually, a few yards at a time, until it enclosed quite a lot of land which had never been in the original deeds and titles.

How and when Swanpool had been acquired by the Zafferys was a mystery which went back a long way. Through centuries there had always been a Zaffery at Swanpool, and Seth's father's claim that his forebears came from Spain had much to support it. In his children there was evidence of Spanish blood. They had inherited nothing from their English mother, and never regretted it. Seth and his brother had much in common, but physically were very different. Seth was tall and angular, but Ezra was short and thick-set. Both could be gay when business was good, and both could be vicious when the wind of good fortune was set against them. They would buy anything which promised a profit, and lift any unattached article which appealed to their incurable acquisitiveness. Like their dead father they were good seamen, and well-versed in the ways of the sea, and the vagaries of the weather. At the worst there was always the sea to fall back upon. One could not starve while fish swam and one had a boat, and knew how to use it. At times they even preferred this way of life — days when the sun poured down on the blue water, and Ezra could take out his guitar and play it while the incredibly stupid denizens of the deep caught themselves on the long traces which they laid. Then, later, Seth's barefooted wife, Hazel, would cook the best of the fish in wine, and the smell of fish and garlic would mingle with the free wind, and Seth and Ezra would get as drunk as their liquid stocks would permit.

On this particular evening, Seth and his brother were in the large, barnlike, draughty sitting room, drinking copious cups of black coffee, into which they tipped abundant sugar. Seth still wore his seaboots, for he had been out laying lobster pots, but Ezra wore a pair of wide corduroy trousers, kept in place by a black sash, and surmounted by a blousey sort of shirt of pea-green colour. There had always been something feminine in Ezra in his love for bright colours, and frills. Unlike Seth, he hated dirt of any kind, and he kept his hands as clean as any doctor's. When playing his guitar he was wont to regard his immaculate hands with such obvious pleasure as to cause Seth to scowl his contempt for such girlish vanity.

Warm as the evening was a peat fire was glowing on the wide stone hearth, radiating more heat over the wide room. The aroma of this mingled with the tobacco and cigarette smoke would have been insufferable to most human beings but these two loved that sort of atmosphere. Indeed, it pervaded the whole house, and seemed in keeping with its amazing collection of junk.

'Time Bolling was here,' growled Seth, as he knocked his pipe out on the leg of the huge mahogany table. 'He's always late, no matter what time he says.'

'That clock's fast,' said Ezra, pouring himself out yet another cup of half-cold coffee. 'Ten minutes at least.'

'It still makes him half-an-hour late,' snarled Seth. 'I think he's losing his nerve.'

'Not him,' said Ezra, regarding his finger-nails. 'He's got nerve enough for ten men. He's holding out on us. Thinks he can wring more money out of us. He'll come and tell us all the difficulties — like he did last time. Seth, I don't trust him.'

'Do you think I trust him?' asked Seth, half closing his dark eyes.

'Then why work with him?'

'Because there was no one else. Without him we couldn't have made any progress at all. He got the — .'

He stopped suddenly and listened, and then turned his head to his brother again.

'I thought it was the old swine himself,' he mumbled. 'It's no use, Ezra, we've got to trust him. Things have gone too far to start making changes. What's all that damned noise?'

It came from the stone-built part of the rambling house, and now the two men could plainly hear high-pitched voices in the throes of tremendous altercation. Seth stood up and advanced with heavy tread towards the communicating door. Before he could reach it it was flung open, and Zillah came to view, her hair tangled and her breasts heaving tumultuously.

'It's Hazel,' she said. 'Tried to keep me out. I'm a member of the fam'ly, ain't I? She's nobody — only your wife. My mother was your own sister. She's not civ'lised — don't even wear shoes. I stamped on her ugly toes I did, and I'll do it again fifty times if she tries to keep me out. See?'

Seth looked his irate niece up and down, and then told her to shut the door, which she did with some gusto.

'Now why do you come here turning the house upside down?' he asked.

'I've run away.'

'Run away from whom?' asked Ezra, smoothing his black hair down with his right hand.

'My old man, of course. I hate him. I've always hated him. Now I've come to live here.'

'That was thoughtful of you, Zillah,' said Seth. 'Quite a compliment, too.'

'I like this house,' said Zillah, looking round. 'I like you too, Uncle Seth, and you Uncle Ezra.'

'And your aunt?'

'Not her. She's a cow. But I can manage her.'

'That's more than I can,' replied Seth. 'And why have you run away from your father?'

'He sent me to work at Nancrannon, just as if I wasn't born to be something better than a dish-washer. I runned away once before, but he belted me and sent me back again. To-night that girl up there hit me in the face.'

'What girl?'

'Her they call Tessa, who's staying there with her brother. He's a nice man is

Mister George, but she's a b — .'

Seth guffawed his amusement. He could always get entertainment out of his fire-brand niece. She was a tonic after his sour wife and his glum brother.

'You're a caution,' he said. 'Just like your mother. She was a bit of a beauty too — like you. She ran away, too, with a better man than Mr. Poltimore, who was never anything better than a butler, who bowed and scraped to the Laverings. What is young Mr. Lavering like these days?'

'He's big and very good-looking.'

'And very rich.'

'Is he?'

'Of course he is. Worth hundreds of thousands of pounds. I must call and see him one of these days. Maybe he'd like to buy a pony.'

'Maybe he wouldn't,' said Ezra. 'A man with all that money would buy a hunter.'

'You know everything,' snapped Seth. 'His father bought our ponies so why shouldn't he?'

'His father had a young son, and he hasn't.'

'Oh, shut up! Now, my girl, what am I going to do about you?'

'Let me live here. I've brought some things in a trunk.'

'Where are they?'

'Hazel kicked the trunk outside. That's why I trod on her toes. I'd like that room upstairs — the one that's got the butterfly picture over the fireplace.'

'They're not butterflies. They're dead moths,' grunted Ezra. 'But that doesn't matter. You can't stay.'

'You shut yer mouth,' snapped Zillah. 'Seth is master here, and he'll let me stay — won't you Seth?'

'I can't,' said Seth. 'You're not of age. Your father can come and take you away at any moment.'

'He doesn't know where I am.'

'It won't take him long to guess.'

'You can hide me in the barn — in the hayloft.'

Seth smiled at her stupidity, and then the door opened and Hazel entered. She was a wide-hipped woman, and as untidy as a woman could be from her straggling black hair to her open blouse which displayed a large proportion of her upper anatomy. She halted a few yards from the group and pointed a finger at Zillah.

'Get that slut out of here,' she said.

'Who you calling slut?' demanded Zillah. 'Oh, you've put on slippers. Well, I can tread on them just as well, and I — .'

'Stop!' cried Seth. 'Between the pair of you you'll drive me mad. Damn all women — everywhere.'

'Damn yerself,' retorted Zillah. 'Are you afraid of that?'

Her contemptuous glance at Hazel produced unexpected results. Hazel suddenly produced a short, black-handled knife.

'I won't have her in this house,' she said. 'She's evil. Not one night will she stay here — .'

She made to advance on Zillah, who showed not the slightest sign of fear, but Seth put an end to it by interposing himself between the two women.

'Give me that knife, Hazel,' he said. 'She's not staying. Give me that knife.'

Hazel reluctantly yielded up the ugly weapon. Seth slipped it into his pocket and swung round on Zillah.

'Get your bag and go back,' he said.

'What!' squealed Zillah. 'You can't do that.'

'I can. I don't want your father coming here and making a scene. He could bring the police if he wanted to, and I don't like the police.'

'No, you wouldn't,' sneered Zillah. 'Well, I'm not going back to wash any more dishes. I've got all the things I like, and I'm going to London.'

'You're crazy.'

'And I want some money,' shouted Zillah. 'Lots of money.'

'You'll get no money out of me.'

'We've got no money to spare,' put in Ezra.

'Oh yes you have — in the leather bag, inside the coffee pot.'

Hazel shot her husband a swift glance, and he looked a trifle embarrassed.

'It's all gone,' he said.

Zillah laughed impishly for a moment, but grew deadly serious as she saw the three tense hard faces of her relatives.

'Twenty pounds,' she said. 'You can sell

Folly to Mr. Lavering and get it back again. He's so rich he might even pay thirty.'

'You're mad. Get out, before I put you out,' snarled Seth, now thoroughly enraged.

'Don't you touch me,' said Zillah. 'I'm not so mad as you think. I know why old Sam Bollin comes here, and what he brings, and why you want it, and if I — .'

There came a banging on an outer door, and a robust voice asking if anyone was at home. Seth, whose eyes had been boring into Zillah, turned his gaze to his equally disturbed brother.

'That is Bollin,' he said. 'Hazel, get into the kitchen, and take Zillah with you.'

'I won't — .'

'Do as I tell you,' snapped Seth. 'I want to talk to her afterwards.'

'Do I get my twenty pounds?' asked Zillah.

'Perhaps. I'll think it over. Go with Hazel, and for God's sake don't start any more trouble. Go on. Hurry!'

'Hey, where's everybody?' bawled Bollin's stentorian voice.

'Ezra, go and let him in,' whispered Seth. 'Blast that girl! But we'll deal with her later.'

Ezra rose and hurried to the door. A minute or two later he came back with an enormous man, who sported a red beard, a reefer coat and a greasy peaked cap. He flung the cap on to a couch as he entered the room, and grimaced as Seth's glance swept him from head to foot.

'No, I haven't got it,' he said.

'So I see,' sneered Seth. 'You promise a lot and perform very little. You said — .'

'I know what I said,' snapped Bollin. 'But I can't produce rabbits out of a hat.'

'I don't want rabbits. Who's talking of rabbits?'

'Let's get to the point,' begged Ezra. 'What's the hitch?'

'Money,' replied Bollin. 'The man I got the last supply from is taking risks. If he were found out he'd lose his job.'

'So the dirty swine is holding out on you?' snarled Seth.

'Call it that if you like. But he wants five quid, and I can't move him.'

'Suppose I tell him to go to hell?'

Bollin shrugged his enormous shoulders.

'Can you afford to do that?' he asked. 'It's not easy for outside persons to lay their hands on that sort of stuff. Without it we're stuck, ain't we?'

Seth didn't reply to this, but Ezra nodded his head.

'Well, then,' said Bollin. 'You've no choice in the matter.'

'Haven't I?' asked Seth. 'I could drop the idea. Maybe the whole thing is a fake.'

'Fake!' ejaculated Ezra. 'You know it's no fake. The old lady knew what she was talking about.'

'I wonder,' mused Seth. 'When people are dying they get strange ideas.'

'You believed it then,' said Ezra. 'Why start throwing doubts on it now?'

'It's costing a lot of money, and taking a lot of time. Money isn't too plentiful.'

'All the more reason why we should go right ahead. It would be crazy to give up now.'

'Who's giving up?'

'You are. You're all excited until it comes to paying out a bit of cash. Better let me handle the finances. I've got a better head for it than you.'

Seth took a violent objection to this.

'You handle money!' he sneered. 'How much did you pay for that silly instrument? More than you earn here in a month.'

He jerked his thumb contemptuously to Ezra's guitar which was reclining in an old chair, and Ezra showed his dislike for this comment on his beloved instrument. Bollin, who had been filling his pipe from an enormous rubber pouch, regarded the two squabbling men with a quiet smile.

'It's up to you two,' he said. 'You won't get any further by throwing mud at each other. Better make up your minds.'

'Mine is made up,' said Ezra. 'My brother's sticky fingers are the trouble.'

'If yours were half as sticky we'd be better off,' retorted Seth.

'Well, five pounds isn't going to break you,' said Bollin.

'All right,' said Seth, resignedly. 'I'll get it. My God, what are you smoking in that pipe — seaweed?'

'I've smoked worse things than seaweed

in my time,' growled Bollin.

Seth left the room for a few minutes and then returned with a wash-leather bag, which was tied round the neck with an attached string. He undid the string, and took out a big roll of notes, from which he counted five. He put the bag into his trousers pocket and handed the five notes to Bollin.

'I want the stuff to-morrow,' he said. 'And I want enough to finish the job, because I'll pay out no more cash until I know for certain that this isn't a wild goose chase.'

Bollin blew out an enormous cloud of dark blue smoke, and watched its evolutions in the air.

'I'm not by nature an inquisitive chap,' he said. 'But I guess I'm being kept a bit in the dark over this.'

'If you're going to start holding out on me — ' roared Seth.

'Not me. I'm a patient sort of fellow. My cut's to come when you get through. That was understood, and I don't go back on a bargain. All the same I think it's time you put me wise on a few points.'

'Such as — ?' asked Seth.

'What's the game — the real game?'

'I told you,' replied Seth, with beetling brows.

'If you did I was dozing at the time. You told me you were after something valuable — but how valuable?'

'We don't know,' replied Seth. 'What does it matter anyway. You get a percentage.'

'Surely. But a percentage can be anything from a penny to a million quid. I'd like to have some idea of the size of what is coming to me.'

'I tell you we don't know,' said Seth, irritably. 'We're all in the same boat. Would I be spending all this money if I didn't feel certain it was worth it. You haven't spent a penny.'

'I've spent a lot of time and labour.'

'Yes — yes. I'm not trying to depreciate your help,' said Seth in a wheedling voice. 'But you've got to trust us.'

'That's true,' put in Ezra. 'This is something we can't talk about. But you'll come out all right.'

'I hope so,' replied Bollin. 'But a fellow

has to tread warily. D'you know who the mine belongs to?'

'Of course. Mr. Lavering.'

'Yes, young Mr. Lavering now that his father is dead. And he's right here on the spot.'

'I know,' muttered Seth.

'Calls for cautious action, don't it?'

'Of course. It always has.'

'Glad you see the point.'

'Only a fool wouldn't. Now you'd better get along, Bollin. Ezra and I have some business to discuss.'

'Okay.'

'Don't turn that money over until you've got what you want.'

Bollin laughed as he picked up his cap and jammed it down on his big head. Then he waved a hand and went out. Seth cursed him as the door slammed.

'There's a man I wouldn't trust two inches,' he said.

'Yet we have trusted him.'

'We had to get help, and we might have got worse. Now for that cunning little snake.'

'Zillah?'

'Yes. Get her in. Don't bully her.'

Ezra went to the communicating door and called Zillah's name. A few moments passed, and then Zillah came to view. Behind her came her outraged aunt.

'Remember what I told you,' she called.

'All right, Hazel,' replied Seth in a pleasant voice.

Zillah, quite sure of herself, came to the large table where Seth was sitting.

'Now listen,' said Seth. 'You can't stay here. Your damned father may turn up at any moment, and he hates us enough to go to the police. What were you saying when Sam Bollin arrived?'

'You know,' replied Zillah. 'If I have to go to London I want the twenty pounds.'

'Why should I give you twenty pounds, Zillah?'

'Because it would pay you to.'

'In what way?'

'When old mother Zaffery was dying I was here — remember? The old man was out fishing so I runned along.'

'Yes. What then?'

'You wouldn't let me see her.'

'She didn't like you. That's why.'

'I never liked her either. She was always quoting the scriptures and telling me about hell-fire. But I'd never seen anyone die so I crept upstairs. The door wasn't prop'ly closed, and I heard — .'

'You dirty little spy!' cried Seth. 'I've a mind to put you over my knee.'

'You can't frighten me,' retorted Zillah. 'You'd better give me the twenty pounds, or I'll make it twenty-five. If that clock's right I've only got twenty minutes to get to the railway junction, and it's over a mile.'

Seth looked at Ezra, and found his brother as depressed as he was himself. This half-wit niece of theirs had the cunning brain of a fox, and a hide like a cow. This chit of a girl held them at ransom. She listened at doors, eavesdropped on dying relatives. Yes, she was dangerous.

'Ten pounds,' he said.

'Twenty,' replied Zillah.

'Fifteen.'

'Twenty. You're not very clever, Uncle Seth, because in one minute the price

181

goes up. I've got a good business head I have.'

'Pay her, for God's sake,' groaned Ezra. 'Let's be rid of her.'

'All right,' choked Seth. 'Here, take your filthy money. Take it and go, and much good may it do you.'

He wrenched the bag from his pocket, opened it, drew out the rolled notes, and counted them in a voice that was thick with emotion and hate.

'Nineteen,' said Zillah. 'One more.'

He flung the last one at her. She rolled the whole lot together and thrust them down the neck of her blouse.

'Now I got to hurry,' she said. 'Us be a clever family — us Zafferys.'

12

Lavering had spent an uneasy night, for he regretted his passage of words with Tessa, who had gone to bed immediately upon reaching the house, without even a goodnight to her puzzled brother. Lavering explained as well as he was able, and placed himself in the wrong.

'I had a bad mood on me,' he said. 'It was too bad after her coming out to meet me. Sorry, George.'

'That's all right, old man,' replied George. 'I expect she scratched you with her sharp little claws. Of course she doesn't mean anything. It's just the way she's made.'

'It was entirely my fault. In any case she's my guest and I've shown myself to be a pretty rotten host. I'll have to put matters right in the morning. That reminds me. It looks as if we shan't have our sweet little Zillah in the morning.'

'Unless Poltimore can lay on the heavy

hand again. Tessa certainly packs a nasty slap. I've never seen anyone look more surprised than Zillah was. I've been reading a book on housekeeping.'

It was while Lavering was lying in bed wondering why his morning tea didn't arrive that he suddenly remembered the domestic crisis. He looked at his watch, and found it was half-past eight. Then he heard noises from downstairs, and concluded that Poltimore had again worked a miracle, although Zillah apparently wasn't serving any more bedside tea. He dressed in leisurely fashion, and finally went downstairs. The breakfast table was nicely laid, and from the kitchen came the smell of something in a frying pan. Opening the casement window he walked out into the garden. There was a heavy dew upon the roses and the lawn, and a slight mist hung over the cove. The spell of the place was no less potent in the morning light than under the moon. The great gulls soaring up the steep face of the distant cliff hurled their plaintive cries at him, bees plundering the flowers sang their interminable anthem — the joyous refrain of the honey-gatherers. Every-where the picture was perfect.

He turned in his perambulation of the long herbaceous border and saw Poltimore standing on the shallow terrace, obviously waiting for him.

'Hullo, Poltimore!' he said, as he drew nearer.

'Morning, zur. I comed to tell you that Zillah won't be coming here any more.'

'What!'

'She's run away.'

'When?'

'Last night. I wasn't in when she came home. When I did get back I found she had packed some of her things in a suitcase and gone. I thought at first that she had gone over to Swanpool, so I walked there and saw the Zafferys. But she wasn't there, and they said they hadn't seen her.'

'But I thought she had come this morning. I heard someone in the kitchen, and — . Wait a moment.'

He left Poltimore and hurried round the side of the house to the kitchen window. Inside he saw Tessa with her hands full of plates.

'Tessa!'

'Good morning!' she said calmly. 'I guessed Zillah wouldn't turn up so I turned to.'

'You — you should have called me.'

'Why? It was I who socked her. Breakfast is nearly ready. I've just called George.'

'I won't be long,' he gasped, and hurried back to Poltimore.

'Was it her?' asked Poltimore, clinging to the slightest shred of hope.

'No.'

'I thought not. She's gone all right. It's always been at the back of her mind. She never wanted to work here — or anywhere else for that matter. It's those film magazines that are to blame — leading young girls to think they can become 'stars' in a few weeks, and live in luxury for the rest of their lives. My cottage is full of the trash. I'm sorry, Mr. Lavering.'

'That's all right. You did your best for us, and it didn't work out. What will you do about Zillah?'

'I'll get her back somehow,' Poltimore

growled. 'I'll do my duty by her until she comes of age. After that she can go her own way.'

'But have you any idea where to find her?'

'No.'

'London's a big place.'

'Surely, but she can't have very much money. Maybe she'll write to me when she finds out that folks are not rushing at her.'

'I hope she will.'

'Thankee, Mr. Lavering, but how are you going to manage?'

'It will do us all good to shift for ourselves for a bit, but all the same if you should find anyone who can help us out, I'll be grateful.'

'I'll do my best.'

He touched his cap and went off at a brisk pace. Lavering went into the house, and ran into Tessa who had a jug of milk in one hand and a toast-rack in the other.

'That was Poltimore,' he said. 'Zillah has run away.'

'I'm not surprised. He's well rid of her. She'll never be any good.'

She placed the milk and toast-rack on the table, and began to check up everything.

'Ah, marmalade,' she said. 'I knew there was something else.'

'Tessa!'

She turned her head.

'I was a pig last night.'

'So was I,' she said. 'The moon got under our skins. Is that noise upstairs due to George's vocal organs or the water draining out of the bath?'

'It can't be the bath, because it's singing 'Love Me and The World is Mine'.'

'The drain-pipe can do that as well as George.'

'So I'm forgiven, Tessa?'

'There's nothing to forgive, Jerry,' replied Tessa in a very soft voice. 'Except me. I had no right to speak to you as I did. You're giving me the best time of my life, and all I do is criticise. George always said I had ants in my pants, which is a vulgar version of bees in one's bonnet.'

'Which isn't true.'

'I'm afraid it is, Jerry,' she replied solemnly. 'I'm the bossy sort of female. I want to manage everybody — you in particular.'

'Why me?' he asked with a smile.

'Because you look so big and unmanageable. Think how swelled-headed I should get if I could say, 'Jerry, close that door,' 'Jerry, come here,' 'Jerry, kiss my hand,' and get them all done.'

'Why not?' asked Lavering, and turned and shut the door. Then he came close to her and caught her right hand. It was a particularly shapely little hand, with an alluring dimple at the back of the thumb. Tessa tugged, but it was ineffective. Very solemnly, Lavering raised it to his lips and kissed it.

'Onions!' he said.

'Oh, you beast!'

'But I've always liked onions.'

'Jerry, you fool!'

'Yes, sometimes I think I am,' he said, seriously, relinquishing her hand slowly. 'I find it difficult to be really happy — to know what makes for happiness. For you it's easy.'

'Why do you think so?'

'Because you know the secret. I've watched you at times — opening invisible doors and letting joy and happiness flow in unimpeded. Somewhere at the back of your eyes there's a kind of radiance which I've only seen once before in my life — and that was very long ago.'

The door burst open and George sailed in. He gave one look at the laid table, and rubbed his hands.

'So she came after all,' he said. 'I'd have given five to one she wouldn't.'

'And you'd have won,' replied Lavering. 'This is Tessa's handiwork. Our late maid-of-all-work left us and her devoted parent last night, for fresh fields and pastures new!'

'My hat!' said George. 'Are you serious?'

'Quite. Poltimore came and told me a few minutes ago. Unless some fairy waves her wand and produces a working woman to come to our aid, I can foresee trouble.'

'Oh, Tessa can manage,' said George. 'She's quite good at that sort of thing when she's driven to it.'

'Who's going to drive me?' demanded Tessa.

'Oh, not me,' replied George. 'I'm on your side. Talk to her, Jerry. Make clear her duties in an emergency like this.'

'I know my duties,' replied Tessa. 'The first of them is to make you two dodgers develop a sense of independence and self-sufficiency. I'll let you off this morning, but after that, watch out.'

Tessa's culinary efforts were most successful, and the two men ate like starving creatures.

'Toss you to see who washes up, Jerry,' said George.

'No need,' put in Tessa. 'One washes and the other wipes.'

'What about lunch?'

Lavering settled the question of lunch by suggesting that they should go out in the car and have lunch in some place.

'That's an idea,' said George. 'Any objective in mind?'

'No, but there are dozens of lovely spots worth seeing. Get the map and work out a route that will bring us to a decent hotel round about lunch time.'

George lost no time in adopting this suggestion. He did the job most thoroughly, planning what promised to be a wonderful trip, which embraced numerous places off the beaten track, and later lunch at St. Ives. He was trying to plan an interesting way home when Tessa yelled 'Washers-up,' and brought a groan from his throat.

Later, when he proudly exhibited the results of his labour, Tessa pouted her lips, and looked quite disappointed.

'I wanted to go to Tintagel,' she said.

'Oh, everyone goes there,' argued George. 'The place will be packed with people — long queues of 'em. Besides, it's right off the route as I've planned it.'

'Change the route then,' said Tessa. 'Jerry, do you particularly want to explore farmyards and pig-styes?'

'Farmyards and pig-styes — !'

George was nearly incoherent. Tessa turned her appealing eyes to Lavering.

'All my life I've wanted to see Tintagel,' she said. 'King Arthur and his Knights of the Round Table, and Merlin's Cave.'

'They don't live there any longer,' said

George. 'Tessa, you can go to Tintagel another day.'

'I should like to go to-day. You and Jerry could do your explorations another day. There never was such a day as this. Say you want to see Tintagel, Jerry.'

'I do.'

'Of course he doesn't,' said George. 'It's just that *noblesse oblige* stuff. Tessa, I'm ashamed of you.'

'We can still finish up for lunch at St. Ives,' Tessa pointed out. 'Then you and Jerry can bog the car just as you planned.'

'Take her away,' pleaded George. 'Really, old man, you should put down a firm foot. It's the only way with women.'

They started half an hour later, with George at the wheel. Once having got himself in that desirable position he quickly recovered from his temporary frustration, and looked as pleased as a boy with his first toy engine.

'Literally sings,' he said.

'What does?' asked Tessa.

'This engine. Aren't you asleep yet?'

Tessa laughed as she stretched herself out in the comfortable back seat, and the car lifted itself over the hill-tops and brought to view at intervals vistas of incomparable beauty.

'If I were a man with homicidal tendencies I think I could cheerfully murder you for possession of this car, Jerry,' he said.

'You don't have to, George. I'll make you a present of it.'

'That would be a joke.'

'It's no joke. It's just what the perfect host does in some parts of the East. You admire something he possesses, and he is in honour bound to offer it to you.'

'Well, we're in the West — not the East.'

'It's yours all the same. Tessa bears witness.'

'Can't you two talk sense for a change,' pleaded Tessa.

'I am talking sense,' said Lavering. 'I've been wondering what I could give you as a souvenir to remember Nancrannon when I'm about five thousand miles away. George has solved my problem. You'll be able to drive him to the station every morning, Tessa.'

George laughed at the crazy idea.

'If I had a car like this my salary would scarcely pay for the petrol and tax,' he said.

'I can't help that. You've wished the thing on yourself. Now you'll have to dispose of Ethel, unless you are sentimental about her.'

George turned his head to gaze at his companion. He found him looking quite serious.

'Forget it, old man,' he said.

'I have. Now I've got to think of something for Tessa.'

'Are you making your will?' asked Tessa. 'If so, I'll have Nancrannon.'

Lavering laughed easily, and for a long time there was silence. Finally they drew near to Tintagel, and Tessa became very excited. She had seen pictures of the place, and had soaked herself with Arthurian legend.

'I hope I shan't be disappointed,' she said.

'You won't,' said Lavering. 'Not on a day like this. It's twenty years since I was here, but the impression it made upon me is as clear and fresh as if it were only yesterday. I can remember my mother telling me about Merlin and the arrival of the babe, as I gripped her hand almost in fear on the threshold of that old cave under the castle.'

'I know,' said Tessa. 'How does it go?'

'And then the two
Dropt to the cove, and watched the
    great sea fall,
Wave after wave, each mightier than
    the last,
Till last, a ninth one gathering half
    the deep,
And full of voices, slowly rose and
    plunged,
Roaring, and all the wave was in a
    flame;
And down the wave and in the wave
    was borne
A naked babe, and rode to Merlin's
    feet,
Who stoopt and caught the babe,
    and cried, 'The King!
Here is an heir for Usher!' '

Lavering turned his head round and stared at her in amazement.

'So you remembered all that?'

'It suddenly came to me.'

'She's got a memory like an elephant,' said George. 'Is that Mallory?'

'No — Tennyson,' replied Tessa. 'Oh, this is too marvellous. There's the castle. I can see it.'

'Crowds of tourists — just as I told you,' said George.

'We're tourists, too, and so we've got nothing to complain about,' retorted Tessa. 'Where are you going to park the car, Jerry?'

'Ask George,' said Lavering. 'It's his car.'

'Oh, give over, old man,' expostulated George. 'But I reckon it will be safer somewhere off the road. Some idiot is sure to crumple up a wing if you leave it in a car park.'

The Bentley was subsequently locked up and left, and from that moment Tessa's dream became a living reality. As the tide was out they visited the cove first, and entered Merlin's Cave. It was open at both ends, and its subdued light threw into brilliant contrast the sunlit sea outside. Tessa gripped Lavering's arm as she let her gaze range over the fantastic scene, and when she spoke it was in an awed whisper which went hissing away over the convolutions of the dark rock. From outside came the incessant thud of the great waves which pounded the beach.

'Not disappointed?' asked Lavering.

'Disappointed! Oh, Jerry, it's worth coming a million miles to see. I can see Merlin and Bleys standing just there, and the great wave sweeping — .'

'The poor child is psychic,' interrupted George. 'Still, I will say it's impressive.'

'That's very generous of you, George,' said Tessa.

Later they left the cave and made their way up the steps which led to the castle. Thrilling as the cave was it could not hope to compare with the view of the castle as seen from the goat track across the narrow neck of land which divided the ruins in twain, and when finally they opened a nailed door and stood on a grassy sward, surrounded by low turreted walls, Tessa was breathless from admiration and pent-up emotion. Wandering through the ruins they came at last to the level expanse at the summit of the headland. Here there were the remains of a small chapel, containing a huge block of stone reputed to be the original altar table. Near this dream-compelling spot they sat down, and let their gaze reach out to the incomparable coastline in both directions. Tessa's eyes were bright as she turned her head slightly towards Lavering.

'Thank you, Jerry,' she said. 'This I shall never forget.'

'I'm glad you like it.'

'You must like it even more, for you were born not far away.'

'That's true. To every man his particular desire. To me Cornwall is always home — the real home.'

'Yet you went to Canada.'

George gave her a sharp look, but Lavering did not seem to mind the remark.

'I had to,' he replied. 'My life was very

empty of certain things. Canada gave me some of those things.'

'Not all?' asked Tessa.

'Not all. Nothing can ever do that.'

'By Jove, I can see the car from here,' said George. 'That bright light is the sun on the headlamps.'

'That's right,' agreed Lavering.

'And there's a fellow prodding the front tyre with a stick. Silly ass! Why on earth does he want to do that. Infernal cheek!'

Lavering laughed at George's indignation.

'Now you're getting the property sense,' he said.

'Don't talk rubbish.'

'I'm not. You took that over when you wished the car on yourself. Owning valuable things has its drawbacks.'

'Now see here, old man, isn't that joke wearing a bit thin?'

'What joke? Don't you realise I am serious?'

'Of course not. People don't give away cars as if they were cigarettes.'

'You'll find they do. I don't want a car. I've got an old Ford in Canada. I saw wood with it.'

'How on earth can you saw wood with a motor car?' asked Tessa.

'With a driving belt placed round a brake drum, and the wheels jacked up. George will be able to supply you with logs all through the winter, Tessa.'

'I could slap you,' said Tessa.

'Because I gave George a car?'

'But — !'

'George can decline the gift if he really wants to, but I don't want him to do that. Soon I shall be back in Canada, and I'd like to think that George is taking you round a bit. I know you have Ethel, but Ethel's remaining life is short. The Bentley is taxed and insured for the rest of the year, so — .'

'But, Jerry,' interrupted George. 'I can't accept a thing like that. It's — well, it's half a fortune. Besides, you'll want it. You won't go back to Canada.'

'Why not?'

'It's not natural. Here you are with everything anyone could desire. What can Canada give you that can't be got here?'

'Certain things that you can't weigh on scales.'

'But you love this country. It's your real background — your inheritance.'

Lavering nodded but said no more, and Tessa gave George a look which said quite clearly that he wasn't to pursue the subject at the moment. A little later they wended their way back to the car.

'You should see Camelford and Dozmary Pool,' said Lavering, to Tessa. 'But we'll do those places another day. Now George, we just have time to get to St. Ives for lunch.'

'Do I drive?' asked George.

'Of course. I'll sit in the back and keep Tessa awake.'

13

The party enjoyed their lunch at St. Ives. The food was excellent and Lavering ordered champagne of the best vintage. The dining room of the hotel offered a delightful view over the small port, and it was pleasant to watch the activity in the little harbour as they sat and satisfied their needs.

'And now,' said George. 'Tessa having seen visions in dark caves, can I choose my own way home?'

'Can he, Tessa?' asked Lavering.

'I suppose so, but heaven help us.'

They were passing through the vestibule when Lavering was attracted to a painting on the wall. It was a very fine piece of work, and showed the small port emerging from a light summer mist, somewhere round about sunrise. Lavering peered at the artist's signature in the bottom corner. It was Austin Sutherland.

'Ready, old man?' asked George,

impatient to get back into the car.

'Er, yes — in a moment.'

The hotel manager seemed pleased that the picture was receiving admiration. He came forward and smiled.

'Nice, isn't it?' he said. 'I couldn't resist it. It was painted from the terrace just outside the dining room, early one morning. I mean it was started then.'

'Very fine,' replied Lavering, in a strange voice. 'So you met the artist?'

'Oh, yes. I know him very well. He lives here in fact. Not at the hotel. He has that nice blue villa up on the hill. The one with the wonderful hedge of fuchsias.'

'Mr. Austin Sutherland.'

'Yes. He exhibited at the Royal Academy last year.'

'I — I think I should like to meet him,' said Lavering.

'I'm sure he'd be pleased. He has some very fine pictures up there, and is making quite a name for himself, especially in the west country. He's a very modest, charming gentleman.'

The manager excused himself as some guests arrived, and then Lavering made a change of plan.

'I'm going to make a call, George,' he said. 'Do you feel like giving Tessa a run along the coast, and meeting me here in about an hour's time?'

'Why, of course. But can I take you to where you want to go?'

'Oh no. It will do me good to walk, and it isn't very far. I'm going to look at some pictures.'

'That's okay with us,' said George. 'See you here about half-past three.'

He watched them enter the car and drive off, and then he looked up at the blue villa on the hill behind the hotel. From where he stood he could see the brilliant display of fuchsias to which the manager had referred. The presence of many 'lights' in the roof gave away the profession of its owner. A few moments later he was taking what was obviously a short cut through the hotel grounds.

The villa, on being approached, lost none of its earlier appeal. It was completely enclosed by its remarkable flowering hedge, and when Lavering nervously opened the wrought-iron gate he found himself confronted by a garden of quite unusual beauty. Never was grass so green nor flowers so riotous. There were numerous elevations, and cunning obstructions to long views. It was all intimate and delicious. He walked up a crazy-pavement, past intriguing alcoves, marvelling at the dozens of butterflies on every clump of bloom. Honey bees zoomed past him, and he caught a glimpse of two hives painted light blue, which explained this abundance of insect life. Out of breath from his long climb he stood for a moment, with his finger on the bell-button, and then, at last, he pressed it.

The door was opened by an apple-cheeked girl, with roguish eyes, whose cap and apron signified her position. Lavering asked her if Mr. Sutherland was in, and she said she would find out. Would the gentleman give his name.

'I'm afraid he won't know my name,' replied Lavering. 'Will you tell him that I am — an admirer of his work. I've just come from the hotel.'

'Please come inside,' she said, in her

soft Cornish voice. 'I'll see if he's in the studio.'

Lavering waited for a few minutes when she returned and said that Mr. Sutherland would be pleased to see him in the studio.

'This way, sir,' she said. 'But it's a long climb. Right at the top of the house.'

'I think I can manage that,' he replied with a laugh.

She conducted Lavering up two flights of stairs, and then along a corridor, at the end of which was an arched door.

She knocked on this, and immediately a pleasant voice said 'Come in!' The girl opened the door, and Lavering passed her and entered the long studio. The artist had clearly been working, for he wore an old blouse and Lavering caught sight of a palette on a table, shining with wet paint. He was a man of about fifty years of age, with a mass of untidy dark hair, flecked with grey at the temples. He had deep-set impressive eyes, a strong straight nose and a firm chin.

'I must apologise for intruding,' said Lavering.

'Not at all. In any case I was just about to finish work, as I haven't stretched my legs since breakfast. I don't think we've met before?'

'If we have you wouldn't remember,' replied Lavering. 'I was attracted by that picture of yours at the hotel below.'

'You liked it?'

'Very much. May I look round?'

'Of course. Cigarette?'

He offered his case, and Lavering took a cigarette, and a light. As he did so the artist stared at him very hard.

'I feel we have met — somewhere,' he said.

Lavering gave his attention to a small study of bright moonlight on a turbulent sea. He knew little about the technicality of painting but here he was sure was a little masterpiece.

'It was a long time ago,' said Lavering, answering Sutherland's remark at last.

'It must have been, for I have a good memory for faces. Yet, when you came in I got the feeling that you were not a complete stranger.'

Lavering now turned and faced him.

'Mr. Sutherland, do you remember Nancrannon?'

'Nancrannon!' Sutherland took the cigarette from his lips, and a curious little hiss escaped from his lips. 'God, it can't be!' he said.

'It is. My name is Gerald Lavering.'

'The small boy with the pony! Yes, I can see him now — like a pale ghost beside you. Strange how quickly the years pass. It was twenty years ago. The small boy is a stalwart man, and the artist must have changed, too. Do I look very old to you?'

'No. But I can only just remember you as you were.'

'It's as well. Mr. Lavering, had you any special reason for calling on me?'

'Had I? I don't know. It was an impulse when I saw your name on that canvas — something I couldn't resist. If I had stopped to consider the matter, doubtless I shouldn't have come.'

'I'm glad you did.'

'Why?'

'Because there are some things you should know. You were too young to understand in those other days. You were kind enough to admire my work. In the first place you should know that but for one person I might never have got anywhere. That person was your mother. May I proceed?'

Lavering nodded, and watched Sutherland crush the lighted end of his cigarette into an ash tray.

'I came to Trewith that summer, ailing in health and in spirit,' he said. 'I came to hide myself away from a world which I thought had treated me badly. The young take misfortune hardly. I saw all my high hopes lying in pieces. Life was no longer worth living, for I saw myself as a failure. Several exhibitions had produced no sales worth mentioning. I swore I would paint no more, but build up my health and then find a job of some sort. For a few weeks I kept that resolution, but then the urge to paint came on me again. It was so insistent I had no power to resist. It was then I met your mother. She came to see what I was doing. I pretended not to see her, and went on with my work. But she stayed, and somehow her presence was not distracting. On the contrary I became conscious of a feeling of power. It was as if my hands were not my own. At last we spoke, and I discovered that she, too, was an artist, but mercifully removed from the necessity to live by painting.'

'Was I with her?' asked Lavering.

'Not on that occasion. It was later when she brought you along. By that time I had told her something of my apparently hopeless struggle — of my resolution to give up painting — to accept defeat. She begged me to go on, not to be discouraged by the lack of public appreciation, but to believe in myself and my destiny. I hadn't much faith left at that time, but very slowly she built it up. I found I was doing better work under her encouragement and inspiration. She was like a goddess in that exquisite garden.'

He paused for a moment, and Lavering saw his gaze reach out into space. Then the focus shortened and he resumed in a low soft voice.

'I sent my pictures to London, but they did not find purchasers. My debts grew and deep depression settled on me again. She knew what was wrong and came to my help with money. I refused to take it at first, but in the end I did. Not all that money was used to pay my debts. A lot went in drink. I think she knew that, but it did not shake her faith in me. During this time I could not be unaware that she was far from happy, but that was a matter we never discussed. Her unswerving faith in my abilities frightened me. I lived in awful fear of letting her down. I tore up canvases because I felt they were not up to the standard she expected. She became to me the infallible oracle. The summer began to wane. My health had been restored. I knew soon that she would go, and that only her influence, and the memory of her would remain. Then — then came the tragedy.'

'Go on,' said Lavering.

'How much do you know — about that?'

'Only that she went out in a boat and never came back.'

'No, you must know more. You must know that vile things were hinted at. Listen, Mr. Lavering, they were damned black lies. What bound me and your mother together was a tie stronger than anything physical. She lifted me up from a black pit of brooding defeatism. If I've ever done anything in painting that is worth while, she was the inspiration behind it — the force which gave it being. It was suggested she loved me, and that when confronted by this secret and illicit love she took the boat — . I shall never forget that morning when the news came that she was missing, and later when they found the abandoned boat. I shall never forget the pain in my heart when the innuendoes were poured into my ears. I tried to see your father, but he refused to see me. Then my wrath rose against him — I regret to say. I wrote him a letter attributing her death to his mad and utterly groundless suspicions. Then I tore it up, and became embittered and disillusioned. All through history, saints have walked this earth, only to be misunderstood and vilified. She was one of those. I have walked round Nancrannon many times since — have seen her face and form in every bush and cloud, have heard her voice in the wind and sea.

Now you come here out of the past to remind me — of everything.'

He lighted another cigarette with a hand that was far from steady, and Lavering noticed that moisture had gathered in the corners of his fine eyes.

'Is that what you really came to hear?' he asked.

'Yes, I think it was,' replied Lavering. 'This is very painful to both of us, but it's something to know that there was no truth in that ghastly story.'

'But the tragedy remains. Nothing can alter that. She who loved the sea so intensely took refuge in its wide embracing arms. Who can we hold responsible for that?'

'Must someone be responsible?'

'Not if you believe in destiny. Not if you believe that human beings have no free will — that we are the playthings of Fate, which cares nothing for personal feelings, for love, affection, and friendship.'

Lavering knew what lay behind Sutherland's carefully chosen words. He was laying the blame on the shoulders of the man who had believed the worst of the woman he had pretended to love — the man who had been so certain of his own conclusions that he had refused to hear the testimony of the alleged wrong-doer. Now came the illogical desire to defend his father.

'Who are we to lay the blame?' he asked. 'Who can say whether we shouldn't have acted in the same way — by similar impulses? He's dead now and — .'

'Sorry,' said Sutherland. 'You're right. I was carried away by vivid memories. Please forget it. Now will you let me discharge a debt of honour?'

'What debt?'

'The money I borrowed — from her. The conditions on which I borrowed it was that I should repay it when I had made good. The total is eighty-five pounds.'

'Please!'

'I should feel happier.'

'She would never have accepted it. Surely human beings are privileged to help their less fortunate fellows?'

'Yes, but it was I who made the

conditions, and I want to fulfil them.'

Lavering shook his head.

'There are many charities,' he said. 'She would approve of that.'

'That's true. I'll square the account that way. Now can I offer you some tea?'

'No thanks. My friends will be waiting for me. I'm glad to have met you, Mr. Sutherland.'

'I, too. One moment. I have something which I want you to accept. One picture which I've never sold, and never meant to sell. Excuse me a moment.'

He left the studio and was absent for a short time, during which Lavering had time to admire the interesting display of finished and unfinished work. Then Sutherland came back, with a small framed picture in his hands.

'This shouldn't require an explanation,' he said, with some emotion.

Lavering took over the painting. It was in oils, and the subject caused him to catch his breath, for there was his mother, as she appeared in his most vivid memory. Her face was radiantly happy, and she was beckoning towards her a

216

small boy seated on a shaggy Dartmoor pony. The small boy was himself. At the bottom was Sutherland's very distinctive signature.

'The best bit of work I've ever done, for what that is worth,' said Sutherland.

'Yes, it's inspired.'

'She could work that miracle with me. Yes, I'm glad you called, Mr. Lavering. Very — very glad.'

'Call at Nancrannon some day — soon,' said Lavering, huskily.

Sutherland nodded, but did not commit himself, and a minute or two later, Lavering was out in the bright sunshine.

14

Lavering had time to get his picture wrapped up before George and Tessa came back in the car.

'Are we late?' asked George.

'Oh, no. Was he careful, Tessa?'

'Very careful,' replied Tessa, with great seriousness. 'The only thing we hit was a handcart.'

'Tripe!' snorted George. 'I missed it by a mile. The idiot was on the wrong side of the road, round a sharp bend.'

Lavering made to get into the seat beside George, but then changed his mind and got into the back beside Tessa, who gave a rapid glance at the wrapped picture. The car began to move, and very soon the exquisite little fishing port was lost to view. George ran along the coast for some distance, and then cut inland.

'Where now?' asked Lavering, lazily.

'I don't know. You don't mind, do you?'

'No. So long as you don't run out of petrol.'

'I've just laid in a supply,' replied George. 'I like these lanes. You never know where they are going to finish up.'

'Never were truer words spoken,' said Tessa.

Whether by accident or design, George certainly found an interesting route. They encountered, at intervals, quaint villages and hamlets which looked as if they had been undisturbed for centuries, and where pigs and chickens wandered across the road. In places the harvest was being gathered, and the stooks in the brown fields made a pleasant sight. Tessa thought Lavering was exceptionally quiet, and again her gaze went to the package which rested beside him.

'So you patronised the arts?' she asked.

'Yes.'

'Can't I see it, or am I too young?'

'Would you like to see it?'

'Of course.'

Lavering handed it to her without undoing it, and after a glance at him she undid the string.

'Oh!' she gasped, as the painting came to view. 'It's — it's — .'

'Yes, the pair of us.'

'But, I don't understand. Did you know — about this?'

'No.'

'Austin Sutherland,' she said. 'That was the name of the man who painted the big picture in the hotel.'

'Yes. I remembered the name.'

'You knew him?'

'He was the painter I told you about the other evening.'

'Oh, Jerry!'

'It was an impulse I couldn't resist.'

'She was a lovely woman.'

'Yes, in mind as well as body.'

'It's beautiful,' she said. 'The whole thing. Did you buy it?'

'No. He gave it to me.'

She was surprised by his calm serenity. It seemed to her that some change had taken place in him — a change most difficult to analyse. Her wide sympathetic eyes were fixed on him.

'You were right in a way, Tessa,' he said. 'She was the victim of groundless

220

suspicion. Of that I am absolutely positive. It was all a tragic mistake.'

'I'm so glad,' she replied fervently. 'Jerry, if I hadn't insisted on seeing Tintagel you might not have met that man. Oh, yes, you would, because in any case you were going to St. Ives. So I don't get any credit out of it any way.'

'Do you want any credit?'

'Yes, if the net result of this is to give you greater peace of mind. George, I'm certain you've lost your way.'

'Why not?' grunted George. 'It's grand to be lost in a small country like England. Right or left — which is it to be?'

'Please yourself,' said Tessa.

George swung the car to the right fork, and then changed gear rapidly as he saw the road rise up like the side of a house. They roared over the summit where the hedgerows closed in on either side, leaving only just enough room for the wide car to pass.

'If we meet anything now we're sunk,' said George. 'Someone will have to go back.'

'And it won't be you,' said Tessa. 'Give

me the map. I bet this leads to a farm.'

A few minutes later the farm material-
ised, and George pulled up the car in the
midst of inquisitive geese and pigs, and
mopped his brow to cover his humilia-
tion. Lavering laughed as he got out of
the car.

'Just what we needed, George,' he said.
'Perhaps they'll give us some tea — also
tell us exactly where we are.'

The farmer's daughter was quite
prepared to do this. She was a finely-built
girl of about seventeen, and she explained
that the rest of the family were 'stooking'
in a distant field. A farmhouse tea was
produced with remarkable rapidity. It
consisted of scones, hot from the oven,
masses of cream and jam, and another
plate of home-made bread and rich
butter. In addition there was a cake of
quite colossal proportions.

'We're in luck,' said George. 'Pity we
can't adopt her — or something. We then
shouldn't miss our late fire-brand. Wonderful spot, isn't it? All a fellow could
desire — chickens and pigs, and cows and
geese. Look, there's a little river down

there. A fellow could do a bit of fishing when he got tired of eggs and bacon.'

The bronzed tall girl came and asked them if they had all they wanted.

'Oh yes, and more,' replied George. 'There's one thing you can probably tell us. What's the best road for Trewith?'

The girl had never heard of the place, so George produced the map and indicated it.

'I've never been there,' said the girl. 'This is where you are now.'

'Oh, surely not!' gasped George. 'We came from St. Ives.'

'You're here sure enough,' laughed the girl. 'You'll have to go back ten miles to get on the main road again. You seem to have come a long way off your course.'

'We rather suspected it,' said Lavering, with a glance at George, who was shaking his head as if he had reason to doubt that they were at the spot indicated.

'I must have made a wrong turning at the bridge away back,' he said finally. 'Well, it won't take long to get back there.'

When finally they re-entered the car

they took with them a dozen eggs, a pound of cream, and two sections of honey. George still made various detours but eventually they drew near Trewith, with its now familiar coastline.

'Thanks for a lovely day, Jerry,' said Tessa. 'I shall dream about King Arthur to-night.'

'He would be flattered,' remarked George. 'Anyway, I believe the chap was a myth.'

'What!' screamed Tessa.

'And there's another thing we have forgotten in the thrill of our excursion — the household chores.'

'You would remember that,' said Tessa. 'I suggest we paint our names on a plate, cup and saucer, knife and fork, and be responsible for our own hygiene.'

'Why not a newspaper and fingers?' asked George.

'Civilisation must be kept going.'

'Perhaps Poltimore has found us a lady-of-all-work,' said Lavering, hopefully.

When at last they reached Nancrannon, they were surprised to see Boozer rushing madly towards the car.

'I shut him in the lounge,' said Tessa. 'How on earth did he get free?'

George pulled up the car as Boozer, in his excitement, raced across its bows. The next moment the dog was on the running board, making attempts to get into the car. Lavering dragged him in by the scruff of his neck.

'You scoundrel!' he said. 'What does this mean?'

Boozer began to bark furiously, but then changed his tactics and laved Tessa's face with his long red tongue. Lavering dragged him out of range.

'You really mustn't take liberties, old fellow,' he said. 'Yes, I know the temptation was almost irresistible, but gentlemen don't do that sort of thing — at least not without some kind of encouragement.'

'Don't you believe it,' retorted Tessa.

The car pulled up before the entrance, and Poltimore came to view from the interior.

'I hope you don't mind, sir,' he said. 'I've been trying to get you some help, but haven't succeeded. So I thought I'd come along and get a meal going. I let the dog out for a run.'

'Thanks, Poltimore,' said Lavering. 'That's very thoughtful of you. We are grateful.'

'Women are difficult to get this time of the year, but I'll see you through. It's no holiday if you have to do your own cooking.'

George was in hearty agreement, and when in due course Poltimore produced the results of his culinary efforts, the party was stricken momentarily speechless. The meal kicked off with hors d'œuvre of endless variety, followed by fish served in shells, delicious roast chicken, fresh fruit salad in cups, and a cheese savoury garnished with red-pepper and something else.

'Shall I serve coffee in the lounge, sir?' asked the imperturbable Poltimore, when this stage was reached.

'Yes, please,' replied Lavering.

'The man's a blessed miracle,' said George, when they were in the lounge. 'Where did he learn to cook like this?'

'Remember, he was once butler here.'

'Gosh, he must have swallowed the whole of Mrs. Beeton while he buttled,' said George. 'That was as good a meal as you could get at the best London hotel. Will he wash up?'

The matter was settled later. Poltimore was ready to take over the whole job, provided he could go on sleeping at his own cottage, and have the afternoons off to attend to his fishing.

'I'm all alone now,' he said. 'And that makes a difference?'

'No news from Zillah?'

'No. But she'll write when her money gives out.'

'And then?'

Poltimore shrugged his broad shoulders.

'What would you do, Mr. Lavering, with a daughter like that?' he asked.

'I don't know,' Lavering admitted. 'I'm glad she isn't my problem. Perhaps she'll outgrow her wild ways.'

'Not her,' growled Poltimore. 'There's a bad strain in that side of my family. I should have known it before I took the step, but when you're young you don't know half as much about human nature as you think you do. Well, if there's nothing else you need, I'll be going now. The stove's banked down, and won't need touching. You'll find plenty of hot water.'

'Thanks again, Poltimore. Good night!'

Later, Lavering hung his newly acquired picture in the lounge, where it was freshly admired.

'That chap can certainly paint,' said George. 'The flesh is marvellous, and that necklace looks so real I feel I could take hold of it. What's the pendant?'

'A small ivory elephant,' replied Lavering. 'She always wore that. I think she regarded it as a mascot. I remember she used to give it to me to play with. It had pink eyes, and I called it 'Jumbo'.'

The telephone, which had recently been installed, rang loudly and Lavering took up the receiver. He spoke for a minute or two and then hung up the receiver.

'Canting,' he said 'The family solicitor in London. He wants to see me about sundry matters connected with the estate, and is catching the night train. I'm afraid he's going to get a shock.'

'Why?' asked Tessa. 'Oh, I'm sorry, I ought not — .'

'That's all right. You see, Canting is labouring under the delusion that I'm going to settle down in this country, and run the Hartford Estate just as my father used to do.'

'Aren't you?' asked George.

'No. I've always hated Hartford. It has memories for me which are like a running sore. Here it was different. All the happiness that I have known was compressed into the holidays I spent here. I never belonged to Hartford — nor what it stood for.'

'What did it stand for?' asked Tessa.

'A kind of feudalism. There was no freedom there for anyone but the Lord of the Manor. I'll have nothing to do with it.'

'But you could stay here,' said Tessa.

'I thought that might be possible. I love this country — the people, the sea, the moorlands. But now it holds a tragedy — something I never dreamed of. I know

229

I should have no real peace of mind. It's something I can't live down.'

Tessa started to say something, but George put in a quick remark and stopped her. It was intended to steer the conversation into a channel less painful, but it did not succeed, for Tessa came back to the attack at the first opportunity.

'You aren't trying to live it down, Jerry,' she said. 'Everything you do tends to make it live again. Everything you omit to do has the same effect.'

'What do you mean by that?' asked Lavering, quietly.

'You aren't really living in the present at all. Your heart aches for the days that are gone. This is a lovely old house, but you prefer to make it a tomb. Change the furniture round. Alter everything. Don't let things scream at you. Go away with George for a few days, and let me and Poltimore ring the changes — .'

'Tessa!' cried George.

'Let me finish,' said Tessa. 'To-day Jerry made a discovery which made the tragedy look less black, but he still has a grudge against the woman who loved him.'

'Tessa! This is beyond — ' interrupted George.

'No, let her speak,' said Lavering. 'In a way she's right.'

'What is hurting you, Jerry, is your mother's abandonment of you at that very early age, apparently to satisfy her own outraged pride. It must be that. You are torn between loving her as you used, and accusing her of desertion of you, who were little more than a baby. You think she should have thought of her baby first and her pride afterwards, but you make no allowance for impulse, for a mind wrenched off its balance by untrue accusations. It might happen to any of us — at any time, much as we like to believe it couldn't.'

She stopped and for a few seconds there was complete silence. George looked most uncomfortable, but Lavering displayed no resentment.

'What would you have me do, Tessa?' he asked.

'Go on believing in her, but not to the complete exclusion of everything else. The world is born afresh every day, and the poet says 'Gather ye roses while ye may'.'

'Where?' asked Lavering, with a smile.

'Here — where you belong.'

'Easy to say, but difficult to perform,' he said. 'You're a clever girl, Tessa — much cleverer than I imagined. Now I think I'll give Boozer a run.'

George made a noise in his throat when Lavering had gone, and gave Tessa one of his penetrating looks.

'It was good to get that off my chest,' she said.

'Don't you think it's a bit of a cheek?'

'Of course it was, but what do I care so long as it does him good?'

'Good! I didn't understand half you were saying. Do you imagine that bullying Jerry will have the slightest effect upon his future actions?'

'I shouldn't be surprised,' said Tessa, sweetly.

15

'Now children,' said Lavering, at breakfast the following morning. 'Father has an important interview with his solicitor. So you will have to do without him for a few hours. There's a dead calm — just the day for the motor boat. Alternatively, there's your excellent car — .'

'My car!' exclaimed George.

'Your car. That reminds me that you should take steps to get the licence transferred. That will prevent you from landing me into any trouble.'

'Now, Jerry,' pleaded George. 'Let's get this straight — once and for all!'

'What is there crooked about it?'

'People don't give cars away like that.'

'This is where we start a revolution. If you can't afford to run it when the present licence and insurance run out, then sell it and buy something smaller. Tessa, can't you make him see I'm serious?'

Tessa looked him straight in the eyes, and nodded her head.

'I believe you,' she said.

Lavering rose and put his hand on George's shoulder.

'Don't be an ass, old man,' he said. 'I took many a gift from you in the old days. Are you too proud to take one from me now. Honestly, I want you and Tessa to have the car, and to get all the fun you can out of it. Canting should be here at any moment, so I'd better get ready for him. See you later.'

George was quite unable to eat the rest of his breakfast. Now, at last, he knew that Lavering was not teasing him, and he was completely overwhelmed.

'We'll never be able to live up to it,' he said.

'If we knock a few dents in the mudguards, and chuck some mud over the bonnet it may be easier,' suggested Tessa. 'Oh dear, I wish I could feel that Jerry wasn't going to make a mess of things.'

'What things?'

'This interview with Canting. It's going

to settle the whole question of Jerry's future.' She banged her hand on the table. 'It's madness — all this socialistic stuff that Jerry talks. Nothing of all this belongs to him, because he never contributed any effort to get it. That sounds like puerile nonsense. People with natural talent never do anything to get it, but they accept it just the same. I can't see any difference.'

'There's something in that argument,' replied George. 'But Jerry wouldn't agree. When he makes up his mind about a thing he's difficult to shake.'

'I'd like to shake him.'

'I can't help thinking about the Bentley,' said George. 'Poke me, to make sure I'm not dreaming.'

Tessa kicked him instead, and brought him to his feet with a howl.

'Now let's do something,' she said.

'Yes, the car,' he replied, with his eyes gleaming.

'Make dents in it?'

'Don't be an idiot. I thought we'd do as Jerry suggests, and get a transfer form.'

'I feel more like a walk.'

'Much too hot.'

'It isn't hot at all — just perfect.'

'All right — you walk and I'll drive.'

Tessa was quite content with this arrangement, and a little later, clad in a pair of 'slacks,' and accompanied by Boozer, she went down to the cove and started a beach walk.

Mr. Canting arrived in a hired car, looking as neat and spruce as if he had come but a few miles instead of spending the whole night in the train. He carried a bulky portfolio, and looked completely out of place in his black coat, high white collar and spats.

'Had a good journey?' asked Lavering, as he shook hands.

'Quite pleasant, and uneventful. How changed the place seems. I haven't been down here for ten years, when I came down to see how things were going. The garden is a wilderness.'

'Yes, but rather nice. Now before we start, can I offer you a drink?'

'It's early to imbibe, but as I had breakfast hours ago I won't refuse.'

'Whiskey or sherry?'

'Oh whiskey, I think.'

Lavering poured out two drinks, keeping his own very thin, since he had no need for it. Canting raised his glass.

'To the future,' he said.

'To the future — whatever it may be.'

'And now let us get to business. I have some good news. I have managed to get probate settled at a very reasonable sum. Owing to the dilapidations at the farms, and here, I had a good debating point.'

'What is the sum?' asked Lavering.

'One hundred and eighty-six thousand pounds.'

'As much as that?'

'The valuations agreed upon are, I can assure you, very low — much below the real values. Most of the land at Hartford is excellent building land. Already I have been approached by a building syndicate for the four hundred acres marked pink on the map. They include Rymer's Farm, and the land on Higher Durton, fronting Sandy Lane. Ah, here it is.'

He unrolled a map and indicated the land referred to. Lavering did no more than glance at it.

'Aren't you interested in such a proposition?' asked Canting.

'What would become of Rymer?'

'He would have to go, of course. As a matter of fact his tenancy expires next year.'

'How long have the Rymer family farmed that land?'

'Seventy or eighty years I should say.'

'Has Rymer ever tried to buy his freehold?'

'No.'

'Why not?'

'He knew that nothing would induce your father to sell. Besides he has no money.'

'Why not?'

'Oh, there's no money in farming.'

Lavering gave a short laugh, causing Canting to frown.

'Sorry,' said Lavering. 'But it's strange to hear that people like the Rymers have worked those farms for over three hundred years and made nothing out of them, while my family has managed to live in luxury on the same farms. There

seems to be something wrong somewhere. Not only have we lived, but have
even contrived to put away at least a
hundred and eighty thousand pounds.'

'Aren't we drifting away from the main
point?' asked Canting.

'Not at all. It's interesting to contrast
three different points of view. My father
wouldn't sell the land, not because he
wanted to grab all the profits, but because
he regarded it as his personal property,
created for him and his ancestors by some
special act of God. You would sell it as a
mere matter of business. But I, having no
business acumen, but a lot of experience
in inducing crops to grow by the sweat of
my brow, find myself opposed to both of
you. How much money can Rymer find?'

'I've no means of knowing.'

'Then please find out. Whatever it is it
will be enough to buy the freehold of his
farm, and leave him a bit over. The same
applies to the other tenants.'

'Good God!' ejaculated Canting. 'What
would your father say?'

'Who knows?'

'But if this thing goes through what is

to prevent the farmers from selling to the building syndicate?'

'Just as you advocated I should do?'

'But — . Really, you leave me breathless.'

'Now about Hartford itself.'

'Are you going to give that away, too?'

'Yes. As a child I was most unhappy there. I should like that ghastly place to be noisy with laughter. Find some charity which will accept it for the welfare of children. With it goes an endowment of a thousand a year for a period — say, twenty years. After that it should be able to look after itself. Have it offered in my father's name. I think you'd better have another drink.'

Mr. Canting seemed to think so, too. He seized his filled glass and drank it in one gulp.

'Have you thought how you are going to live?' he asked.

'Probably as I've lived for the past seven years.'

'You mean — you're not staying here?'

'I think not.'

'Oh, but there's a limit to what you can

do with your inheritance.'

'Only limits of sentiment and respect. Mr. Canting, why didn't you tell me what happened here twenty years ago.'

Canting twisted his thin fingers together.

'I was merely carrying out your father's wishes,' he said. 'Would it have benefited you to have known the truth?'

'Truth is truth.'

'Even truth can be very painful. It soured your father's outlook. It hardened his heart against everyone. He was never the same after that.'

'He believed the worst without hearing the defence.'

'I know very little about that. All I know is nothing would induce him to come here again, nor to sell the property. It might be made a very nice home — for someone. What do you want me to do with it?'

'Sell it.'

'Are you — serious?'

'Why not?'

'But you were born here — .'

'I had to be born somewhere. But there

are certain things I want to retain. I'll make a list of them later.'

Canting shrugged his shoulders. What could one do with a fellow like this, who had no respect at all for tradition?

'It's all very depressing,' he said. 'I appreciate that the tragedies and disillusionments of youth are hard to forget, but you come of a long line. I had hoped you would carry on — .'

'And perpetuate the Laverings? I don't think we deserve to be perpetuated. It gives me a sense of satisfaction to know that I am the last Lavering.'

Mr. Canting shook his head sadly. He had come there in great fettle because he believed he had done a good stroke of business for the estate. Now he was cast into the depths of depression.

'I can't help feeling you are making a great mistake,' he said. 'But the decision is yours. I shall carry out your instructions to the best of my ability.'

'Thank you. Are there any other points?'

'Not now. You have made the whole issue painfully simple.'

'You'll stay to lunch?'

'Oh, no. I can get a train back, and reach London this evening. May I telephone for that hire car again?'

'There may be no need. I think my car — I mean my late car — is still here. Excuse me a moment.'

George was still flicking dust off the bonnet of the Bentley when Lavering appeared.

'Oh, George,' he said. 'Are you going for a drive?'

'That was the idea.'

'Then will you take Mr. Canting to the station? Our business is over, and he wants to get back to London.'

'I'll be glad.'

'Good.'

A little later Canting was seated by George's side, grasping his portfolio tightly and looking rather like an undertaker.

'You got through that quickly,' said George brightly.

'Yes. The Laverings have always been rather strange people,' replied Canting. 'But up to now they have always had a very shrewd idea on which side their bread was buttered. Never have I seen a valuable and historic estate so shockingly maltreated.'

'Really?' said George.

'Really!'

From which George gathered that Mr. Canting had received the shock which Lavering had promised.

16

At Swanpool, Seth Zaffery was in a curious mood. Two days had passed, and Bollin had not turned up. This enraged him, for he began to believe that Bollin was holding out on him, and that when, and if, he did come again it would only be to ask for more money. But he had other troubles too, which were not concealed from his observant, bare-footed wife — troubles that caused him to wake up suddenly in the night, and to cry out in his sleep. He drank even more than usual, and neglected the fishing, which was so essential to them all. So Ezra went out in the boat alone, and complained bitterly about it.

'I'm going over to see that swine,' said Seth, finally. 'I'll either get the stuff or bring my money back.'

'You can't take the trap,' said Ezra.

'Why not?'

'Betsy wants shoeing.'

'I told you to get it done.'

'I've had my hands pretty full. What's eating you up, brother?'

'Stop that damned strumming,' cried Seth. 'My nerves won't stand it.'

Ezra scowled as he laid aside his guitar. Personal insults he could stand, but he hated ignorant criticisms concerning his musical gift.

'You'll have to use the 'bus,' he said.

But Seth was prevented from going by the arrival of Bollin, who announced himself with his usual stentorian call. He came into the house without waiting for the door to be opened, and was empty-handed.

'You promised, — ' commenced Seth, savagely.

'I know — I know. I came to tell you that I'll have the stuff to-morrow. That's all fixed up. But here's a bit of news I got at the inn on my way here. There's been a murder.'

'Eh!' ejaculated Seth.

'So the police haven't been here yet?'

'Why should the police come here?' asked Ezra. 'And who has been murdered?'

'That niece of yourn — Zillah.'

Ezra drew in his breath with a hissing sound, and Seth closed both his big hands on the arms of the chair in which he sat, until the knuckles shone white under his dark skin.

'Found her body under a bush about a mile this side of the railway. She had been strangled.'

'Are you telling the truth?' asked Ezra.

'I'm telling you what I heard. They say the body had been lying there for days.'

Hazel came in with a jug of coffee and some cracked cups. She was as untidy as ever, and heard the last part of Bollin's remark.

'What's this about a body?' she asked.

'Hazel, Zillah has been murdered,' said Ezra.

Hazel put down the tray, and rested her hands on her ample hips. Then she laughed.

'Don't do that,' snapped Seth.

'Why not? People laugh when they're glad, don't they? Who's going to cry over that vixen? She was no good. If she'd been my daughter I'd have drowned her long ago. She stamped on my foot when she was last here and wanted to — '

'Shut up!' snapped Seth.

'When was she last here?' asked Bollin.

'Two — ' commenced Hazel.

'Yes, two weeks ago,' interrupted Seth. 'She wasn't happy at home, and having to work for young Lavering. I wonder why anyone should want to kill her? Must have been on her way to the railway station when it happened. Poltimore told me that she had run away — to London. Going to be a bit awkward for him.'

'Why?' asked Bollin.

'The police will find out how he used to beat her. She told everybody.'

'She liked being beaten,' snapped Hazel. 'How was she killed?'

'Strangled,' replied Bollin. 'They found a suitcase and a handbag. There was no money in the handbag, so it looks as if that was the motive. She must have had some money or she couldn't have hoped to get to London.'

'Coffee?' asked Ezra, as he took up the coffee jug.

'Can't bear the stuff,' replied Bollin. 'But I wouldn't object to something with a bit of a kick in it.'

'I'll join you,' growled Seth. 'Hazel, bring that bottle.'

Hazel brought the whiskey, and poured out liberal doses for the two men. Ezra stuck to his black coffee.

'All right, Hazel,' said Seth. 'We can manage now.'

His wife took her dismissal with a shrug of her plump shoulders. Bollin's glance followed her as far as the door.

'Don't she ever wear anything on her feet?' he asked.

'No,' replied Seth.

'Economical sort of wife. Can't help thinking about that gal. In a way she was mighty attractive.'

'In a way,' agreed Seth.

'Well, it'll certainly give the police something to do. They haven't had a decent sort of case since that fellow broke out of jail and cut two throats — and that was years ago. Now I'm going to beat it, but I'll be back to-morrow with the stuff, and then we can go ahead.'

'I'm relying on you,' said Seth, with a glare.

'You can — this time. Cheers!'

As the outer door was heard to close, Ezra looked at his brother with great intensity.

'What are you staring at?' growled Seth.

'Didn't you want Hazel to say that Zillah called here two nights ago?' asked Ezra.

'No. That was the night she was murdered. We might even be the last persons to have seen her alive. We don't want to get ourselves mixed up in it. Safer to say we haven't seen her for two weeks. That fool of a wife of mine nearly put her foot in it.'

Ezra drank his third cup of coffee, and his brother tilted the whiskey bottle again. Then after a long silence, Seth got up.

'I'd better talk to Hazel,' he said. 'If the police do come and ask a lot of questions, we had all better tell the same story. We haven't seen Zillah for two weeks, see? Not since she came here and wanted to stay. That's right, isn't it?'

'Is it?'

'If you want to avoid trouble that's the way to avoid it.'

'Maybe, you're right.'

'When his brother had gone, Ezra picked up the guitar, and drew his fingers across the strings quietly, producing a series of broken chords. But he did not appear to be listening to them, nor to be conscious of having produced them. His brow became wrinkled into sharp straight lines, and then the music stopped. He laid down the guitar and then got up and stole across to the chair on the back of which Seth's coat was draped. Diving his fingers into the inside pocket he drew out a tattered wallet. He opened it quickly and drew out a somewhat bulky bundle. They were one-pound notes — twenty-two in all, and twenty of them had been rolled up together. The remaining two were separate, and folded neatly. Ezra's hand shook. He hesitated for a moment, and then put all the notes into his own pocket, and returned the wallet to the coat. He had scarcely done so when he heard the sound of an approaching motor car. It stopped outside the house, and after a moment or two the bell rang sharply. Catching his breath he went to the door, and came face to face with two men. One was in ordinary clothes, and the other was in the uniform of a police Sergeant.

'I am Inspector Warren,' said the plain-clothes man. 'Of the County Constabulary. Are you Mr. Zaffery?'

'Yes.'

'I am investigating the death of a Miss Zillah Poltimore, who, I believe, was your niece?'

'That's right,' said Ezra. 'I heard about it only a few minutes ago. Come inside.'

The two men followed him into the room which he had just vacated, and as they reached the table Seth entered through the door which communicated with the kitchen.

'Seth, the police,' said Ezra.

'Ah, about poor Zillah?'

The Inspector nodded at Seth, and asked their relationship, also what other persons lived in the house. Seth satisfied him on these two points.

'When did you last see your niece?' asked the Inspector.

'About a fortnight ago,' replied Seth. 'I think it was exactly a fortnight. She called here — in the evening.'

'For what purpose?'

'She wanted to know if she could stay with us, because she was unhappy with her father.'

'Did she stay?'

'No. That would have caused trouble with her father.'

'Did she tell you why she was unhappy?'

'We knew. She didn't like having to do domestic work. She was always hankering to get away from the district.'

'Did she ever say she would run away when she had a chance?'

'Yes — several times.'

'Did her father call here recently?'

'Yes, two nights ago — about ten o'clock. He asked us if we had seen Zillah that evening, and we said we hadn't. He seemed to have the idea that we were hiding her up, and looked round the house. Finally he went away.'

'Did the girl ever complain about having been beaten by her father?'

'Yes.'

'Why did he beat her?'

'She was always getting into trouble. Once she stole a cycle, and was nearly sent to a reformatory. She was a very self-willed girl, and a terrible liar.'

'Do you know where her mother is?'

'No. She ran away from her husband many years ago.'

'Was he cruel to her?'

Seth hesitated and then shook his head.

'She was a bit wild, too,' he admitted. 'Poltimore made a mistake in marrying her. They could never have hit it off. She liked life and excitement, and Poltimore is a dull sort of fellow.'

'Had the girl — Zillah — any boy friend?'

'Every boy was her friend,' said Ezra. 'She liked men, and being admired.'

'But had she any particular male friend?'

Seth didn't think so, and Ezra concurred.

'And that was the last time any of you

saw her — when she came here a fortnight ago?'

'Yes,' replied Seth. 'That's right, Ezra, isn't it?'

'That's so,' replied Ezra.

'I should like to speak to Mrs. Zaffery,' said the Inspector.

'I'll call her.'

'No, please, don't bother. Is she that way?'

The Inspector indicated the kitchen door, and Seth nodded his head. The two men then left the room, and Seth sat down.

'That was bound to happen,' he said.

'Of course,' replied Ezra. 'Did you tell Hazel what to say?'

'Yes. Good job I did.'

But he still appeared to be uneasy, and Ezra knew why. They sat in silence for a long time, and then at last the two officers came back.

'That's all, I think,' said the Inspector. 'Your wife hasn't much of an opinion of her niece.'

'No. They never got on together.'

'Is it true that the girl once ran

away from Nancrannon, where she was employed?'

'Yes.'

'Did she go back again?'

'Yes. Her father made her. That made her more discontented than ever.'

'How do you know if you haven't seen her for a fortnight?'

Seth frowned but had wit enough to meet this thrust.

'It was the talk of the neighbourhood,' he said. 'You can't move a finger here without everyone knowing it.'

'Somebody told you?'

'Yes.'

'Who?'

'I can't remember. I think it might have been Lawton, the dairyman.'

'Hm!' said the Inspector, and made a note.

A minute later the car was roaring up the bumpy road. Ezra looked at his brother.

'He caught you there,' he said.

'Shut up! Curse that girl for bringing the police here.'

'Curse the man who strangled her, you mean.'

'Yes — him, too.'

'Think they'll leave us alone now?'

'Why not?'

'I'm only asking you. Seth, why did you go out on Wednesday evening soon after Zillah had left?'

'Go out? I never went out.'

'Oh yes, you did.'

'Ah, yes, I went to haul the boat up higher. There was a high tide, and — '

'That couldn't have taken an hour.'

'What the hell does it matter how long it took?' roared Seth. 'What's on your mind, eh? What's on your mind?'

'Nothing.'

Seth turned and put on his coat. Then he bawled his wife's name, and after a pause she came from the kitchen, wiping her hands on her apron, and chewing something.

'They've gone,' said Seth. 'What did they ask you?'

'Lots of things,' replied Hazel.

'Yes, yes — but what sort of things?'

'About Zillah — when I last saw her.'

'What did you say?'

'Two weeks ago. That was what you

told me to say, wasn't it?'

'Yes. What else?'

'They asked me where we were all Wednesday evening. I said we were all here, until we went to bed.'

'Good! Anything else?'

'Oh, yes.' She went on chewing.

'Empty your mouth,' said Seth.

Hazel turned and spat a plum-stone into the fireplace.

'What else?' Seth insisted.

'Did I think she was a nice girl? I told him plenty.'

'You would.'

'And then — then he asked me if I had any idea who strangled her. I said I didn't know and didn't care. The man in uniform wrote it all down. I showed him my bruised toe — where she had stamped on it. Nearly broke the bone she did.'

Hazel raised her bare foot for her husband to see. He appeared to be quite disinterested, until Ezra made a quiet comment.

'Looks a mighty fresh bruise to have happened a fortnight ago,' he said.

Seth nearly howled with mortification.

He seized his wife's quite shapely foot and peered at the damaged toe. No one but a fool could believe it had been inflicted so long ago, and the Inspector didn't look like a fool.

'What did he say to that?' he asked.

'He said I had nice toes,' replied Hazel, quite unconcerned.

'You fool! You lunatic!' he raved. 'You've made me out to be a liar. Why in God's name did you have to display your filthy feet?'

Hazel raised her head proudly. For a moment her dark eyes flashed angrily, and then she turned and hurried away.

17

At Nancrannon, the holiday party got the amazing news straight from Inspector Warren himself, after his visit to Swanpool. Poltimore had left two hours before, and the trio was engaged in a three-cornered darts battle when the Inspector, and his Sergeant-assistant, made their near presence known. As Tessa was throwing, and George was watching her to make sure she didn't cheat, Lavering answered the door himself. The dart-players heard some conversation at the door, and then Lavering came back with the two visitors.

'My guests, Miss Lashing — Mr. Lashing. George, this is Inspector Warren of the County Police. He's brought some bad news.'

'I'll bet George has been driving the Bentley too fast,' said Tessa.

Lavering shook his head, and Tessa knew that she was miles from the mark.

'It concerns a young woman, named Zillah Poltimore,' said the Inspector. 'Her dead body was found this evening. There is evidence that she was strangled.'

George gulped and laid aside the three darts which he had in his hand. Tessa stood quite still, expressing incredulity.

'Good God!' gasped George. 'How ghastly!'

'Inspector Warren wishes to ask us some questions,' said Lavering.

'Yes — yes. Of course,' replied George.

The Sergeant asked if he might use the small table, and having received permission, he sat down, and produced a large note-book, some of the pages of which were held together with a rubber band. The questions which followed were of a routine order. When they had last seen the girl? Did they know that she contemplated leaving them — and her home? Had she, while in their service, mentioned any man with whom she might have become familiar? Did she receive any callers? Such questions were easily and promptly answered. Tessa explained the circumstances which had caused Zillah to run out on them — for the second time.

'Did her father call here the following morning?' asked the Inspector.

'Yes,' replied Lavering. 'He told me that his daughter had left home.'

'Did he appear to be distressed?'

'Yes, but he told me that he wasn't greatly surprised, as she had always wanted to get away from him — preferably to London.'

'Did she ever complain about her father's treatment of her?'

'In what way?' asked Lavering, cautiously.

'Did she ever allege cruelty?'

Lavering hesitated, and looked at Tessa.

'You must answer the question, Mr. Lavering,' said the Inspector.

'Yes, she did complain, but it's only fair to her father to say that she was a particularly stubborn and provocative girl.'

'I can endorse that,' put in Tessa. 'She could drive one mad at times.'

Then suddenly she realised that her

interjection was not going to aid Poltimore, since it might help the argument that Poltimore too had been driven 'mad.' It was a little mortifying to watch the Sergeant write down the remark in shorthand.

'Did Mr. Poltimore take his daughter's place here after she had gone?' asked the Inspector.

'Yes.'

'Did he mention his daughter again?'

'Oh yes. He thought she had little money with her, and that she would communicate with him when she needed money.'

'Would you say his behaviour was normal?'

'Quite normal,' said Lavering. 'Inspector, may I ask a question?'

'Yes.'

'Is Poltimore under arrest?'

'Not exactly. He is under detention — temporarily.'

'But Poltimore is no more capable of murder than I am. He is a man of the highest principles — trustworthy and decent.'

'No doubt,' replied the Inspector. 'But all that matters at the moment is evidence.'

'Isn't that evidence?'

'Of a kind — yes. Did any of you see him on the day when his daughter went away?'

'No,' replied Lavering, while George and Tessa shook their heads.

'Did you pay her any money for her services?'

'Yes, but not directly. In fact, no actual money has passed yet. I have a general bill to settle with Poltimore. He has been looking after this house for a long period, and I'm not sure how matters stand. My intention was to make a settlement before I leave, as I am only here for a short stay.'

'I suppose you haven't missed anything from the house?'

'No. As a matter of fact I haven't troubled to find out. Are you suggesting that Zillah — ?'

'She must have had money if she intended going to London. The source of that money has not yet been divulged.'

'All she got from me was five shillings,

which I gave her for a puppy which she wanted to get rid of.'

'H'm! That wouldn't get her far.'

The two officers stayed but a few minutes longer, and then Lavering let them out, and hurried back to George and Tessa who, like himself, were staggered by the grim news.

'Poor old Poltimore!' said George. 'He's in a nasty spot. Not arrested — only detained. I like the fine distinction. Jerry, you don't think that he — ?'

'Of course not.'

'But somebody did it.'

'Don't make obvious remarks, George,' said Tessa. 'Of course someone did it. But there would be no sense in Poltimore strangling her. He only had to give her a little money and tell her to go to hell, and she would have gone there fast enough.'

'Aren't you a bit hard, Tessa?' asked Lavering. 'After all, she was little more than a child.'

'Child! There was nothing about life which she didn't know. Murder is horrible, and I hope they'll find the brute who did it, but I refuse to sentimentalise over Zillah. What sympathy I have is reserved for her long-suffering father. Do we finish this darts game?'

'Definitely no,' said George. 'This is the first time I've been close to a murder, and I can't say I like it. Think we shall be called to the inquest to give evidence?'

'I hope not,' replied Lavering. 'Well, we seem to be thrown back on our own resources again — unless they decide to set Poltimore free.'

'Some of us will have to roll up our sleeves and — .'

The telephone bell rang, and Lavering went to the instrument and picked up the receiver. There followed a conversation which was quite unintelligible to George and Tessa, and finally Lavering hung up the receiver.

'Canting, from London,' he said. 'Incurable habit that man has of doing his business in the evenings. Must work all night. He has certainly got a move on — bringing down a man on Friday to see this place.'

'Only to see it?' asked Tessa.

266

'Perhaps to buy it — if he likes it enough.'

'Jerry!' gasped Tessa. 'You're not serious?'

'Why not?'

'You mean — you've made up your mind to go back to Canada?'

'Yes.'

'All this doesn't mean anything any more?'

'It doesn't mean what it once meant.'

'But I thought — .'

'What did you think, Tessa?'

'Oh, I don't know. But — but if it were mine I wouldn't give it up — not to any stranger. There's something about it that is appealing — a kind of spirit that calls for — for aid.'

'Aid?' asked George. 'What on earth are you talking about?'

'I don't quite know. But Jerry should know. His roots are here, and he should be able to see that Nancrannon is something more than mere stone and mortar. There's more in it than that — all the joyous days of youth — all the precious moments you don't really wish to forget. You won't be able to bear the thought that some stranger is here. You won't be able to think of Nancrannon without having his shadow falling across your thoughts. I know you love it — even when you pretend to hate it.'

'How do you know?' asked Lavering, with a smile.

'How does one know anything? Half by observation, and half by intuition. Don't sell it Jerry — don't.'

George managed to steer the conversation into less embarrassing channels. It amazed him that Tessa should so consistently venture to give Jerry free advice on the management of his own affairs, and he registered a resolution to talk to her seriously at the first opportunity. That opportunity came early the next morning, when he discovered that his host had gone for a very early bathe. George tapped on Tessa's door, and entered on a sleepy invitation.

'Hey, wake up you!' he said, and pulled the pillow from under Tessa's head.

'Oh you want to get rough, do you?' she retorted, and scrambled out of bed on the further side.

'No, I don't. I want to talk to you.'

'You could have done that without any monkey tricks. What do you want to talk about at this time of the morning?'

'Jerry.'

'What about him?'

'Why do you keep butting in on his private affairs?'

Tessa turned away, went to the dressing table, seized a hair-brush and began to brush her tangled locks with tremendous energy.

'Do you realise I'm talking to you?' asked George.

'You're talking where you always talk — through your hat,' retorted Tessa.

'Anyone else but Jerry would have told you to mind your own bloomin' business,' grumbled George.

Tessa turned her head, and showed her exquisite profile.

'It's my business to prevent him making a fool of himself,' she said.

'Your business! Why you've only known him a couple of weeks. All that time you've been his guest — remember that.'

'What difference does that make? You may have known him for umpteen years, but already I know him better than you do.'

'Women always think they know men — .'

'Jerry isn't a man. He's just a child — who has been slapped and doesn't like it. He thinks he knows what he wants, but he doesn't. All this business about his mother is holding him back from the serious business of life.'

'What do you think is the serious business of life?'

Tessa turned right round and shook her glorious hair free. George peered at her. She looked different now. He thought the girl of yesterday had gone — that he was looking at a comparative stranger. She had always been a resolute young person, but now there was more than mere resoluteness about her.

'Don't glare at me like that,' he complained.

'And don't lecture me, big brother,' she retorted. 'The battle is on.'

'What battle?'

'You'd be surprised.'

'Can't we drop this cross-talk comedian stuff?' pleaded George. 'I'm responsible for your being here, and — .'

Tessa laughed and caught both his hands.

'Your responsibility ends here and now,' she said. 'In future I'll be responsible for anything that happens. George, you remember that self-portrait done by Jerry's mother?'

'Yes. What — ?'

'Don't you think I'm just a little bit like her?'

'No,' said George. 'She was a beautiful woman.'

'Beast! Am I so frightful?'

'I'm not throwing you any bouquets. Look here, what's your little game?'

'Just the old game, George. It started in the Garden of Eden ages and ages ago.'

George drew in his breath with a little hiss of astonishment. With a tug he drew his sister towards him, and stared into her eyes.

'My hat!' he gasped. 'You don't mean — that you — that you — ?'

'Is there any reason why I shouldn't fall in love?'

'No, I suppose not. Even quite intelligent people do it. But you're wasting your time with Jerry. He's not that sort of chap. All you'll do is hurt yourself.'

'I don't mind being hurt in a good cause. Now run along. I want to get dressed. Have you forgotten that there's work to be done? Breakfast won't cook itself.'

George went back to his bedroom, shaking his head. This holiday which had promised to be one long uneventful laze was producing results of remarkable variety. The murder was a big enough bombshell, but what Tessa had just revealed seemed even greater.

'Poor kid!' he muttered. 'I should never have brought her here at all.'

18

In view of the lack of domestic help, both Lavering and George voted for lunch out, but Tessa was against this.

'Time you two dodgers got away from those bachelor ideas,' she argued. 'I'm going to cook you a meal, and you're going to like it — I hope.'

'Can you do it without dirtying a lot of dishes?' asked George. 'Why can't all the vegetables be chucked into one pot, instead of miles of saucepans, and what not — masses of knives and forks, and plates and things?'

'Because we're civilised.'

'I haven't noticed it. Now, all we have to do is find a nice pub — .'

'Nothing doing,' interrupted Tessa. 'You two go and play tennis, and leave me in peace.'

'Look here, can't we help?' asked Lavering.

'No. I hate the sight of you both.

Besides, George is putting on tons of weight. Too much lounging in the car. Make him run about on the tennis court.'

'Shall we?' asked Lavering.

George was more than willing, and very soon the air was full of resounding bangs, and occasional expletives, as George failed to take some of his opponent's terrific services. Boozer scouted for balls which went over the wire netting, and had to be chased before he would surrender them. Very soon George was shirtless, and within half-an-hour he discarded his vest as well. Finally, when he realised that they were out of sight of everyone, he took off his trousers, and played in what was left.

'Disgusting!' said Lavering.

'I've always wanted to go native. Oh, you swine — that was a dirty one.'

Lavering laughed as he smashed back George's very feeble 'return' and sent him racing across to the far corner, where he missed the ball by a good yard. This sort of thing went on until George was staggering about the court like a drunken man. At least he was game, but completely outclassed.

'Well, that's set,' he said. 'Gosh, it was good. Why did you let me win the first set?'

'I didn't. You won that fair and square.'

'I wish I could think so. Goodness, someone is coming!'

George rushed to the seat, and made frantic efforts to get into his trousers. He had got tangled up in them when the oncoming person came into view from behind the obscuring bushes. It was Poltimore.

'Well!' gasped George, easing up on his efforts.

Lavering hurried to the entrance gate.

'Hullo, Poltimore!' he said. 'It's good to see you.'

'Aye, they let me out this morning, and I reckoned you'd like to know,' replied Poltimore.

'I'm delighted. But we're all terribly sorry to hear the very bad news.'

'Bad it be,' said Poltimore, clenching his fists. 'And to think that they believed I might have — might have — .'

He passed a horny hand across the eyes.

'That was a ghastly experience,' said Lavering. 'What is the position now?'

'I was told not to leave my place without telling them where I was going. Nice thing to happen to an innocent man in a free country. My girl was savagely murdered and the only person they arrest is me. Why can't they find the real murderer?'

'Perhaps they will. Have they any clues?'

Poltimore shook his head.

'They're so close,' he said. 'They won't say anything — only ask questions — thousands of questions. I'm not denying she was a bad girl, but bad as she was she didn't deserve that fate.'

'No. It was dreadful. We were all questioned, too, but of course, we weren't able to assist them. Haven't you any suspicion against anyone?'

'Not a thing. It's all a complete mystery. Perhaps it was just a tramp who saw her carrying that suitcase and her handbag, and reckoned she was going away, and must have money. She wouldn't have given up without a fight

— you know the sort of girl she was? Then, perhaps, he had to catch her by the throat to stop her from screaming out. I wish I knew who 'twas. Yes, I wish I knew.'

'We may in due course. In the circumstances I suppose you won't feel like continuing here?'

'Why, of course, Mr. Lavering. This is a bad business, but it won't do me any good to brood about it. I've got to go to my cottage, but I'll be back in an hour or so.'

'Good man,' said Lavering. 'We can use you.'

So Poltimore came back to the house, just in time to deal with the mass of washing-up due to Tessa's gargantuan meal.

'Now we can snooze in the garden, Jerry,' said George. 'I'll be honest. I hate work.'

'As if Jerry hadn't noticed that by this time,' said Tessa. 'Oh, yes. I've a job for you both, and that goes for you, Boozer. There are rats in my bedroom.'

'What!' gasped Lavering.

'Not exactly in the room, but just above. I can hear them scuttling about at nights. Here's a chance for Boozer to prove that he's worth his keep. What is there above my room?'

'An attic,' replied Lavering. 'We used to keep old junk in it. If it hasn't been touched in all these years it must be in a mess. George, you'd better get your rompers on.'

'All Tessa's rats are mice,' complained George. 'Jove, I could do with a nap after the way you kept me rushing about. Cruelty to animals I call it.'

'Rats, Boozer,' said Lavering. 'Ever caught a rat? No, I don't suppose you have.'

Boozer, scenting that something was in the wind, began chasing all over the room, looking for anything which might give him a run for his money. He found only one thing which appeared to be evading him most effectively, and he concentrated on that. It happened to be his own tail, but that was no deterrent. His efforts to put an end to its cowardly retreat were tremendous.

'You idiot!' said Lavering. 'That will get you nowhere. Stop it!'

Boozer finally collapsed in a quite ridiculous attitude, and after getting his breath back he followed Lavering and George upstairs to the attic.

'Sooner you do your stuff the better, Boozer,' yawned George. 'I get no kick out of ratting.'

Lavering opened the door of the attic, and gazed at the accumulation of junk. An attempt had been made to tidy the place up, but the quantity and variety of the articles rendered this vain. There were old tennis rackets, a huge meccano set, sundry old pictures and playthings. A trunk full of ancient magazines, a pile of newspapers, a large wardrobe full of clothing, and innumerable other things, some of which brought back memories of other days.

'What a mess!' said George.

Boozer began to sniff loudly at a big pile in one corner, and then to scratch at it.

'What is it, boy?' asked Lavering.

'I'll bet he's leading us up the garden

path,' said George, who foresaw work ahead.

'We'll see. Pull some of that stuff down.'

'Theirs not to reason why,' quoted George. 'Foo — dust! I'm suscep — susceptible to — atichoo!'

'What a pansy you are,' complained Lavering, as George dusted his hands together. 'That won't hurt you.'

'I loathe dirt.'

'What is dirt?' asked Lavering, as he dumped a pile of junk in a vacant spot. 'Matter in the wrong place. Stop that noise, Boozer! You'll scare the enemy.'

But Boozer was now getting worked up. He dashed about, got under their feet and between their legs, and finally brought George down with a crash, and with a clothes-horse on his chest.

'To think we're doing all this chiefly for your benefit,' grumbled George, as he scrambled to his feet.

The big pile was being slowly reduced, and then suddenly something dashed from the rear of a hat box. Boozer nearly fell backwards with surprise. It was a tiny brown mouse, and it made for a cavity between two boxes.

'Stop it!' yelled Lavering.

George flung a book at the creature, but missed it by two feet. The mouse — diverted from its course — made for another opening at a tangent. Boozer, with a terrifying wail, fell on it. His wet muzzle made a trail all over the floor, but he missed the mouse.

'There it is!' cried Lavering.

'Where?'

'Just behind you.'

George swung round, and the mouse leaped for safety. This time it was successful in getting behind what remained of the pile of junk. Lavering pulled out a box, and Boozer, now worked up to a state of hysteria, dashed into the space created, from which only his rear parts projected.

'Come out,' said Lavering.

But instead of obeying Boozer went further in, with such gusto as to bring about a collapse of the pyramid above him, which completely cut off his means of exit. He began to howl about it.

'He would go and do that,' complained George. 'You know, I think he's a bit lacking upstairs.'

'So were you when you were his age,' retorted Lavering. 'Let's get him out. Lend a hand.'

Boozer was successfully extricated, and then the last layer of articles was carefully dealt with. George, armed with a tennis racket, kept on the alert while Lavering removed the articles one by one.

'S-sh!' hissed Lavering. 'We've got him. Look, there's his nest — right in the corner.'

'And the hole which leads — '

'Stop the hole.'

George put the racket over it, and Lavering disturbed the heap of chewed newspaper, and bits of cloth. There was a quick movement towards the covered hole, upon which George, with a quick movement, turned the racket over and held the mouse a prisoner under the strings.

'Got him!' he gasped. 'Boozer — here boy!'

Boozer looked everywhere but where

he was needed, and finally Lavering had to drag him forward and push his nose down to the racket. Then he seemed to go clean mad, performing a kind of canine 'can-can' around the improvised cage.

'Let it go, George,' said Lavering.

'He'll miss it.'

'No he won't.'

'I'll bet you.'

'I'm not a betting man. Give him a chance — now!'

George turned up the racket, and the mouse ran for its life. Boozer immediately ran in the opposite direction, and George struck out with the racket. More by luck than judgment the wood caught the fleeing mouse, and knocked it out. It uttered a little squeak, and Boozer turned round and expressed his astonishment. Then he saw the cause, pounced on it and shook it between his teeth.

'Yah, you cheat!' said George. 'Why you haven't the gumption to catch a common cold. Who's that?'

It was Tessa, come to see how the ratters were progressing. George pointed his finger at Boozer, who was still posing for applause.

'Oh,' she said. 'A dear little mouse.'

'Your rat all the same.'

'But that little thing couldn't have made all the noises I heard. Boozer, drop it, you beast!'

'Well, I like that,' complained George.

Boozer, realising he was unpopular, and that there were designs upon his capture, sneaked out of the open door, and went bounding down the stairs.

'Oh look, a clever little nest,' said Tessa. 'Are you sure there was only one mouse?'

'It looks like it,' replied Lavering. 'A bachelor by all the evidence. Boozer was a bit slow in the uptake, but he'll learn.'

Tessa looked round at the strange assortment of articles.

'Time you had a spring cleaning here, Jerry,' she said.

'There'll be one soon enough. But I can make a start with that pile of newspapers and the magazines. The rest will probably appeal to people who attend jumble sales.'

Tessa opened the wardrobe and peeped into it.

'Dresses and shoes,' she said. 'Oh, they're lovely. Genuine Edwardian. Oh, just look at this lovely lilac — .'

She stopped as she caught George's glance, and realised that the wearing apparel could have belonged to none other than Mrs. Lavering. With a nervous little cough, she let go the lilac-coloured blouse and closed the door of the wardrobe.

'Shall I help you tidy up?' she asked Lavering.

'Thanks.'

'Does that let me out?' asked George.

'Yes, you can go and sleep away the precious hours,' retorted Tessa. 'But you can take that bundle of newspapers down with you.'

'Wonderful how you think of things,' groaned George. 'What do I do with them? Make a bonfire?'

'No, leave them in the library,' said Lavering.

Later, while George was enjoying his siesta, and Tessa had gone to her room,

Lavering brought down a vast number of magazines and placed them with the newspapers. On the terrace, outside the window, Boozer was stretched out, surveying something very small which lay about two inches from his whiskers.

'What is it, Boozer?' asked Lavering, bending over the worm-like article.

It was the tail of a mouse.

'Taking care of your digestion, eh?' asked Lavering. 'Well, I don't blame you.'

He came back to the library, and turned over some of the newspapers. The top issues had been nibbled by generations of mice, but lower down they were clean and undamaged. They were in chronological order, with the later issues at the top. Suddenly he found himself gazing at a large headline — 'CORNISH SEA TRAGEDY.' Then he saw the name — LAVERING. As he worked backwards the space given to the affair increased. Here was a statement made by Mr. Poltimore, there another by the cook employed at Nancrannon. What had caused this beautiful young woman, and mother, to have taken a boat out on such a night? Had she an exaggerated opinion of her power to control it in such a storm as threatened? A widespread search had been made for her body, but without success. A young artist, named Sutherland, who had known Mrs. Lavering fairly well, gave it as his opinion that the victim had an incurable infatuation for the sea. She was a woman of great courage, for whom the roughest sea held no terrors. Yet another article pointed out the coincidence of the second local victim of the same storm. He was a neighbour of Mrs. Lavering — a Mr. Zaffery. Like her he had taken out a small boat and never been seen again, but in his case the boat too had been lost.

Nowhere was there a suggestion that Mrs. Lavering might have committed suicide, but it was clear that the police had asked questions regarding the state of Mrs. Lavering's mind at the time. Lavering read on, issue after issue, almost against his will. The whole drama, in its serial form, extended over weeks. He was still engaged at it when there came a tap on the door and Poltimore entered.

'Excuse me zur,' he said. 'Shall I lay tea indoors or on the terrace?'

'On the terrace, Poltimore.'

Poltimore's sad eyes had gone to the newspaper, but he said nothing, and was leaving when Lavering stopped him.

'Poltimore, why were all my mother's dresses taken up to the attic?' he asked.

'Your father told me to do that,' he said. 'Just before he left here.'

'Did he give any reason?'

'No. If I may say so, sir, he never gave any reasons for anything he did — or ordered to be done.'

'I found these old newspapers, too.'

'Aye, he put them there himself. I'd have burnt them long ago, but my orders were to touch nothing. I'm sorry, sir, if — '

'That's all right. There's a lot about — my mother, but very little about Mr. Zaffery, and yet he was drowned, too.'

'What newspaper would waste time on him?' asked Poltimore. 'He was no better than his children.'

'I can't remember him.'

'I should have thought you would, zur.

He was round here often enough trying to sell or buy things. He was big and dark, with a face like a hawk, and he wore large velvet trousers, and a funny little hat. Your father bought the pony from him which you used to ride. Paid far too much for it, too. I could have got it for half the price if he had left it to me, but it wasn't to be. He was too proud a man to bargain with that wheedling scoundrel. That was over twenty year ago, but it seems only yesterday.'

'Yes — it does,' mused Lavering. 'This house is like a petrified forest. All the joys, all the sorrows — everything frozen into permanence. I should never have come here. But I didn't know. Why wasn't I ever told the truth?'

Poltimore stood dead still. He looked as if he had something to say, but lacked the boldness to say it.

'Well?' asked Lavering.

'I said nothing, sir.'

'No, you said nothing, but you've been here all these years, tending the ghosts of the past. They must have said things to you. What things?'

Poltimore stirred uneasily.

'There have been times when I've imagined things,' he said. 'Times when I've seen him walking down the long corridor — stiff like he always was, and proud and unforgiving. I beg your pardon — '

'Go on, Poltimore.'

'Folks are as God made them. Nothing seems to change them — not even their own wishes. He was like that — hard yes, but praying not to be. I believe he knew you would come back here one day, and that is why he would have nothing changed. He wanted you to know — as you could not know then — that she had abandoned him and you. It could have been different — made clean and pure by time, but he wanted it to tell you what he could never tell you himself.'

Lavering was breathing heavily. It was astonishing that Poltimore, with all his natural simplicity, and humility, should be able to speak in that fashion — to endorse what was already formulating in Lavering's own mind.

'To perpetuate my mother's guilt,' he

muttered. 'That was to be part of my inheritance. No wonder Zillah said this place was haunted. It is — with the spirit of unrest.'

'She was psychic was Zillah. It was in her gipsy blood. My ghosts were imaginary, but hers were real. She said she had seen — '

'Yes.'

'Your mother, walking down the staircase. It was when I brought her here long ago, to play while I looked over the place. That happened twice, and she wouldn't come again — not until she was grown up. Poor Zillah! To think — .'

He stopped abruptly, and then muttered that he was talking too much about what didn't rightly concern him. He would go and get the tea ready.

Lavering put aside the newspaper which he had been reading, and walked out on the terrace, with Boozer prancing about, interesting himself in bees and butterflies. His antics had the effect of chasing away the gloom which had fallen on his master. At least Boozer had no complexes. For him it was the morning of life in all its richness of interest and experience. A few moments later, George came whistling from the house. He had had his nap, and, as usual, was on top of the world again.

'Where's that sister of mine?' he asked.

'Making herself beautiful.'

'Funny how that comes first in their calculations,' said George. 'A year or two ago she didn't care too hoots what she looked like. Then suddenly she started daubing stuff over herself. The longer you live with women the more mysterious they become — like cats.'

'They probably think the same about us.'

'But, hang it, we do behave rationally. They make me ill when they kiss and call each other darling. Hey, Boozer, what have you done with that poor little mouse?'

Boozer came and smelt the end of George's trousers.

'He thinks you're hiding another one in your turn-ups,' said Lavering. 'The other one is now undergoing the natural processes of digestion.'

'You uncivilised animal!'

Boozer barked a protest, and then made a terrific leap at a bee, which he narrowly missed.

'One of these days you're going to get a nasty surprise,' said George. 'Oh, there's Poltimore with the tea. Cheers!'

19

It was George who suggested the 'pub-crawl,' after the evening meal, and Lavering concurred. Both Boozer and Tessa were invited, Boozer because it was his privilege to be taken for a late walk, and Tessa because of common politeness.

'Oh, no,' she said. 'Three males, a pub and a woman don't mix. Besides, I want to wash my hair. It's got a sandstorm in it. Then I'm going to light a fire, and sit by it.'

'A fire!' gasped George.

'To dry my hair, idiot.'

'You certainly do get ideas. But you could save all that trouble by cutting a yard off it. Shall I do it for you?'

'I need no masculine aid in this little matter. I'm glad you're taking Boozer. He'll be able to guide you home.'

As soon as they had left Tessa lighted a wood fire in the lounge, opened up the hot-water boiler, and started on her ablutions. By the time she had finished the wood fire was blazing in the lounge, filling the place with a smell that she loved. She spread out a number of cushions, shook out her mass of wet hair and reclined in pensive mood, with a hair brush beside her. It began to grow dark outside, and the fire grew brighter by contrast. At intervals she brought the stiff brush into use, humming to herself in desultory fashion. Her reflections embraced all that had happened since she arrived at Hartford in George's old car — the trip by road — her first sight of Nancrannon — every little incident since, even to scraps of conversation. Amid all this, Lavering stood out like a giant silhouette against a moving background. Surprising as some of his acts had been, at heart she was not greatly surprised. Intuitively she was led to put her finger on the root cause of his trouble. In his moodier moments this struggle within him was like a play to her, enacted in full limelight. The past which he had nurtured with such ferocity had proved to be but an illusion. He wished now to get away from it, but was held back by chains of his own devising. His solution was to sell the house in the belief that this act would cut the Gordian knot.

'No,' she muttered to herself. 'It would bring you no relief, Jerry darling.'

Half dozing in the heat of the fire, she let her imagination reach out. Now she was in Jerry's boat, racing through those marvellously blue seas, with the salt wind in her teeth, now climbing those verdant slopes where Arthur had built his fantastic castle, now in the car passing through flowerdecked lanes. How good it had been — and was — these days by the sea, and in the sunshine. True there had been tragedy to mar the otherwise perfect vacation, but that would pass. What would remain for all time was the memory of this holiday, in this strange romantic house, with George and Jerry — even when Jerry was thousands of miles away, and strangers passed up and down the stairs and the long corridor. This last reflection caused her to sigh and shake her hair vigorously.

'No,' she muttered again.

Satisfied that her hair was dry enough to be 'done' in some fashion, she rose to her feet, took the towel and the hair brush, and went upstairs. As she was about to pass the door of Lavering's bedroom, the door was open, and the light in the passage shone full on a picture beside the window. It was the self portrait painted by Mrs. Lavering, which Lavering had removed from the lounge. Tessa's glance went to the beautifully painted lilac coloured blouse, and the broad-brimmed straw hat. But it was the blouse which took most of her attention, for it was edged by a lace fichu of unusual design. She knew that she had seen that self-same fichu only a few hours before. It was in the wardrobe in the attic where the rat-hunt had taken place.

She went back to the place where the second flight of stairs commenced, and then, after a hesitation, she climbed to the attic, and switched on the light. The wardrobe doors were now free of clutter, and she opened them and looked inside. There was the blouse on a wooden hanger, looking as fresh as the day on which it was made. On the shelf above she found the hat, replete with ribbons. Her hands seemed to burn as she fingered the articles, and the desire to bring the picture to life was irrepressible. Without allowing herself any second thoughts on the matter, she hurried downstairs and slipped into her own room. There she did her hair in the style of the painting, as she remembered it, not forgetting the straying coil behind the right ear, which lent such charm to the painting. Choosing a skirt which would hit off the blouse, she then put on the blouse itself, and found that it fitted her perfectly. The effect was most pleasing, and with great trepidation she put on the hat, and tied the ribbons. The angle was wrong so she gave it a tilt — and there sat the late Mrs. Lavering.

'Not bad,' she said. 'But I haven't got her milk and cream complexion. Perhaps she never sat in the sun for hours on end.'

Another long look into the mirror, and she took off the borrowed articles, and quickly did her hair in the accustomed style. Again she mounted the attic stairs, and she was putting the blouse on its hanger when she noticed that the little watch-pocket was stiffer than the rest of the garment. She put her fingers into it and drew out a folded piece of paper. She unfolded the paper, and came upon a curious plan, beautifully drawn in pencil. She took this down into the lounge for closer examination, but no sooner had she got there than she heard Boozer barking outside the house, and knew that Jerry and her brother were in the offing.

Now she found herself in a dilemma. If she showed the plan to Jerry he would naturally ask where she had found it, and that, in the circumstances, was embarrassing. She could, of course, tell a fib, but that course was repugnant to her. Before she could make up her mind what to do George and Lavering were in the house, and Boozer came dashing into the lounge, wagging his tail.

'Get away,' she said. 'You smell of beer.'

'You're right,' agreed George, as he entered the room. 'The little beggar does drink beer. I tried him.'

'What a disgusting thing to do.'

'Oh, he only had a sip — at the bottom

of the tankard. But was he pleased!'

Lavering came in and gave a glance at Tessa's gleaming hair, and the red embers of the fire.

'Dry already?' he asked.

'Oh, yes. You've been a long time.'

'The inn was packed, and everyone was talking about the same thing.'

'The murder?'

'Yes. The police appear to have been very busy. It was difficult to find anyone who hadn't been questioned.'

'Let's not talk about that,' she begged.

'Agreed. What about playing something on the piano?'

'I — I don't feel much like playing.'

'Oh come, do your stuff,' said George. 'And drive the blues away.'

'I haven't any blues to drive away.'

'If you won't play, I'll sing,' threatened George.

'All right. Anything to prevent that. What would you like me to play — or try to play?'

'I leave it to you.'

Tessa searched among the music, and finally found a volume of Grieg. She switched on the standard lamp, and tilted the shade a trifle.

'Ah, Chopin,' said George, as she commenced to play.

Tessa gave him a withering look. At times you could never be sure whether George was engaged in the art of leg-pulling or not. But after that he was as silent as Lavering, who, as usual, gave himself completely to the entertainment. Boozer was the only member of the audience who seemed to have any doubt about the quality of the music. Once he stretched his neck upwards and opened his mouth with the obvious intention of expressing his feelings, whatever they may have been, but George pushed him over on his back, and the surprise attack silenced him.

Lavering was sitting with his elbows resting on his knees, and his hands supporting his chin. His eyes were half-closed, and Tessa, when she stole him a glance, knew that his thoughts were not with them. From one piece she went on to another until she came to the last page of the series of short pieces.

'I think that should be enough to charm you to sleep — or murder,' she said.

'That was fine,' said Lavering. 'What a lot of hidden talent you have.'

'The girl's a marvel,' George said, with great seriousness. 'She can walk on her hands, too.'

'I can believe it,' laughed Lavering. 'Well, I feel like going to bed.'

'Me, too,' said George. 'What about an early bathe in the morning? The tide should be just right about seven o'clock.'

'You know you can't get up at seven o'clock,' retorted Tessa.

'I'll bet you I'm up at seven to-morrow, and in the sea by a quarter past.'

'All right. Sixpence on it.'

George shook hands with her solemnly. They were walking up the staircase when, again, came the phenomenon which they had experienced before. It was not a noise so much as an earth movement, which caused rattlings in the house. George stopped dead and looked at Lavering.

'Did you feel that?' he asked.

'What a silly question,' said Tessa. 'Anyone but a corpse must have felt it. Jerry, is the house safe?'

'It's been here for about three centuries,' replied Lavering.

'That's not much of an argument. Pompeii was safe until one day. Do you think the sea has undermined the cliff?'

'No. At the moment it is low tide.'

'Then how can you account for it?'

'I can't account for it, unless — ?

'Unless what?'

'The old tin-mine was extensively worked. Part of it may even run under the house. A fall of rock down there, due to water percolation and rotting props might create that effect.'

'Then you still think the house will stay put?' asked Tessa, with a smile.

'Good heavens — yes. Well, it appears to be all quiet now, so you can sleep in peace.'

'Did anything like this ever happen in the old days?' asked George, as they proceeded to their rooms.

'If it did I've forgotten all about it. Poltimore's the man to know. I'll raise the matter in the morning. Well, good-night, George! Good-night, Tessa!'

George had scarcely entered his bed-room when Tessa slipped in and closed the door gently.

'Hey, what's this?' asked George.

'S-sh!'

'Bed time stories? All right, you can kiss me and leave out the story.'

'Idiot! This is serious,' she whispered.

'All right. I'll buy it.'

Tessa produced the plan which she had found in the blouse pocket, and handed it to George. He turned it several ways until he was sure it wasn't upside down.

'Some sort of a plan,' he said. 'Do you know what it is?'

'No.'

'Then what do you mean by saying it was serious?'

'Because of the circumstances in which I found it.'

'What circumstances?'

'I've got a confession to make. I tried on that lilac-coloured blouse which I saw in the wardrobe upstairs.'

'What on earth for?'

'I don't know. It was just a — a whim. Mrs. Lavering painted herself in that blouse, and a large floppy hat. Anyway, I tried them on — while you and Jerry were soaking.'

'Soaking!' ejaculated George. 'I like that. At least we were minding our own business.'

'S-sh! Don't shout.'

'I'm not shouting. But what has all that to do with this drawing?'

'It was in a little pocket of the blouse, folded up neatly.'

'Mrs. Lavering's blouse?'

'Of course. That's why I couldn't very well give it to Jerry.'

'At least you have a conscience. All the same, I can't see that it's the least bit serious. It might be any old thing. The most sensible thing to do is creep upstairs and put it where you found it, unless you want to confess to Jerry that you have been nosing into his private affairs.'

'Oh, no. He'd be terribly annoyed.'

'So would you in similar circumstances. He invited you to his house, gives us both a royal time, and the best you can do in return is to go snooping — '

'Oh, stop it! You have no imagination at all. Look — what do you make of that pair of vertical lines on the left-hand side of the plan. There?'

She indicated the place with her fingers, but George shook his head.

'Mightn't it be the shaft down which Boozer fell — the old mine shaft?'

'It might, but — '

'Then that would make sense of all the rest of the lines. It can be a plan of the underground workings of the tin mine — or part of it. Where the lines all converge on the right into one long gallery might be the place where Jerry took us in the boat. Jerry said there was an old mine working on the further side of the big cavern.'

'That's right,' said George.

'The plan was obviously drawn by Mrs. Lavering herself.'

'How can you say that?'

'Because the lines are the lines of an artist.'

'Poor argument,' scoffed George. 'But what then?'

'It suggests that she had been there several times. You can see where she has altered the lines.'

'Suppose she did? I can't see what you are driving at. Jerry told us that the mine belonged to his father, and grandfather.'

'You certainly are slow in the uptake. Why should Mrs. Lavering take the trouble to make this plan, long after the mine had been abandoned? Some parts of it are flooded, and she would have to approach it from the sea. Even at low tide you can only get there by taking a boat.'

'Then she took a boat.'

'Yes, George — and she took a boat on that evening when she never returned. We know it was going in that direction when she was last seen.'

'And left that plan behind her,' said George quickly.

'Yes — and never returned,' retorted Tessa.

'You said that before.'

'And I'll say it again. My theory is that she went to the old mine on that evening, and because she had forgotten the plan she got lost in it. That would explain her leaving when a storm was brewing. She thought she would get back long before there was any danger. Her body was never found — remember, but the boat was. That all supports the theory.'

'You'll drive me crackers,' said George, pushing his hands through his hair. 'Why should she want to rush off to the old mine late in the evening? Tell me that.'

'I can't. If I could, perhaps we should be able to solve the whole mystery of her death. What are we going to do about it?'

'Nothing. It's all baloney, as the poets say. You're making a three volume novel out of the mere fact that Mrs. Lavering — or somebody — was interested enough in the mine to make a plan of part of the workings — if indeed it is that. It might be any old place.'

Tessa looked at her brother intently. All his arguments were fudge. She knew he was now as intrigued as she was herself, but George had his own ideas about propriety, and he still regarded her discovery as very improper.

'Take my tip and put the plan back where you found it,' he said. 'Perhaps

— on another occasion — you can find it again in less felonious circumstances.'

'That may be your last word, but it isn't mine,' she said. 'I'm going to think it over. Good-night, sweetest!'

20

George lost his bet the following morning. He came to consciousness to realise that someone was in the room — someone in a bathing-wrap, and white cap. It took him quite a few moments to identify this curious apparition.

'Tessa!' he said.

'It is now exactly a quarter-past seven — at which precise moment you were going to be in the sea. That's sixpence you owe me and I'll have it now.'

George sat up and rubbed his eyes.

'How long have you been here?' he asked.

'About ten minutes.'

'Then why the devil didn't you wake me?'

'What — and lose my bet!'

'What bet?'

'You know what bet. Come on — out of it. Jerry will be waiting. He's gone to start the engine.'

'What engine?' asked George sleepily.

'The engine that charges the accumulators.'

George got out of bed and staggered across to the window.

'I don't believe it's a quarter-past seven,' he argued. 'It feels more like midnight to me. Where's the sun?'

'Staring you in the face. Can you get into your bathing suit or shall nursie lend you a hand?'

George reeled back from the window, picked up sixpence from a pile of coins on his dressing table and gave it to her.

'Take your filthy lucre and leave me alone,' he said.

Tessa foresaw his miserable intentions. She dashed to the bed, flung all the bedclothes on to the floor, and threw the pillow at the opposite wall. Then from below Lavering's voice boomed out.

'Oh Lord!' groaned George. 'It's a conspiracy. What are you waiting here for? How can I get into a bathing suit with you dancing about. Clear out!'

'We'll give you two minutes,' said Tessa.

George joined them a little later. He

311

wore a brilliant blue dressing gown over his swim suit, the long tassel of which nearly reached the ground. Boozer, who included himself in the party, made flank attacks on this as George walked. Finally, he succeeded in getting it between his teeth, upon which he stuck all four feet into the sand and pulled his utmost. The dressing gown came undone, and George let loose a blood-curdling cry. Boozer scuttled for his life, but came back again to the attack.

'You were swindled out of five bob, Jerry, when you bought that animal,' said George. 'He doesn't know a thing. B-r-r-r! The wind is quite fresh. I bet the sea is like ice.'

Tessa stopped on the edge of the incoming tide, and the next wave broke over her ankles.

'Ow!' she screamed. 'It's freezing.'

'I knew it,' said George. 'The proper time to bathe is when the sun — .'

He stopped as Lavering slipped off his dressing gown, rolled it up and flung it well up the sandy slope, and then ran into the sea. A few steps and the water was up to his waist. He then did a shallow dive, rose to the surface about ten yards further out, and commenced a tremendous crawl, until finally he turned on his back.

'Lovely!' he bellowed.

'Coming!' cried Tessa.

George dodged the garment which was flung at him, and caught a glimpse of Tessa's brown limbs as she ran and dived into the sunlit blue sea, and tore through it until she reached Lavering.

'Come on!' they both shouted in chorus.

George took off his dressing gown very deliberately, rolled it up, and placed a large stone on it, and then advanced down the beach like a man going to the scaffold. The cold water advanced up his round calves to his waist. He took a great gulp of air, but still went on until only his head remained above the water. Then came a wave and completely submerged him. When he next appeared he was close to Tessa and Lavering.

'Warm as toast,' he said. 'All that fuss!'

'Liar!' cried Tessa. 'It's freezing cold, but lovely. Jerry, I'll race you to that rock.'

'Too far,' replied Lavering.

'You, George.'

'Not me. I know my limitations.'

'I'll go myself, then.'

She swam away at once, towards the projecting slab of rock which offered a suitable place for sun-bathing, and which was at least a quarter of a mile away.

'Tessa, don't be an idiot!' called George.

Tessa did not — or would not — hear, but went on her course with a powerful overhand stroke.

'Can she make it?' asked Lavering.

'I don't know. She's pretty good in a swimming bath, but — '

'I'll go and head her back.'

Tessa turned her head and saw Lavering coming after her at speed. He waved a hand to induce her to return, but the only effect was to cause her to swim even faster. Lavering put his head down and went all out. He was a magnificent swimmer, and moved through the water with the ease of a fish. But before he could reach Tessa she had made the rock, and scrambled on to the flat surface.

'It's lovely here,' she gasped. 'No wind at all.'

'But dangerous,' replied Lavering, as he pulled himself out of the sea. 'You can't take liberties with the tide round these coasts. When did you learn to swim?'

'Soon after I left my cradle. Look how clear the water is. I can see right down to the bottom.'

Lavering shook the water from his hair, and sat down beside her, with his back supported by a barnacled pillar. The water had been cold but the sun was comfortably warm, and from their present position they were afforded views along the coast in both directions. Looking back Tessa saw Poltimore on his way to the house. She waved a hand and Poltimore waved back.

'But for him I'd probably be wrestling with the kitchen range,' she said.

'He's a good fellow, and deserves something better than what has happened to him. Oughtn't we to swim back?'

'Oh not yet. It's lovely sitting here — feeling the sun going right through you. Look, there's a boat out there!'

Lavering turned his head a little and saw the boat come into view from a concealed bay. It was a long way off, but he could distinguish two men in it, and could just hear the throb of a motor engine.

'Fishing, I suppose,' he said. 'Behind that little promontory is Swanpool. They are probably the Zaffery brothers.'

'Poltimore's relations?'

'Yes. He hates them.'

'They can't be much good if Poltimore dislikes them. Jerry, when is it the man comes to see Nancrannon?'

'To-morrow.'

'I hope he'll find fault with everything.'

'That's a nice thing to say to the prospective seller.'

'You've no need to sell. You'll be a rich man without Nancrannon.'

'You would prefer to see it standing there — empty and derelict?'

'I'd prefer to see you living there.'

'A landed gentleman — sitting in idleness?'

'Why sit in idleness?'

'I've always understood that was the

special privilege of landed gentlemen. It gets you a place in the social reference books, and entitles you to call yourself 'county'.'

Tessa sighed, and threw a piece of rock into the colourful sea.

'You know, Jerry,' she said. 'You can be quite stupid at times.'

'So you have discovered that, too?'

'How can I help it with you standing on the proverbial soap box and talking a lot of hot air. You're a bit of a hypocrite, too.'

'Are you trying to start a fight?' he asked, with a smile.

'Yes.'

'Any rules about it?'

'None.'

'Then come on,' he said, suddenly, and laid her swiftly on her back, with her arms pinned down on the rock. With his legs astride hers she was herself absolutely helpless.

'You — you trickster!' she gasped.

'Take back all you said.'

'I won't. I meant what I said. You are hypocritical because while you pretend to hate the idea of being a landed

317

gentleman, you're quite willing to sell the place to someone who probably won't have such scruples. That's inconsistent and cowardly. Let me go.'

Lavering looked down at the tanned face and neck. The sunburn was now of a deeper shade than her hair, and the contrast was most attractive. Then he observed — not for the first time — that she had remarkably fine eyes. He had thought they were deep brown, but now he saw that there was a suggestion of violet in them, and one or two other colours impossible to name. When she laughed, two intriguing little dimples appeared at the corners of her shapely mouth, and those incomparable eyes became illuminated from within.

'Don't stare,' she said. 'It's rude.'

'You know, you're quite pretty — in a way,' he remarked.

'Which way?'

'I can't quite make up my mind — yet.'

'Then you'd better be quick, because there's a sharp piece of rock boring into my back. Ooh!'

Lavering pulled her up quickly, and saw

318

that her complaint was genuine.

'I'm sorry,' he said, soberly. 'I'm really too old to engage in horseplay. I suppose it's the morning air. You've got seaweed in your hair.'

'You've got bindweed in yours,' she retorted. 'Oh, Jerry, it's lovely here. Look at the colour on those rocks, and the strange light on the white beach.'

Lavering looked in the direction of her pointing finger.

'That's the beach where we landed, to see Father Neptune's cave,' he said.

'Why, so it is. Oh, Jerry —.'

'Yes.'

There came a sudden impulse to tell him about the drawing she had found the previous evening, but he took his eyes off her for a moment and the impulse went. George was standing on the beach waving a towel at them, and shouting something.

'The worms are beginning to bite, I expect,' said Lavering. 'We had better swim back. What were you saying?'

'Nothing.'

'Then let's go.'

'Yes. Come on!'

She stood up and made to dive off the edge of the rock. Laverton gave a little cry and seized her from behind — his arms encircling her breasts. She turned her head.

'You can't do that,' he said. 'You could easily hit a rock with your head.'

'Yes — perhaps you're right,' she replied, breathing heavily.

'Better lower yourself down.'

She nodded, and did as he suggested. A minute later they were both swimming strongly towards the beach, with the tide in their favour.

'About time, too,' said George. 'I thought you were going to spend the day there. I'm starving.'

'Glutton,' said Tessa.

'What's wrong with a good healthy appetite?'

'Indigestion and obesity. What's Boozer got hold of?'

'The tassel of my dressing gown,' grumbled George. 'He chewed it off while I was swimming. Think he'll have the sense to bring it home?'

'Hey, Boozer, bring it here!' shouted Lavering.

Boozer stopped tossing his trophy into the air, but made no attempt to obey. He placed his two paws beside it, and rested his chin on it.

'Come on, boy,' pleaded Lavering. 'Good boy — bring it!'

'You see,' said George. 'He doesn't even know the English language. Hi, you mongrel, bring me my tassel!'

But Boozer had none of the retriever in his make-up, and he stayed where he was until they started back to the house, then he brought up the rear with the tassel in his mouth.

'Don't you dare bury it!' shouted George, wagging his finger.

The early morning breeze died away as the day progressed, and by noon the sun was blazing down on a dead flat ocean. Poltimore served an excellent cold lunch on the terrace, and George had his siesta in a long chair, with a newspaper spread over his head to keep away the flies. They woke him up at tea time, and he sighed at the sight of home-made scones, cream and jam.

'Just my idea of Paradise,' he said.

'Disgusting,' retorted Tessa. 'Jerry and I have cut down two trees and weeded a mile of path. I thought you were going shopping.'

'By Jove, so we were. What about it, Jerry?'

'There's plenty of time. We'll take the car — after tea, and run into Bodmin.'

'What about you, Tessa?' asked George.

'Leave me out,' said Tessa. 'I'd prefer to play about here.'

'Sure?'

'Quite sure.'

'That's okay, then.'

'Don't be so pleased.'

'I'm not pleased. But don't get into any mischief.'

'Don't you,' retorted Tessa.

Tessa saw them off later. Boozer had jumped into the car, and was settling himself down for a nice ride, but George pointed out with some truth the detestable habits of certain untrained dogs in respectable shops, and so Boozer was dumped into Tessa's arms, from which he scowled at the lucky tourists.

'Never mind, Boozer,' said Tessa. 'You shall come for a nice walk with me.'

Boozer obviously didn't think that was the same thing. He, too, liked bachelor parties, especially when they included 'pubs,' as they invariably did.

21

'I've laid the table for supper,' said Poltimore, later. 'There's some soup on the stove, and plenty of cold meat and salad. If you want sweets, there's a bowl of junket and some fresh raspberries on the larder floor, with a cloth over them. Mr. Lavering knows I'm leaving a bit early this evening, but you can leave the washing up for me to do in the morning.'

'Oh, we won't do that.'

'It's no trouble, Miss Tessa. I never could understand the objection some folks have for washing up.'

'You should tell that to my brother,' said Tessa, with a laugh. 'Is there going to be a storm?'

'No, Miss. It's just heat, and nothing more. Low tide this evening. One of the lowest of the year.'

'Could I get as far as Trewith along the beach?'

'Aye, if you went now. Maybe you'd

have to climb over some rocks near Penhale, but there's no danger there. Just a lot of shallow pools. Anything more, Miss Tessa?'

'No, thank you!'

Tessa, who was in her sun-bathing suit, changed into a pair of slacks, with Boozer as an impatient observer. Then, as a last thought, she took the plan which she had so recently found. Here was an opportunity to check up the drawing, and at the same time to see again that amazing cavern which had impressed her so deeply.

'Come on, Boozer!' she said. 'Now we're all set.'

Boozer went leaping ahead of her, apparently impervious to the heavy heat. At intervals he would stop and look back as if to say 'for the love of Mike get a move on.' From the cove, Tessa made the western turn on a stretch of fine white sand which was so hard that it scarcely registered her footprints. Here and there were islets of rock, in the surrounding pools of which swam shrimps and tiny fish. Boozer was not interested in these, but the great blue circular jelly-fish which were scattered along the whole length of the beach was another matter. The dog pranced round them, sniffing and barking, snapping his teeth close to them, without actually touching them.

'No good, Boozer,' said Tessa. 'Not edible, and they've got nasty stings when they're annoyed.'

Below her, parallel with her advance, the lazy rollers could do little more than lave the gleaming beach. How different to the occasions when that same blue ocean was piled in mountains of careering white-capped waves, which thundered like cannonades and flung the spindrift over the frowning rock bastion. She felt she had been transferred to Southern Italy — some dream isle in a dream sea, where dryads lived and sirens sang. She went to where the waves were breaking and walked ankle-deep, with her trousers turned up to her knees. Boozer didn't like this. Nothing would induce him to cross into another element.

'You big baby!' she said. 'This is where life began. I was an amoeba, and so were you, but you must have had a tail. Leave that jelly-fish alone!'

The beach narrowed as she proceeded, and soon there was little of it left as she approached the rock obstruction at Penhale. But as Poltimore had said, the shallow pools left by the sea were easily negotiable, and she reached the flat promontory over which she scrambled, to find dry, hard sand on the further side. From here she could see the marvellous rock configuration which framed Neptune's Cavern, and the spot on which she and George and Jerry had landed from the boat. Seen in the western light it was even more romantic than on the former occasion, and she caught her breath in her speechless admiration.

'Why aren't I a painter, Boozer?' she asked.

Only now was the tide approaching its lowest ebb, and she saw that she had plenty of time, for away towards Trewith there was a comparatively wide expanse of open beach. At last she approached the entrance to the cavern, and she felt in her pocket to make sure that the little electric torch was still functioning.

'Here we go,' she muttered. 'Come and hold my hand, Boozer.'

Boozer appeared not to like the tunnel which led to the large cavern. It was not easy to avoid those pools of still, cold water, and there were drips coming from the roof. But for Tessa the going was easier than on the previous occasion, because she had not to scramble over the higher rocks as she had then. Ultimately she reached the cavern which previously had been flooded, and here as before she stopped and let the scene sink deep into her consciousness. Now there was a variation of the lighting effects and the oblique rays of the declining sun no longer reached the sandy floor, but struck through the crevices of the roof across to the fantastic walls, painting them orange and violet, interweaved with subtle and bewildering tints which changed as she watched them. At the far end she could see dimly two tunnels, running left and right, and these were in accordance with the plan, which showed that both these tunnels converged further on. She chose the right one, because it looked easier of access, and walked across to the opening.

'Scared, Boozer?' she asked.

Boozer, who was staring into the tunnel, turned his head and showed his green eyes, which were eerie enough in themselves. Tessa flashed the electric torch into the tunnel, and then began to move forward over the wet and uneven floor.

Very soon the other gallery came in from the left, and the main tunnel widened out. Here and there were old timbers shoring up the roof, and twice she passed workings which were not shown on the plan at all, but the main gallery and its connections corresponded exactly with the plan, and no longer was there the slightest doubt that this was the place depicted.

The long gallery finally joined a cross working. To the right the plan was a blank, except to indicate that a working ran in that direction. She turned to the left, and climbed a slope where the roof was almost completely boarded up, and supported by stout beams. Again she made a turn, and then another. According to the plan she should now be approaching the vertical lines which she had taken to be the main shaft. Boozer was walking at her heels, apparently suffering from chronic claustrophobia.

'All right,' she said. 'We'll soon be in the fresh air again. I don't like this queer smell any more than you do. Clever of Mrs. Lavering to remember all these turnings and to draw this neat plan. Good gracious, just look at that!'

Ahead of her was a curious patch of light — almost nebulous in its form. She switched off the torch in order that she could see better what it was, and then she realised that it was daylight filtering down a vertical working, and being reflected by the rock wall.

'The mine shaft!' she said. 'That's where you fell down — you nitwit. This is the end of the journey, and I can't say I'm sorry. Steady now!'

She switched on the torch again, and went forward cautiously, Boozer sneaking up behind her. The gallery narrowed until it was only a few feet wide, and finally she stepped on a wooden platform of solid construction which seemed to go to the very edge of the pit. In actual fact it went beyond this, and overhung the main shaft by a foot or two. Clinging to an upright support she looked up the shaft and saw the open end of it. Below her was water — so still that the surface looked solid.

'Phew!' she said. 'No wonder you're scared, old boy. It's a marvel you're alive to tell the tale. Well, I've seen enough. Thank God for sunlight and fresh air.'

She turned and made her way back across the slippery planks. Then suddenly she saw something partially hidden by a loose boulder. Closer inspection showed that it was an empty cigarette packet, not of great age. This caused her to remember that Lavering had picked up a half-smoked cigarette on the landing platform when he had made his historic descent in the bucket. So someone else had been here recently! But it signified nothing beyond the universality of human inquisitiveness.

'Home, Boozer,' she said.

Nothing was more to Boozer's liking.

He gave a bark, which went echoing strangely through the strange place, and leaped up at her in his excitement. That leap was most unfortunate for it knocked the electric torch out of her hand, and brought darkness except for the nebulous light which came from the shaft. This was just sufficient to cause the chromium-plated torch to be visible. She picked it up, only to discover that the lens and bulb were broken, and that it was now utterly useless.

'Now we're in a mess,' she muttered. 'Unless I can manage to read that plan — .'

She found the plan and held it close to her eyes, but not a line of it was visible. Then she felt her way back to the shaft, but by this time the light was worse than before, and it was with the utmost difficulty that she could see even the surface of the sheet of paper. She tried to remember the many turnings which she had taken since she left the big cavern, but found it a hopeless task.

'You got me in this mess, Boozer,' she said. 'And it's up to you to get me out.

Boozer, where are you?'

She looked for the dog's green eyes, but saw nothing but ever-increasing darkness.

'Boozer!' she called. 'Come here, boy!'

She caught her breath as she realized that Boozer was no longer in the vicinity. This should not have astonished her since she knew that that untrained animal seldom came when he was called, or did anything one wanted him to do. For the first time in many years she began to feel afraid. Perhaps luck might favour her, but if so it had to be quick, for soon the tide would be sweeping up that narrow tunnel and into that big cavern — rendering escape impossible until the sea receded.

'Boozer!' she cried again, and then strained her ears to catch any sound. None came. Only the monotonous dripping of water from somewhere.

Resolutely she began to move forward, feeling the right wall with her hand. After covering a few score yards, the blackness was complete. Then her right hand went into space and she knew there was a turning. Which way to go now — right or left? She believed it was left, so she went in that direction, groping all the time, and dragging her feet slowly for fear of obstruction. She made another turn left — after considerable reflection — and after advancing for a long time she got the impression that she was descending. This was frightening as she could not remember having climbed any gradient at that end of the workings. Then suddenly her foot went into water, and she knew she was wrong.

Back she went, with her heart thumping madly, to the place where she had made the turning. Here she crossed a gap and went straight on — groping as before. After a few minutes she found another turning, and by this time she had not the slightest idea whether to take it or go straight on, for there had been a number of turnings which she had neglected on the outward journey. She went straight on. A long time passed, and still there was no gap in the solid wall on her right. Now she began to fear that she might have missed a turning on her left. She reached out with her left arm, but could find no wall there. Panic began to assail her. Doubtless this ancient mine was honey-combed with such workings, and that Mrs. Lavering had only plotted a fraction of the endless tunnels. She had heard that some of the oldest tin mines had been worked by the Phoenicians. That reflection was devastating. She might go on like this for days, getting deeper and deeper into old and forgotten passages. There might be gas. There might be anything.

She stopped and listened to the tremendous beating of her heart. What was the best thing to do? Was it better to go back and attempt to reach the main shaft again, where at least there was some connection with the outer world, and where the air was undoubtedly fresher than it was here? She began to imagine she was choking, and that caused her to choke and gasp until she was nearly exhausted. Then commonsense came to her aid. That way lay madness. She had to keep her wits. Clear thinking was an essential. The thing to do was find a spot where the air was fresher than it was here, and there to rest for a while. Soon the tide would be rushing into the cavern. In this sepulchral silence that noise should be heard. It would — or should — be some indication of the direction she must take.

So she went on — very slowly now, breathing heavily and painfully. At last there came a turning on her right. She took this and became aware of a decided up gradient. Soon there was a noticeable improvement in the atmosphere. Breathing became much easier, and her mind seemed clearer. She decided to rest for a while.

Now came unprofitable self-reproach. Why had she been so idiotic as to make this visit — alone? She might have known that Boozer would be useless in such an emergency. How much more sensible it would have been to have told Jerry that she had found the plan, and in what circumstances. What sense was there in making the trip at all? Oh, to be safely back at Nancrannon, playing the piano, or enjoying the sunset from the terrace. By this time George and Jerry would probably be back from their shopping expedition, and wondering where she was. How long would it take them to reach the conclusion that some calamity had befallen her?

What a strange thing complete darkness was! The visual part of her brain would insist upon conjuring up colours. These colours were chiefly of the pinky-red order. They seemed to float before her like a cloud, to disappear and then come again. Her ears, too, were tuned as never before. Every little sound was enormously magnified. Her beating heart, her lip movements, the contact of her hand with her clothing — all were incredibly loud. Then, after a long while, there came another sound — from a distance. It caused her to sit bolt upright and listen intently. Yes, it was the sighing which she had heard before in the outer tunnel which led to the big cavern — the sound caused by the influx of the sea, and the expulsion of the air.

But in what direction was it? At one moment it appeared to come from ahead of her, and at another from behind. But wherever it came from it was a relief from the terrible silence. Surely it must grow louder as the tide rose higher, and then perhaps she would be able to locate it with some degree of accuracy. Her hopes were soon fulfilled. The sighing and gurgling, and booming increased in volume. Now she felt sure that she was going away from the sounds. The only thing to do was to go back, and attempt to use them as her guide. A little less fearful and depressed she began to retrace her footsteps.

22

Lavering and George came back from their shopping expedition with a wonderful array of parcels. George had remembered all sorts of friends and relations who, in his opinion, were entitled to expect souvenirs of his Cornish holiday.

'My Aunt Fanny will go dippy over this necklace. She's mad on gee-gaws, and when she knows that these stones were found on Marazion beach — .'

'Perhaps,' said Lavering.

'Oh, I say, old man, don't spoil it all. You know that these stones can be picked up on many Cornish beaches.'

'Yes, but were they?'

'My Aunt Fanny is going to believe they were. Tessa must have gone for a walk. Taken out that quadruped of yours, too. By Jove, it's hot. Do we eat now or wait for her?'

'We wait.'

George sighed. He took his presents to his bedroom, and then came down and occupied a chair on the terrace.

'What a life!' he sighed. 'Ghastly to realize that in a few days' time I'll be back in the damned bank, shovelling out money to worried customers.'

'Why worried?' asked Lavering, as he sat down beside George.

'Those who run overdrafts are worried about being able to repay them, and those who have large credit balances are worrying about the share market. No one is entirely free of worry. Gosh, what a sunset!'

Time passed and the last reluctant bars of the sunset faded out. From the garden there stole the pungent odours of the night-scented blossoms, lingering long on the still air.

'Tessa's making a world tour of it,' complained George. 'That's the worst of women — they're so darned energetic — at the wrong moments.'

Lavering laughed, as he stood up and stretched himself.

'You win, George,' he said. 'It's a cold

meal, anyway, so we had better go and fend for ourselves.'

They did this to good purpose, and were soon sitting before the miscellaneous cold fare. By the time they had finished it was quite dark, and still there was no sign of Tessa or the dog.

'I hope she hasn't been silly enough to take the boat,' said George. 'The sea's calm enough, but if anything went wrong with the outboard motor she'd be in a mess.'

'If she took the boat she wouldn't take Boozer.'

'She might. I'm going to have a look for the boat.'

'I'll come, too.'

They left the house and walked down to the cove. There was the small boat, above the tide level, with its anchor thrust into the sand.

'That's a relief anyway,' said George. 'She'll probably come back, calm as you like, and say 'Am I late?' Just like a woman.'

When eleven o'clock came, and Tessa had not appeared to say 'Am I late?' both

George and Lavering were showing signs of anxiety.

'At what time did Poltimore leave?' asked George.

'Early this evening. He told me he had some business to do.'

'Perhaps he knows where Tessa intended going.'

'That's possible.'

At that moment there was a noise outside. Both men heard it and George looked at Lavering.

'The front door,' he said. 'Sounds like Boozer.'

Their doubts were then removed by a sharp barking.

'Ah, she's back,' said George, in a relieved voice.

But there was no sign of Tessa's arrival, and Boozer commenced barking again — this time under the lounge window. Lavering opened the window wider, and the dog bounded through it on to the corner of the big couch. Lavering looked at the animal's furry coat.

'Why, you're all wet,' he said. 'I thought you hated water. Hey, where's Tessa?'

Boozer succeeded in looking heartily ashamed of himself. He crawled down to the floor and lay on his stomach, with his gaze fixed on Lavering.

'I don't like this,' said George.

'Nor do I. He would never get wet of his own accord. She might have gone for a bathe, and — . Let's go and see Poltimore. Come on!'

Poltimore was going to bed when they arrived at his queer shanty. It comprised but two rooms, the smaller of which was a bedroom. The larger room was a veritable museum, but it was tidy and clean. The owner was surprised to receive guests at this time of night, and he seemed to sense that something was amiss.

'Poltimore, was Tessa in when you left Nancrannon?' asked Lavering.

'Aye, but she was just going for a walk when I left.'

'Did she say where she was going?'

'Aye. She asked me if it was possible to walk along the beach to Trewith. I told her it was if she started right away.'

'Did you actually see her start?'

'No, but I'm sure she was just going to.

She was in her bedroom when I left — changing her clothes, I reckon.'

'She hasn't come back,' said George. 'But the dog has just come in, and his coat was wet.'

Poltimore stroked his jaw with his big hand, and his tanned brow became wrinkled.

'There was plenty of time for her to get safely to Trewith,' he said. 'She couldn't come to any harm along there with this low tide. But now, of course, the tide is making pretty fast.'

'Too fast,' said Lavering, grimly. 'I wonder if she can have been cut off. She may have tried to walk back and got caught in that nasty patch by the cavern.'

It was here that George remembered Tessa's intense interest in the plan which she had found.

'We're wasting valuable time, Jerry,' he said. 'Let's get the boat out and cruise as far as Trewith. There's that big electric lamp in the Bentley with the long-range lens.'

'Why not take my boat?' asked Poltimore. 'She's not afloat yet, but she will be before long.'

Lavering declined the offer, since it would involve waiting an indefinite time, for Poltimore's boat was too heavy to manhandle. George's suggestion seemed to be the better.

'Will ye be needing any help?' asked Poltimore.

'I don't think so, thank you,' replied Lavering. 'It's possible that Tessa has arrived home during our absence. I hope that proves to be the case.'

But when he and George reached Nancrannon they found Boozer alone in the house.

'Well, the boat's our obvious next step,' said Lavering.

'Yes,' agreed George. 'Jerry, I've got an idea about all this.'

'What do you mean?'

'Tell you as we go. Come on.'

As they hurried to the cove, George related the incident of the finding of the plan, and Lavering was not slow to realise what was in his friend's mind.

'You think she may have gone to the cavern?' he asked.

'It's possible, isn't it? We know her intention was to go to Trewith by the beach. That would bring her right up against the cave entrance. Apart from the plan, the place intrigued her. She has often talked about it.'

Lavering nodded. They had reached the boat, which was now floating in shallow water. The motor was lying in the bottom of it, but Lavering soon got it attached to the stout stern. The petrol tank was nearly full, and there was a spare tin in the locker. The engine fired at the first pull on the starter cord, and the craft began to move forward.

'Curious about that plan,' said Lavering. 'But even if Tessa went to the cave there was plenty of time for her to get out of it. Boozer must have got out, and he doesn't cut much of a figure in the water. Keep a good look-out. I'll cruise inshore as far as possible.'

There was as yet no moon, but the sky was so clear and full of stars that the foreshore could be seen with considerable clarity. George presided over the electric hand-lamp, but as yet there was no occasion to use it, for there was still a strip of sand for some distance.

'Penhale is the first danger point,' said Lavering. 'There'll be water right up to the cliff, and some nasty holes. We'll be there in about ten minutes.'

But for their mutual anxiety the trip would have been pleasant in the extreme, for the composition of the nocturnal picture was incomparable. The gaunt cliff seemed higher and mightier in the starlight, and its vague immensity was silhouetted against a sky that was full of stars. To the north the larger stars were reflected in the sea, where they moved to the rhythm of the tide.

'I'll try to get the boat close in at Penhale,' said Lavering. 'Perhaps one of us can scramble up the rocks and take a look round, with the aid of the hand-lamp.'

George nodded, and watched the phosphorescent water stream from the bows of the boat. The camel hump of Penhale drew closer and closer. Lavering altered course a little to avoid a spot where he knew there was a jagged reef, but finally the place he wanted came up at him. He stopped the engine, and let the boat drift in to a landing place.

'I'll go ashore,' said George.

'Come on then, and mind how you step.'

George clambered on to a flat rock, with the electric hand-lamp clutched to his chest. Lavering could just distinguish his movements in the darkness, until George got the hand-lamp into action, and made himself very obvious. The long bright finger of light jabbed into every hole and corner, and twice George changed his position. Finally he came back.

'Not a sign of anyone,' he said. 'The water is right up to the cliff, just as you said.'

'Jump aboard then.'

Lavering pushed himself off with the boat-hook, and started the engine again. A few minutes later they passed round the end of the promontory and struck across a little bay. Beyond that was the jumbled mass of rocks which framed the cave.

'Pretty grim,' said George. 'There doesn't appear to be any foreshore at all. Nowhere to anchor the boat — at least no safe place.'

Lavering had already realised this possibility. The going soon became more dangerous. He reduced speed and finally he took off the outboard motor and resorted to rowing.

'What are you going to do?' asked George. 'There's the tunnel right ahead of us.'

'Much movement of water?'

George got the torch working again.

'No. It's pretty calm at the entrance.'

'Then we'll take the boat right in.'

'What — through the tunnel?'

'Yes. If the tide is high enough there should be plenty of room. We'll soon know.'

George now kept the ray of the hand-lamp focused on the entrance to the tunnel. Yard by yard the boat went forward, and once or twice her bottom was grazed by rocks, but finally the great roof was over them, and the walls enclosed them. An eerie effect was now created by the powerful lamp. It struck down into the green water, and brought to view dark masses of rock which looked closer to the surface than they really were. There was not sufficient room to use the oars so Lavering took one of them and worked it from the stern in figure of eight motion.

'That's cunning,' said George. 'Oh, look out!'

A backward surge of the tide had uncovered a jagged edge of rock, but the next moment incoming water lifted the boat over the temporary obstruction. Slowly the great inner cavern came to view, until they drifted from the tunnel clean into it. George swept the wide expanse with the hand-lamp.

'Not here,' he said. 'What was that?'

'Father Neptune breathing again. Uncanny, isn't it?'

'I'll say it is. There's that booming, too. Ever been here before at night?'

'No.'

'You know, I believe Tessa was right about the plan. It did represent this place. There are the two outlets from the old mine.'

He directed the ray across the water to indicate both entrances. 'I remember they both reached the same spot.'

'Pity we haven't got the plan,' mused Lavering.

'If we had Tessa wouldn't have had it, and then she wouldn't have come — if she has come — here.'

'That's true.'

'What about raising a shout?'

'I can't see that it would do much good. But let's try — together.'

Their combined voices rolled and echoed round the cavern in the strangest manner, but it produced no response.

'That's that!' said George. 'What's the programme now?'

'We'll make the boat fast near the left-hand entrance, and have a look inside. What's the state of the battery in that lamp?'

'Nearly new. It should last for hours.'

'Got a piece of paper and a pencil?'

'I think so. What's the idea?'

'This place may be a regular honeycomb. If we mark every turning, as we take it, or pass it, we shall stand less chance of getting hopelessly lost.'

'What a brain!' said George. 'Here we are — the back of this foolscap envelope, from his hatefulness the Collector of Income Tax. Pencil — now where the blazes — ? Ah!'

Lavering rowed the boat across the unique lagoon, and finally beached it just below the steep patch of sand which terminated at the mine working.

'I don't think she can come to any harm,' he said. 'We'll take the anchor right inside the entrance, to avoid having to swim back later. 'Ready?'

'Yes,' replied George.

23

The two men proceeded up the narrow working, in the full light of the powerful hand-lamp. After covering a short distance, George pointed to the ground excitedly, and brought the ray of the torch lower.

'A footprint!'

'That's right,' agreed Lavering. 'There's another further on.'

'So she did come here. In that case we ought — .'

He stopped as he came to the second footprint. It was clearer than the first, and was almost perfect.

'I spoke too soon,' he said. 'That can't be Tessa's footprint. It's miles too big. What do you make of that?'

'There's nothing to prevent anyone from coming here — especially at low tide.'

'That's true.'

Very soon they reached the spot where the two workings met, and from that point, for a long distance, the ground was dry. George couldn't remember how the plan went so they took turnings at hazard, after marking them clearly on the back of the envelope.

'We don't seem to be getting anywhere,' complained George after a long time. 'Let's give another shout.'

Again their combined voices were raised, and went rumbling away in ghostly fashion.

'Not a sound,' muttered George. 'No sign that she came here at all.'

'Yes there is,' said Lavering. 'If I'm not mistaken there are Boozer's imprints.'

George moved the ray of the hand-lamp, and saw two clear impressions of a dog's pads, but they were facing towards them.

'Now what do we do?' he asked. 'No sign of Tessa, yet she would have to step on this damp stuff if she was with the dog. Think he got scared and ran away from her?'

'No use speculating. We'd better go right on. She may have sprained her ankle — anything.'

They went on through the bewildering maze, shouting loudly at intervals, only to be met by the same echoes and then stony silence. Twice they came to water and had to retrace their footsteps, and George's rough plan was now so long that he had to slit the envelope and continue on the inner side.

'We must be on the wrong track,' he said ultimately. 'Did you bring any cigarettes with you?'

'Yes.'

'Let's have a smoke. This is getting a bit spooky.'

They both lighted cigarettes, and then Lavering had a look at George's lengthening plan.

'Pretty complicated,' he said. 'Whatever you do, hang on to that, or we may be here for days. By the way, did Tessa have an electric torch?'

'Yes — just a small thing.'

'I can't think she would have been so crazy as to come as far as we now are from the entrance.'

'You don't know Tessa.'

'Well, are we to go on, or turn back

until we reach the place where we saw the dog's imprints?'

'Turn back,' replied George. 'Perhaps even the dog may not have been Boozer, but the fact remains that Tessa is missing. That's not easy to explain.'

'No, it isn't!' agreed Lavering. 'I think we should have rung up the police before we came here. Tessa may have got to Trewith, and have met with an accident on the road.'

'In that case, wouldn't they have telephoned the house?'

'Not if Tessa were unconscious.'

George winced at this hypothesis, causing Lavering to wish he hadn't put it forward.

'Alternatively there may be a simple explanation, and she may now be at Nancrannon,' said Lavering. 'In that case she'll wonder where on earth we are. We should have left a note for her. Not very bright, are we?'

But George was far from being consoled, and he walked on in silence, with the plan in his hand, taking all the turnings by which they had come — or at least doing his best.

'Sure you're right?' asked Lavering.

'Pretty certain. The next turning to the right should bring us to the spot where we saw the dog imprints. Yes, here's the turning.'

They turned right, and fifty yards further on they came upon the impressions. Here George stopped.

'I think we ought to investigate that turning on the left,' he said.

'All right. But if that fails we'll go back to the boat, and run as far as Trewith. There's a police station in the village, and we may possibly hear something.'

The turning was investigated for a considerable distance, but it yielded nothing, and finally they turned back and eventually reached the cavern where the boat was floating. Lavering pulled on the anchor line and slowly brought the craft inshore. Again they made the passage through the tunnel, and emerged into bright moonlight.

'Trewith?' asked George.

'Yes.'

'I didn't know there was a police station there?'

'Actually it's only a cottage, housing a constable. He's the sole guardian of the law in these parts. But at least he has a telephone, and we can ring up Nancrannon and find out if Tessa is back.'

George nodded as the boat was pushed between the treacherous rocks. Then Lavering got the engine going, and put the nose of the craft towards Trewith. In a very short time they were under the stone jetty of the little port. Lavering tied up the boat, and mounted the flight of steep stone steps. It was a lovely sight as seen from the jetty itself. The little harbour was flooded with moonlight, and a dozen or so of pleasure craft, plus a few trawlers, threw deep shadows on the calm water. Not a living soul was in sight, and everything seemed sunk in sleep.

'Where does the policeman live?' asked George.

'Up the main street. Come on!'

★ ★ ★

In the meantime Inspector Warren had not relaxed for a moment his efforts to solve the local murder. His portfolio, appropriately marked 'Poltimore (Zillah)' was now bulging with neat typewritten copies of depositions. Separately there was a summary of all this, and a time-table. The Inspector now had no need to consult any of the depositions, for he knew them by heart. It was now very late, but he was still waiting in his office for the return of his assistant — Sergeant Cummings, who had motored over to Trewith on a special mission. He was smoking his pipe reflectively when Cummings came in.

'Well?' he asked.

'Luck's in, sir,' said the Sergeant. 'Here's the pound note. It was paid over the counter of the inn this evening.'

The Inspector took the note, and checked the number against that on one of the depositions. He also took note of the small red ink mark on the back of it.

'Who tendered the note?' he asked.

'Ezra Zaffery.'

'Not Seth Zaffery?'

'No sir. Seth hadn't been to the inn to-day. The landlord remembers the red ink mark. He is absolutely certain it was Ezra.'

'Well, it makes no difference, for I have already secured a warrant against both of them.'

'Think we have a good case, sir?'

'Good enough to frighten one of them into squealing on the other. Even if this shouldn't happen I still think the evidence against them is strong.'

'Just the fact that one of them possessed a pound note which we know was in the possession of the girl a few hours before she was murdered?'

'No. Not merely that. There's the footprint, which we have traced to the boot which you cleverly stole from Swanpool to-day. That obviously belongs to Seth Zaffery, for his initials are inside it.'

'The footprint was a good way from the corpse.'

'I know that, but there's one point which you missed when we were taking evidence from Seth's wife.'

'Was there?'

'I think so. She, like her husband, swore that she hadn't seen Zillah for a fortnight, but a little later she referred to a quarrel and showed us a bruise on her foot caused by her hated niece. That bruise hadn't been there a fortnight, nor even a week. She was lying.'

'You think Zillah had called there shortly before she was murdered?'

'In my own mind I'm convinced she did. She sold her bicycle to Ned Harmer earlier in the evening and received that ink-stained pound note for it. Young Harmer did us a service when he religiously kept a record of his saved pound notes. The girl must have had other money as well, or she could not have hoped to get to London. But there was no hope of tracing that, as we had no idea of the source of it. That doesn't matter now. Ezra will have to explain where he got that note, and that isn't going to be easy. Likewise, Seth will have to explain how his footprint came to be near the place where the corpse was found. And all of them will have to give a satisfactory explanation of why they lied when they said they had not seen Zillah for a fortnight.'

'Yes, they're certainly in a jam, sir,' said the Sergeant. 'But there's just one point, if I may mention it.'

'Go ahead.'

'Are the Zafferys so hard up that they would commit a murder for the comparatively small sum of money which their niece could have had on her person?'

'That's a point,' agreed the Inspector. 'But I don't think it's strong enough to outweigh the other evidence.'

'What about Mrs. Zaffery? Why aren't you arresting her, too?'

'Because I intend to bring pressure on her when her husband and his brother are in jail. She may try to save her husband by attempting to pin the actual murder on his brother. If she does that we are bound to get some more facts — if not the whole truth.'

The Sergeant nodded, and smiled appreciatively at his chief's cunning.

'When do we make the arrests, sir?' he asked.

'Now. I don't want to give them any more time to fake up some sort of story which might sound plausible. I'm hoping that Seth hasn't yet noticed that his boot is missing. Is the car outside?'

'Yes.'

'Then get Watson to come with us. I'll join you in a few minutes.'

A little later the police car was moving swiftly in the direction of Swanpool, and when at last the queer house came to view a light was seen shining from a back window.

'So they're still up,' said the Inspector. 'Little do they guess where they are going to sleep to-night.'

The car was soon outside the entrance to the house. Watson stayed with it, and the Inspector and the Sergeant went to the door. Hazel answered the summons and stared at the two visitors.

'Good evening, Mrs. Zaffery,' said the Inspector. 'Is your husband at home?'

'No.'

'Nor your brother-in-law?'

'No.'

'Where are they?'

'Out fishing.'

'When did they go?'

'An hour ago.'

'When do you expect them back?'

'I don't know. Sometimes they stay out until dawn — and after.'

'I'm afraid I shall have to satisfy myself on that point,' said the Inspector.

'You've no right to force your way in here, with my menfolk away,' Hazel protested.

'As I hold warrants for the arrest of your menfolk I think I have every right,' retorted the Inspector.

'Arrest!'

'That's what I said.'

By the time Hazel had recovered from her incredulity, the Inspector and the Sergeant were marching down the passage. Hazel slammed the door and came hurrying up behind them.

'You must be mad,' she said.

'Remember your manners!' remonstrated the Sergeant.

'Remember your own,' she snapped.

'How's your foot?' asked the Inspector, glancing down at her injured toe.

'That's no business of yours.'

'On the contrary it may prove to be very much my business. No one in here. Take a look round, Cummings. Go into all the rooms.'

Cummings went off, but Hazel remained, glaring at the Inspector and hitching up her skirt.

'I'm not lying,' she said. 'You'll find I told you the truth. You'd better come back in the morning.'

'We stay here until we see them.'

'But I want to go to bed.'

'Then go to bed. We shan't set fire to the house.'

'I don't believe you're telling me the truth. You can't arrest my husband and Ezra.'

'Why not?'

'They've done nothing wrong.'

'In that case they have nothing to worry about — nor you either. I thought you wanted to go to bed?'

'So I do, but I can't with that man upstairs.'

The man upstairs came down a little later, and reported that the house appeared to be empty, except for Mrs. Zaffery.

'I told you so,' said Hazel.

'All right. We'll wait here.'

Hazel spun round on her bare feet, and walked out of the room.

'See where she goes, and lock the door after her,' said the Inspector. 'That is — if you can.'

The Sergeant came back a minute or two later to say that he had found a key outside the bedroom door through which Hazel had gone, and that he had locked it quietly.

'Good. Now draw those curtains, and tell Watson to move the car where it can't be seen.'

The Sergeant went out and was absent for a few minutes. When he returned he reported that the car was well concealed behind a rock.

'Good!' said the Inspector. 'Now you can relax. There's nothing we can do until those fellows come home.'

24

Constable Horton's cottage was a rose-clad affair in limewashed cob, and no one would have guessed it housed a policeman but for the steel plate over the front door. It required three rings of the bell to bring the Constable to the door, where he stood and blinked at his unexpected callers.

'My name's Lavering, and I live at Nancrannon — '

'Of course,' interrupted Horton. 'I remember you now, sir. Is anything wrong?'

Lavering explained the situation, and Horton said that he had been in Trewith all that evening. He hadn't seen Tessa, and there had been no kind of accident.

'It's possible she was delayed and has now managed to get home,' said Lavering. 'May I use your telephone?'

'Whoi, certainly, sir. This way.'

They were shown into the 'office,'

which was office-cum-sitting room. Horton was given the telephone number, and he himself put the call through. Exchange seemed to be asleep but at last the call was taken. There was a long silence, and then he was informed there was no reply. George's face fell at the significance of this.

'Evidently she hasn't got back,' he said. 'What's the next step, Jerry?'

'Inform the County Police Headquarters. Will you do that Mr. Horton?'

'Certainly, sir. Will you give me the details. Time she left home, and description of the young lady.'

Lavering did this with such detail of the physical part that George was surprised. Horton then got on to Police Headquarters and passed on the information.

'They'll do what they can, Mr. Lavering,' he said. 'Exciting times for Trewith. First a murder and then a disappearance. Looks like they've solved the murder, too.'

'You mean — there's been an arrest?' asked Lavering.

'By this time I should say.'

'But I thought there wasn't a single clue.'

'The police don't broadcast their information. Maybe there's more than one clue. Anyway, there was one found to-night — at the inn.'

'Really,' said Lavering.

'Just an ordinary pound note. Our people were pretty smart about that. You see, that poor girl sold her bicycle before she left home, and the young chap who bought it gave her a pound note. He's only a lad, and he happened to keep the number of that note. Well, to cut a long story short, it was handed over the counter at the inn this evening. The landlord had been told by us to watch out for a note with that number on it. Everyone in the district had, too — at least all the tradespeople. Well, there it was. Sergeant Cummings was sent down to get it.'

'Do they know the man who paid it over?' asked George.

'Aye. It was Zillah's own uncle — Ezra Zaffery. The Sergeant told me he reckoned that would fix the Zafferys for good.'

'But Zaffery might have got the note from someone else.'

'For sure he might, but there was other things as well. Well, gentlemen, I hope the young lady will turn up safe and sound.'

Lavering and George went back to the harbour, both greatly exercised in their minds by what they had just heard, but their own intimate trouble relegated the grimmer tragedy to second place. They were both silent as they entered the boat and got it moving again. The tide was now on the ebb, and in their favour as they ran down the promontory, on the further side of which lay the cavern, and in the bright moonlight there was no need to use the hand-lamp to see every detail of the foreshore.

'Think the police will really get a move on, Jerry?' asked George.

'Yes.'

'The whole thing is incredible — especially — .'

He stopped suddenly, and gripped Lavering by the arm.

'What's the matter?' asked Lavering.

'Look — over there — just near the entrance to the cave. It's a woman — on that little bit of exposed sand. It's Tessa.'

Lavering looked and saw the distant figure. She seemed to be drenched with water, and he realised that she must have been in the sea to have got where she was. Then suddenly she dived and swam towards the cave entrance.

'It wasn't Tessa,' said Lavering.

'Who else could it be?'

'I don't know. But it's a curious way to behave. I'm going to put the boat round.'

'You mean make a landing?'

'I mean — find out who that woman is, and what she's doing here. Keep your eye on her.'

This was easier said than done, for while Lavering was getting the boat round, a cloud obscured the moon, and when it had passed there was no sign of the woman.

'I believe she swam into the cave!' said George.

'That seems incredible.'

'Everything's incredible to-night. She

must have seen us, but she didn't make any signal. Steady, old chap! You missed a rock by about an inch.'

'I saw it. See any sign of her now?'

'No.'

'Strange! She must have climbed down the cliff.'

'But is that possible?'

'Not at this point, but it could be done nearer Penhale, and from there she could wade and swim to this place.'

'But why?'

'Perhaps she'll tell us when, and if, we see her again.'

'Perhaps it was just a hallucination.'

'A pretty solid one. No, George — it wasn't the effect of the moon on two light brains. It was a woman and she was very much alive. We'll shove the boat up on that spit of sand, and have a look round. If she isn't there we'll take the boat through the tunnel and into the cavern.'

'Will there be enough water there?'

'Plenty, for another hour at least.'

Lavering got the boat on the high sand ridge, and he and George then investigated the neighbouring rocks, and minor caves. They soon came to the conclusion that their quarry was not about.

'She swam straight for the cavern,' said George.

'All right. Let's follow suit — but we won't swim.'

The boat was easily pushed off, and as the entrance to the tunnel was so close, Lavering used the oars instead of the engine. Once more they entered the uncanny place, and again George had to use the hand-lamp. The water had fallen a little since they were last there, but it was still quite deep, and the ebb was slow and steady.

'Not a sign of her,' muttered George.

The boat went slowly on her course, Lavering using a single oar from the stern. Possible hiding places in the rock above the water-level were investigated, but without result. Soon the entrance to the large cavern came in sight.

'She must have gone through,' said George.

'But she would scarcely have had time.'

'It would be small beer to a woman who could climb down that cliff. Here we go!'

The boat came out of the narrow tunnel into the wide cavern, and the ray of the hand-lamp went reaching out over flood water. Suddenly George gave a little gasp, and the bright ray of the lamp ceased its wandering and stayed centred on one object on the further side of the cavern. It was a stoutly built boat painted deep orange, with black lines round the gunwales.

'That's queer!' said Lavering.

'I've seen it before somewhere,' said George. 'Recently, too.'

'That is my impression also. There's something mysterious going on here.'

'There certainly is. Jerry, can you hear anything?'

'I can hear the old breathing sound.'

'Not that. There it is again — a kind of metallic sound.'

'Yes, you're right. Someone is at work in the mine. But let's have a look at the boat.'

They drew very close to the larger

craft, and peered into it. There was a small cabin forward, and in the large cockpit an engine house, some fishing nets, and odd lines neatly coiled up. She appeared to draw about two feet of water, and it was remarkable that she should have been brought through the tunnel. One thing was clear — if she didn't leave very soon she would have to wait for the next tide.

'Jerry!'

'Yes.'

'I've just thought of something. Those explosions we heard from Nancrannon — always at night. Here's a possible solution.'

'You mean men at work — blasting?'

'Yes.'

'But why?'

'Your guess is as good as mine. What are you going to do about it?'

'Tie up the boat and investigate.'

'Suppose we're not welcome?'

'You think there may be trouble?'

'Don't you?'

'Yes.'

'Then the sensible thing would be to

get back to Nancrannon and telephone the police.'

'That would give these fellows a chance to get clean away. They must leave shortly if they're going to use this boat. A better plan would be for you to take the boat and get on to the police, and leave me here.'

'No, I'm damned if I will,' said George. 'There's no knowing what may be in the wind.'

'All right. Here's another idea. Land me and take the boat across to the tunnel. I'll do a bit of scouting, and if there is any dirty work going on I'll come back, and put their boat out of action. Then we can get on to the police, without much risk of their getting away.'

'I don't like it.'

'Then what's your alternative?'

'We stick together.'

'That would be childish. No, George, I'm going to have my own way about this. Give me the hand-lamp.'

George did so with much grumbling, and the small boat was propelled close to the entrance of the left-hand working.

Here Lavering got out.

'I'll light you across to the tunnel exit,' he said. 'Wait over there. Get going!'

'Jerry — take care!'

'I will. After all this is my tin-mine, or what's left of it, so I'm entitled to know who's trespassing and why.'

'Well, don't be long.'

Lavering said he wouldn't, and George picked up the oars and commenced to row in the beam of the light which Lavering directed across to the cavern entrance. When he reached it the illumination disappeared, and he could just see the dim form of Lavering climbing into the mine working, before he disappeared from view.

25

Tessa, in the meantime, had had a terrible experience. In the inky darkness she had traversed passage after passage, climbing and descending, reaching water and obstacles which sent her scuttling back. The air was bad in places, and she was racked with headache, and haunted by increasing fear of being hopelessly lost. The hard rock under her feet raised painful blisters, until at last she tripped and fell, and had neither the strength nor will to get up again.

In this particular spot the air was comparatively fresh, and the floor dry. After the fruitless wandering it was a pleasant relief to rest quietly, and allow her mind to function normally. How long she had been in the mine she had no means of knowing, for although the watch on her wrist was ticking away loudly the dial of it was as invisible as everything else around her. She guessed that her hands were black from groping along the unending walls, and that altogether she was a sorry sight. To go on was useless — a sheer waste of physical energy. All she could do was wait until the dawn. It might be that even then there would be no daylight, but there was always a chance of finding a spot where this giant rabbit-warren connected with the outer world, and a chance that a search would be made for her. In that event surely the mine would receive attention.

She removed her shoes and found that this was beneficial. What she needed now was a draught of clear, cold water, and the more she concentrated on that need the worse her thirst became. At last she thrust it from her mind, and tried to get some sleep by resting her back against a sloping slab of rock. Despite the horror of her position, she succeeded, but how long in actual time this sweet oblivion lasted she did not know. What she did know was that she had been suddenly awakened, and that in her mind there lingered the impression of a violent noise, like an explosion. Now she became aware of a movement of air, and a curious acrid smell which caused her to cough. She felt round for her shoes, and slipped them on. Something was happening at the end of the tunnel in which she now was. The darkness was less intense. Light was coming from somewhere, which had the effect of throwing projecting spurs of rock into relief. Standing up, she moved towards the source of the light.

After progressing about a hundred yards, she found that a very wide working joined the tunnel from the right, and this was quite well illuminated. Then she heard noises and men's voices. She turned into the working and crept forward slowly. The thud of some implement fell on her ears, and the unmistakable clanging of a shovel. Then came an audible voice.

'We're nearly through.'

'Aye, that last charge did the trick. Give me a hand here.'

Her need was so great that she put aside her qualms, and pressed on through heavy dust, which was choking in its intensity. Suddenly a turn in the widening cavern brought her on the scene of operations. In a broad space, littered with piles of rock, two men were working furiously in the light of two hurricane lamps. They were moving great pieces of rock, with the pick and their bare hands, and it was fairly clear that at some time there had been a big fall of rock from the roof, and that the main object of the two men was to drive a path through it. There was evidence that this had been going on for some time, for the obstruction had formerly been large. Tessa then remembered the strange underground effects experienced at Nancrannon, and for the first time the possibility of danger entered her mind. But now it was too late to do anything, for the man with the pick had suddenly turned his head and seen her. He dropped the implement and made a sharp ejaculation. The other man — equally horrific, with his blackened face and arms — turned and saw what his companion had seen.

'Who are you?' he growled.

'My name is Tessa Lashing, and I got lost here this evening.'

'Oh you did, did you? Why did you come here?'

'I was just curious to see what sort of a place it was.'

'Where do you come from?'

'I'm staying at Nancrannon.'

'Mr. Lavering's house?'

'Yes. I shall be glad if you'll show me how to get out of here. By this time my brother and Mr. Lavering will be anxious about me.'

The two men looked at each other, and it was clear to Tessa that she was the cause of considerable embarrassment. Then the larger man shook his head.

'You can't leave here yet,' he said. 'There's eight feet of water in the cavern.'

'Then how did you get here?'

'We've got a boat down there.'

'Then tell me how I can get to the boat and I'll wait until you are ready to leave.'

The taller man reflected for a moment, and then nodded his head and wiped some of the grime from his face.

'You take her, Ezra,' he said. 'And hurry back.'

'But — !'

'Take her!'

The name 'Ezra' knocked at the door of Tessa's memory as she stepped across the rubble, and joined the second man. There was nothing very unusual in the name, but she had the impression she had heard it quite recently. Then, as they were passing out of the wide excavation into a narrow working, she remembered where she had heard it.

'You must be Ezra Zaffery?' she said.

'Why?'

'Well, surely there can't be two men of that name in a small place like this?'

'You're right,' he said, after a pause.

'Your niece worked for Mr. Lavering until — .'

'Aye, until she was murdered. Mind that water. Keep close to the wall.'

Tessa avoided the deep pool by squeezing in close to the left wall. It was difficult to see any distance for Ezra's torch gave no more than a wan ray of light.

'Are you mining for tin?' she asked, innocently.

'Looking for it. We're busy all day, and night is the only time we have.'

'But I thought this mine was completely worked out.'

'You never know,' he replied, evasively.

The thin ray of the torch disclosed a turning to the right, and Ezra took this.

'Are we far from the cavern?' asked Tessa.

'Quite close. If you — '

He stopped suddenly as there emerged from the blackness a figure. In the miserable light it looked most unreal — a woman, whose clothing clung to her ample limbs, and whose wet hair was trailing over her shoulders.

'Hazel!' he gasped.

'Is that you, Seth?' asked the advancing woman.

'No — it's Ezra.'

Now the two parties met, and Tessa found herself under the stare of a pair of large dark eyes.

'How did you get here?' asked Ezra.

'Swam. I had to. Who's she?'

'A young lady who got herself lost. What are you doing here?'

Hazel deliberately drew her brother-in-law further away from Tessa, and a whispering ensued. Tessa couldn't hear a word of what was said, but she sensed a crisis of some sort. Finally the pair approached her.

'We've got to go back,' said Ezra.

'But you promised — '

'Can't help what I promised. This way.'

'No,' Tessa protested. 'I'm thirsty and exhausted. Tell me how to get out and I'll go on alone.'

Ezra hesitated, so Tessa made a move forward, but the next moment Hazel gripped her by the arm.

'No, you don't,' she said, grimly. 'You do as you're told.'

'Let go!' said Tessa, angrily.

Then Ezra came and joined Hazel, and Tessa was compelled to bow before superior force. Back they went to the place where she had joined the two men. In the short time which had elapsed, Seth had been busy, for at the end of the passage which had been cleared in the great pile of debris was the top of an iron door. It was rusted but Tessa could just distinguish some old paint marks. They spelt 'DANGER. EXPLOSIVES.'

Seth stood staring at the trio in astonishment. He was breathing heavily, having only just shifted a great boulder which had supported half a ton of rubble, whose collapse had revealed part of the iron door.

'What's all this?' he gasped.

'Something's happened, Seth,' said Ezra.

'What has happened?'

Ezra gave a glance at Tessa, and then moved close to his brother and whispered something in his ear. The effect of this upon Seth was electrical. He strode across to Hazel and gripped her fiercely.

'Are you lying?' he asked.

'Why should I lie? Why should I risk my life swimming here?'

'Then — then — . How's the tide, Ezra?'

'Running out pretty fast, I guess. We'd better get out now, or it may be too late.'

'No. I'm going to finish here. We can shift the rest of that stuff in a few minutes. Come on. You, too, Hazel.'

But Hazel gave Tessa a glance, and Seth saw what was in her mind.

'Yes — keep a watch on her,' he growled. 'We'll soon know whether mother told the truth.'

The two men then commenced to work furiously on the obstruction. Some of the pieces of fallen rock were large and heavy, and Ezra suggested another charge of the explosive, but his brother objected. Tessa watched them straining their muscles in their tremendous efforts, and little by little the iron door became cleared. A large padlock was now visible. It was hanging loose and open in the staple.

'See!' said Seth, pointing to it. 'He must have got caught inside. Lend a hand, here, Ezra!'

Tessa found herself fascinated by what was taking place, but she was fully aware that she was in danger. What was it these two determined men were after. Who was it who had been 'caught inside?' The two men were shifting the last great block away from the door when Hazel gave a little hiss of alarm. Seth's blackened face came round.

'Someone's coming,' she said.

They all listened intently.

'Dripping water,' said Seth.

'No, footsteps,' said Hazel. 'There, didn't you hear that?'

'She's right,' whispered Ezra.

Seth uttered a low curse and picked up a short crowbar from a heap of tools near him. Then he came close to Tessa and caught her firmly with his left arm.

'Now douse the lights,' he hissed. 'You Hazel!'

His wife moved noiselessly with her bare feet, and the two hurricane lamps were extinguished one by one. Now the noise of the oncoming person could be heard quite clearly, but after a few moments the sound diminished again, and finally died away.

'Only one man — and he's gone,' said Seth. 'Light one of the lamps, Hazel, and then keep your ears open. We'll soon be out of here.'

The scratching of a match was heard, and again the place became faintly illuminated.

'Now,' said Seth. 'Let's get a move on.'

'How are we going to get out?' asked Hazel. 'The boat must have been seen and — '

'Shut up!' snarled her husband. 'One thing at a time. Ezra, don't stand dreaming. Lend a hand here.'

Ezra gave his brother a glance which had no love in it, and then put his hands to the big rock. Inch by inch it was moved until the iron door could be opened wide enough to permit a person to enter the chamber beyond. Ezra was the nearer man.

'Go on!' whispered Seth.

'No,' said Ezra, with a gulp.

'Why, you're afraid,' sneered Seth.

'Yes, I am.' Ezra passed a dirty hand across his sweating brow. 'I wish I'd never come.'

'Get out of my way, you fool!' snarled Seth, and pushed his brother aside.

He squeezed himself through the narrow opening, and a moment later Tessa heard an exclamation from within. This was too much for Ezra, who promptly overcame his fear and followed his brother. It was the opportunity which

Tessa had been waiting for. Hazel, taken off her guard, was staring towards the iron door. With a wild leap Tessa rushed past her, reached the door and slammed it, and then secured it with the heavy padlock. There was no key in sight, but while she stood there the door was safe. Down at her feet was the crowbar which Seth had recently wielded. She picked it up, and faced the other woman.

'Keep away if you don't want to get hurt,' she said, and then commenced to bang the door with all her might.

'You little fool,' said Hazel. 'They'll kill you for that. Better run while you've a chance.'

'I'm not moving from here until help comes. There was someone quite close just now.'

From the other side of the door Seth's voice could be heard asking what the devil they were up to. Tessa banged all the harder with the crowbar, and the noise was terrific.

'Open the door!' yelled Seth. 'Hazel — can you hear me?'

His wife made no reply, but she showed

she was not lacking in brains, by seizing the hurricane lamp, and blowing out the feeble light. Tessa's heart bounded. She had felt safe enough while she held the iron bar, and could see her adversary, but now everything was different. Those useful bare feet of Hazel made no sound, but she knew that from somewhere in the darkness an attack was coming. To protect herself she swung the iron bar in front of her and suddenly she hit something, and heard a gasp of pain.

'Keep away!' she said.

The next moment a large piece of rock crashed against the door, within a foot of her. She moved away — close to the pile of debris, and heard a second crash. In the tense silence which followed there came another sound from a distance. It was undoubtedly the noise of a walking man. The intruder — whoever he was — was closer again. Filling her lungs with breath she screamed out 'Help,' several times, stopping only when she was seized by a pair of strong arms. So close was the fierce embrace that the crowbar was quite useless as a weapon. So she dropped it, and fought back as well as she was able. Young and strong as she was she was no match for Hazel, and finally she found herself on the floor, and heard Hazel groping for the padlock, while Seth was shouting like a madman.

Then she became aware that the intruder was closer. In the darkness she could see a faint glow down the passage into which she had recently been escorted by Ezra. Scrambling to her feet she ran down the tunnel, the sides of which were just visible. A sharp turn at the end brought her to a standstill, for dead ahead of her was the blinding ray of an electric torch.

'Help!' she called weakly, and felt her knees crumble under her.

'Tessa! Thank God!'

'Jerry!' she gasped, and managed to stay on her feet. He came close to her and lent her a supporting arm.

'Are you all right, Tessa?'

'Yes.'

'But there's blood on your face.'

'Is there? I didn't know. It must have been that ghastly woman. We — we had a sort of scrap. Oh, but I can't explain fully. Something is happening back there. There are two men — the Zaffery brothers, and they've been blasting their way towards an iron door which was obstructed by a big fall of rock. The woman came, and told them something, which caused them to hold me by force.'

'What was her name?'

'Hazel. A big barefooted creature.'

'She's Seth's wife. Now I'm beginning to understand. She came here to warn them. A little while ago, George and I learned that there were warrants out for their arrest. They are believed to have murdered Zillah.'

'Oh! Let's go Jerry,' she begged. 'I've got the jitters badly. In a minute or two they are bound to come back, to get their boat out, while there's enough water. I heard them talking about that.'

'That's what we have to prevent before the police can get here. Come on. George is in the cavern, keeping watch in our boat. Hope I can remember the turnings. Left — right — right — left.'

He went off at a great pace, with Tessa

trailing closely behind, slowly losing ground, for the blisters on her feet were causing her agonising pain. Then he stopped.

'Trouble?'

'Blisters. I've walked for hours, and — '

'Hold the lamp.'

She did so, and he lifted her in his arms and went on, making the turnings which he had mentioned, but to his surprise he suddenly found himself up against a dead end.

'The last turning must have been wrong,' he said. 'It must have been right instead of left. Have to go back.'

'I can walk.'

'No you can't. Keep the lamp steady. They mustn't be allowed to get to their boat. If they do they might make an attempt to get across the channel.'

'I can hear them. Jerry, put me down. We can go faster — .'

She caught her breath as another light came to view, dead ahead of them, and in the powerful ray of the hand-lamp she saw the Zaffery trio standing at the junction of another gallery. There was a hiatus and then the two men came forward, with Hazel bringing up the rear. Seth carried the crowbar, and Ezra was armed with a short spade, the shining blade of which gleamed in the light. Lavering drew in his breath with a little hiss as he put Tessa down.

'Going to be a spot of bother, I think,' he said. 'Keep well back.'

'What do you take me for?'

'Do as I say. These fellows have a rope half round their necks. They're desperate.'

'So am I,' replied Tessa, and limped towards a handy piece of jagged rock.

Seth was now just ahead of his brother, and he stopped within six yards of Lavering, while he sized him up. What he saw was not an inviting sight, for Lavering looked enormous in the strange light, and his right hand was in his coat pocket, with two fingers poking the corner of the coat out and up.

'Right about turn,' said Lavering. 'You're wanted alive.'

'If that was a firearm you'd show it,' growled Seth. 'Very clever, Mr. Lavering, but it won't work.'

'Come and see if it will work.'

Seth gave his brother a glance. Apparently Ezra was for taking no risk, but Seth was built differently. Warrants for arrest weren't issued without good grounds, and if Lavering really had a gun in his coat pocket, he was lost whatever he did. Bold action was undoubtedly called for. He took a few more steps forward, while his frightened brother stayed where he was, and then he lunged out with the crowbar. Lavering side-stepped and as Seth's body came forward, a large hard fist struck outwards and upwards. It sent Seth crashing backwards into the hard rock wall, but he still kept a grip on the crowbar, and with a roar of pain and rage he returned to the attack, calling to his brother for support. Tessa, outraged by the unequal combat, hurled her piece of rock, and then got mixed up in the fight. Three times she saw that awful bar of iron fall, and three times Lavering avoided it, and got in punishing body blows. Then, at last, the bar fell across Lavering's left arm. She saw him wince and knew that the arm was out of action. With a cry of fury she flung herself at Seth, and clawed him round the neck.

'Get rid of this hell-cat,' cried Seth.

Ezra tried to do so, but found it difficult as Tessa had no compunction about biting him in the forearm. He let go of her and raised the spade, but Lavering sailed in and hit him full in the face. Unfortunately it left him wide open, and Seth hit him a short, hard blow on the head with the crowbar. He fell sideways and lay still. The next moment Tessa's hands were wrenched apart and she was flung unceremoniously to the ground, with every ounce of breath knocked out of her body.

After that everything was hazy to Tessa, until she found herself in complete darkness, and was conscious of the clang of iron, and the sound of hurrying footsteps. Her back ached, and she groaned as she tried to straighten it.

'Tessa!'

It was Lavering's voice, from close beside her.

'Oh!' she gasped. 'I didn't know — . Jerry, are you all right?'

'Not — too bad. That crowbar caught me on a vulnerable spot, and my head's like an alarm clock. Golly, my arm, too.'

She reached out painfully and touched his arm. A hand came up and gripped hers.

'This is the good one,' he said. 'Where are we?'

'In the place they were investigating, I think. I'm sure I heard the iron door slam. Have you got any matches?'

'Yes — in my side pocket.'

She found the matches, and struck one on the side of the box. The tiny flame showed Lavering, sprawled on the floor, with his shoulders against an iron-bound chest. His hair was awry, and down the left side of his face was a smear of blood.

'You — you look ghastly!' she said.

'I could retort that you have lost a large amount of the glamour you always had.'

'There's a cut in your head — under the hair. Damn! The match is going out.'

She threw the burnt end down as it reached her fingers, and was about to strike another when Lavering touched her hand.

'Try this,' he said. 'I forgot I had it. Ah!'

There was a flash and a flame, and Tessa saw that he was holding an automatic petrol lighter in his right hand. She took it and was setting it up on a level part of the rock floor when she gave a little scream of terror, and dropped the lighter, causing it to go out.

'What's the matter?' asked Lavering, concernedly.

'Did — didn't you see?'

'See what?'

'Two skeletons — opposite.'

'Tessa!'

'I'm certain of it. That's what Ezra was afraid of. I remember Seth saying something about someone who got caught inside — when the roof fell apparently.'

'We'll soon settle the matter. Can you find the lighter?'

'It was here — somewhere. Oh, here it is.'

'Press the catch.'

'I can't feel any catch.'

'Give it to me. Where are you?'

Their hands connected again, and Lavering found the catch easily from long usage. Again the flash and the resultant light — and then the proof of Tessa's statement. The two complete skeletons were side by side, one in a recumbent position, with arms folded, and the other curled up like the letter 'S.' Covering the white bones in places were bits of clothing, the details of which could not be seen in the poor light. Tessa, horrified by the sight, crept close to Lavering. He put the lighter on a safe spot, and placed his uninjured arm around her.

'Come,' he said. 'They're grisly enough, but harmless. I always had the impression you were as hard as nails.'

'Well, I'm not,' she murmured.

For a few moments Tessa stayed where she was, breathing heavily, with her face half-buried against him, and this position was so comfortable to Lavering that he made no attempt to change it, until suddenly he noticed something striking about the smaller skeleton. In the dim light he could see the remains of footwear — and they were small and mildewed.

'Stay still a moment,' he said.

'What are you going to do?'

Wincing with pain he dragged himself to his feet, and moved across to the skeletons. Then he came back and picked up the petrol lighter, to carry it closer to the grim remains.

'My God!' he ejaculated.

'Jerry, what's the matter?'

He did not seem to hear her, but was kneeling on the floor picking up something from the skeleton itself. Unable to curb her curiosity, she moved towards him, with her heart thumping. In the palm of his hand he held a small ivory elephant on a thin silver chain.

26

'My mother's mascot,' said Lavering, in a hushed voice. 'It was round her neck. She wasn't drowned after all. She was trapped in here when the roof caved in outside that door. By some means the Zafferys must have known — '

'No, Jerry. Seth mentioned only one person. He didn't expect to find two.'

'Then the other must be his father. Don't you remember that old Zaffery was supposed to have been drowned in the same storm? He was an enormous man, and that skeleton is enormous.'

'Yes — yes.'

'The boat which my mother used was seen to come in this direction. She and old Zaffery met here. But why — why?'

Tessa's brain was now working again after her temporary fright.

'Jerry, the Zafferys wouldn't have gone to all the trouble they went to merely to look for a skeleton. They worked at night and used explosives. There must have been something here — something of value. Your mother may have become suspicious of their father. Remember, she had already visited the mine workings, and drawn that plan. Oh, but I haven't told you about that.'

'George told me.'

'Well, the plan didn't include this part of the mine. So it looks as if up to the time when she made the plan she hadn't been here. That night she must have seen old Zaffery and followed him — to see what he was up to.'

'There's nothing wrong with your imagination.'

'But doesn't it fit all the circumstances?'

'Yes. I think it does. There's that chest which I was resting against. Let's have a look at it.'

They moved across to the large iron-bound box. It bore an elaborate old-time lock which at some time had been forced and broken. Lavering pulled up the lid and gazed inside. It appeared to be quite empty, but as he was about to close the lid, the light from the lighter was reflected by something which gave a bright green light. Lavering thrust his hand down and extricated an object from a crack. It was a small emerald, which had once been in a setting.

'Jewellery,' he said. 'It looks as if your theory is correct. Old Zaffery must have stolen it from somewhere, and kept it here because he feared his house might be searched. But how did his sons get to know about it — after all these years?'

'Didn't Poltimore say that old Mrs. Zaffery had died a short time before we came to Nancrannon?'

'Yes.'

'Isn't it possible that she knew, and that she kept the secret until she was dying because to tell anyone would show up her husband? If Zillah got to know it would explain her death.'

'By Jove — you've got it,' exclaimed Lavering. 'It was difficult to find a big enough reason for one of the Zafferys to have killed her, but now we have it.'

'Do you think the Zafferys have got

away with what was left of the jewellery?'

'It looks like it. Let's try that door.'

On reaching the iron door, Lavering put his foot to it, but found it was immovable.

'I saw a stout padlock on the other side,' said Tessa. 'But there was no key, unless Seth found it in here.'

'Looks like a waiting game.'

Tessa gave a glance at the two skeletons, and realised that they had waited for over twenty years.

'Suppose — suppose they overpowered George?' she asked. 'No one would know then where we were.'

'George would see them and have sense enough to get away.'

'Their boat would be faster than the outboard.'

'That's doubtful. They left it very late. They may not have been able to get their large boat through the tunnel.'

'Then it rests with George?'

'To a large extent. You look worn out, Tessa. Go and sit down.'

'What about you?'

'I'm going to stay here and make a din

on the door. What I need is a chunk of rock.'

He managed to loosen a piece of rock, and then commenced to beat on the iron door with it. The clanging made curious echoes, and Tessa noticed that now the lighter was getting short of petrol. Very soon they would be plunged into darkness again.

She sat by the old chest, and removed the shoes and stockings from her aching feet. The light of the torch burned lower and lower, and Lavering continued his monotonous clanging. At last the tiny flame vanished.

'Jerry!' she called.

'Yes.'

'Please come and sit down. You must be tired.'

'All right. I'll try again later.'

Once more he was beside her, and she sighed to feel the warmth of his body against her own.

'Is your arm very painful?' she asked.

'Not too bad.'

'Not broken?' she asked anxiously.

'Oh no. Now try to get some sleep.'

'No use. My mind is too active. I can't help thinking about George. He's not much good in a fight. Jerry, what did you do with the mascot?'

'In my pocket.'

'You don't mind talking about it?'

'No — not now.'

'Now you're together again — you and she — after all these years. At last you know that she didn't fail you — that all the foul things that were said were untrue. That must be good to feel.'

'Yes.'

'You're a strange man, Jerry.'

'How?'

'Demanding so little of life — loving the memory of a beautiful woman, long after she had passed, to the exclusion of everything else.'

'That's not true.'

'Isn't it?'

'No. I want what most men want. Friendship — honest work — time to play.'

'A home, to come to.'

'I have that.'

'Until when?'

'What are you driving at?'

'Aren't you proposing to sell Nancrannon to-day?'

'I was thinking of another place,' he said, slowly.

'Yes, I know,' she murmured, and then lapsed into silence.

Lavering closed his eyes and tried to compose his mind, but this he found very difficult in view of the situation. His head ached and his arm troubled him. On top of these discomforts was the realisation that something might have happened to George. He had been sanguine enough on that matter when Tessa had mentioned it, but the Zafferys were desperate people, as he had recently had cause to know. Seth, at least, wouldn't stop at a second murder, if he saw his retreat in danger of being cut off. Suppose that had really happened — what then?

The Zafferys, under cover of night, might get half-way across the channel before the police started a widespread search. Even then they would almost certainly select the sea as the most promising hunting ground, since they would discover that the fishing boat was missing. Days might pass before the mine was searched — if indeed it was ever searched.

He listened intently, but all he could hear was Tessa's soft breathing beside him. At last she seemed to be asleep, and he was glad. Then somehow his mind became concentrated on her. George had been most careful to insinuate that she would be an unmitigated nuisance, but events had proved the contrary. Without her the holiday would have been a far less pleasant thing. It might even have turned out a bore. Tessa had prevented such a catastrophe. It was astonishing — now he thought about it — how big a part of the picture she was. Like George, he had been disposed to take her for granted — at first, but no longer was that possible. There was something indescribably vital about her — the way she spoke, moved, smiled. Day by day the 'kid sister' had been vanishing. He had been witnessing a strange and intriguing metamorphosis, but he suspected the change was in him and not in her. She had been what she was all along.

Yes, the change was in him. He came back to that conclusion after wild wanderings in a world of half-dream, and it was never more marked than now when within a few yards of him lay the mortal remains of the woman who had given him life, and happiness, and from whom he had been prematurely parted. She had taken with her all that he knew about love, but had left with him a vision of beauty. He had lived too much upon that vision, and Providence had hit back at him. Earth to earth — ashes to ashes. Everything ended that way. Here before him lay the bones of the angel and the probable robber. They had gone their respective ways into the unknown. What they had been was part of the past. But life went on just the same. Outside, even now, a new day was about to dawn. Within him, too, something was stirring — something which seemed to give a new meaning to existence.

'Jerry!'

Tessa's soft voice startled him in the stillness and darkness.

'I thought you were asleep,' he said.

'Oh no. I knew you weren't either.'

'How could you know that?'

'I don't know. One of my intuitions I suppose. George always laughed at them, but sometimes they come true.'

'Have you any intuitions at this moment?'

'Yes.'

'What are they?'

'Secret ones.'

'Why be so mysterious?'

'No one would think anything of a woman if she weren't a bit mysterious.'

'I suppose not,' he ruminated. 'How are the feet?'

'What a question, when we should be thinking of our lives.'

'But I'm very concerned about your feet. They're rather nice appendages.'

'The same remark applies to your head. But seriously, Jerry — if George is all right he should have been back by now.'

'He may be, but you should know that this place is a regular honeycomb. We can't expect him to walk straight here.'

'If there were only some water to drink — '

'Water! You shall drink champagne once we get out of here.'

'I'd rather have a wine-glass of water now than all the champagne in the world to-morrow.'

'To-morrow will come all the quicker if you will only go to sleep.'

'Easy to say — hard to accomplish,' she said huskily.

He changed his position, and drew her up more closely to him.

'Is that better?'

'Yes,' she murmured. 'But goodness — how your heart beats!'

'That's not my heart — that's my wrist watch.'

'It's your heart even if it has got a tinny sound,' she said, and then, to his surprise, laughed.

'That's better. Now start counting sheep.'

'Going through hedges,' she said. 'I'd like to see a hedge just now, or the sunshine on the sea. Don't take your arm away, Jerry.'

'I've no intention of doing so.'

She gave a little sigh, and again there was silence. Nearly an hour must have passed when Lavering heard a sound. His heart seemed to stop for a moment as he strained his ears. Then again came the sound. Tessa was now really sleeping. He tried to disengage himself without waking her, but failed.

'Oh!' she exclaimed. 'Where — what —!'

'It's all right,' he whispered. 'Someone is coming. Listen!'

Tessa became wide awake in an instant.

'It's George,' she cried excitedly. 'Bang the door again. Oh, you won't be able to find it. Where are those matches?'

She found the matches, but before she could strike one a thin ray of light appeared from under the iron door. Its variations in strength indicated that it came from a moving electric torch. Then came louder footsteps, and a booming voice.

'Anyone there?' asked the voice.

Lavering looked at Tessa, for it was certainly not George's voice. While Lavering was hesitating the voice spoke again.

'You there, Seth?'

'Yes,' replied Lavering, as he picked up his knocking-rock. 'Come inside.'

As he moved to the door there was a jangle of metal, and then the door was pulled open, and a big bearded man came to view behind an enormous electric torch. Lavering dodged round him and effectively barred his retreat.

'Who are you?' he demanded.

The big intruder did not reply for a moment. He was evidently taken aback by the sight of the two skeletons which the ray of his torch had brought to view.

'My name's Sam Bollin,' he said at last. 'Captain Bollin they call me.'

'Mine's Lavering. You may have heard it before.'

'Aye,' replied Bollin. 'You must be Mr. Lavering from Nancrannon.'

'That's right. Now perhaps you'll explain why you came here expecting to find Seth Zaffery?'

Bollin was obviously embarrassed.

'It — it was a private matter,' he stammered.

'The matter of stolen property?'

414

'I know nothing about that.'

'You'll have to explain to the police just why you came here, because warrants are out against the Zafferys for murder.'

'What!' gasped Bollin.

'The murder of Zillah Poltimore.'

'My God! Did they do that?'

'You didn't know?'

'Know? Do I look like a bloody murderer? Have they been arrested?'

'I don't know. They came here last night and locked us in this place.'

'Came here!' gasped Bollin. 'The dirty double-crossers! They promised to meet me here just before dawn. I might have guessed they'd try to cheat me at the end.'

'Cheat you of your share of the booty?'

'They said it was theirs — belonged to their father. I've done nothing wrong. It was when old mother Zaffery died that the whole thing started. She told them that their father wasn't drowned at sea. She knew that on that night when he was missing he had come here to get something from a secret hoard. Later she had found the entrance to this room blocked by fallen rock. She knew he was trapped in here. They told me there was a fortune to be picked up, and they wanted my help because as a young man I worked in this mine. I knew where the explosives room was, and I knew how to use blasting powders, and erect safe-guards. We've been working at nights for months, getting nearer and nearer. Then you came down to Nancrannon, and we had to take more care. I was promised a share in the proceeds, but I could never get them down to a real agreement. They kept mentioning treasure but were mighty vague about what it really was, and where it came from. The last time we were here we got close to it, and I reckoned that this morning we'd complete the job. That's why they came last night — to get it for themselves and then pretend there was nothing here. Did they get it?'

'It looks like it. That chest is empty.'

'Who is the second corpse?'

'That's another story,' replied Lavering abruptly. 'Did you come by boat?'

'Yes. I borrowed Ned Webster's boat from Trewith. Told him I was going to do a bit of fishing.'

'Then you can take us back.'

'I'll be glad to. Mr. Lavering, what I told you is God's truth. I'll admit I was willing enough to make a bit of easy money, even if it did involve trespass, but — '

'Your best course is to tell the police everything.'

Bollin nodded, and then led the way through the various galleries to the great cavern. It was now completely free of water, and the first signs of the dawn were appearing through the holes in the roof. They made their way through the tunnel, and finally stepped out into the roseate light of a perfect dawn. Tessa stood on the sand, facing the rising sun, with her hands outstretched.

'Oh glorious day!' she said. 'Heaven help those who live in darkness. This air!'

'This everything,' said Lavering. 'Even my head has ceased to ache.'

'You look dreadful,' said Tessa, regarding him with horror. 'Blood all over your face and shirt.'

'Wait till you have a good look at

yourself. All right, Bollin — we're ready.'

They entered the small motor boat, and were soon making round the headland to Nancrannon cove. The sun was now up and flooding the whole marvellous scene, Nowhere was there a sign of another craft. Finally, Bollin put them ashore.

'I'd better get back to Trewith,' he said.

'No. Go round to Swanpool and see if Inspector Warren is there. Tell him what has happened — in case he doesn't know.'

They watched Bollin get to sea again, and then Tessa drew Lavering's attention to one very obvious fact — their boat was not in evidence. Lavering nodded and led her to the house. It was empty, and silent. George's bed had not been slept in.

'Don't worry,' begged Lavering. 'Go and lie down, and I'll try to get a meal.'

Tessa nodded, and limped to her bedroom.

27

An hour made all the difference to Tessa. With sleep out of the question she had devoted the time to removing all the signs of her recent adventure, and in this she was successful, for even the blood on her face had not been her own. Lavering, too, in the meantime had brought about desirable changes in his appearance.

'My scalp won't need stitches,' he said, 'And my arm is already easier. The loveliest bruise you ever saw. See, I can move it.'

'Not without wincing,' she replied. 'You'll have to wear a sling.'

'Nonsense.'

'I'll fix you up after breakfast. No news, I suppose?'

'Not yet.'

They were just about to make a start on the eggs and bacon when Lavering glanced through the window, and gave a wild howl. There was George swinging up the garden, with his clothes hanging on him like a wet sack. The window was pushed open.

'Hey, George!'

'Morning, Jerry. Is Tessa there?'

'Yes.'

'Any breakfast going?'

'You're just in time.'

George staggered into the room, and collapsed on the couch.

'I'm all right,' he said. 'Just wet, and starving. What a night! Was there ever such a night? Gosh, our little boat did marvels. We had her all out for hours, but had to row her back the last two miles. Ran clean out of petrol.'

'But tell us what happened?' pleaded Tessa.

'Oh, I waited at the entrance to the cavern, just as Jerry advised me to do. Jerry didn't return and I was getting anxious and wondering whether I should put across to the workings, when the gang appeared, and got into their boat. I decided it was time to clear off, and so I got the engine going, and took a chance through the tunnel. Once I thought I had

420

busted the propeller, but she still went on. I took her round to Swanpool, and there I found the Inspector and two men. I told them what had happened, and thought they would go to the mine, but the Inspector had other ideas. He said the Zafferys came first, and that if the woman had joined her husband, they would all probably try to get across the channel. So off we went, full pelt, me, the Inspector and the Sergeant, and sure enough we picked up the fishing boat. Hour after hour we went on, scarcely gaining a yard on her. At first it was good visibility, and a calm sea, but as we got further and further away from land there was a heavy sort of swell, and some low-lying patches of mist. We pitched about a lot, and water came in. Then we began to gain on them, and the Inspector kept shouting to them to stop, but it made no difference. Gosh, what a grand smell!'

'Never mind the smell. What happened?'

'Oh, ghastly! We were getting closer and closer, and the Inspector had pulled out a big automatic, when they vanished in a patch of mist. Then a foghorn sounded — dead ahead of us. Most eerie it was. I could hear the heavy thresh of engines, and didn't like it much. Nor did the Inspector. He told me to ease off, and I slowed down to a crawl. Then suddenly I heard a crash, and the foghorn went off at full blast. We crawled on, and suddenly we emerged from the mist. There was a big cargo boat, hove to. They were lowering a boat, and men were running along the deck. Well, we pulled up close to her. The Captain said they had hit something. They didn't know what. Later, a few things were found floating. That was all.'

'You mean — they were all drowned?' asked Tessa.

'Looks like it. We hung about for some time, but no bodies were seen. Then we came home. The Inspector found a man waiting for him — a chap named Bollin. He told us that you were safe. Now perhaps I can have some breakfast.'

'But you're all wet.'

'All right. I'll rush up and have a rub down. Give you time to do a couple more eggs and some rashers. What's wrong with your arm, Jerry?'

'Mosquito bite. Hurry up. We're hungry as well as you.'

During the meal which followed, experiences were exchanged in fuller detail. According to George, Hazel's escape from Swanpool had been achieved by an amazing feat of athletics, after which she had accomplished the difficult descent of the cliff to the tunnel which led to the cavern.

'The Inspector had no idea she had left the bedroom in which she was locked. Was he annoyed!'

'We thought you had been attacked,' said Tessa.

'I might have been if that old outboard engine hadn't fired at the first pull.' There was a brief silence, and then George said 'Oh, Bollin mentioned two skeletons. He knew one was that of old Zaffery, but — '

Tessa shot him a swift glance and he subsided.

'That was my mother,' said Lavering quietly.

'Good Heavens! Oh, I say, old man, I'm sorry — .'

'There's no occasion for regrets. It's a solution that is infinitely more acceptable than some. I shall have to see the police later, and the Rector.'

'I suppose so,' said George reflectively. 'You're going to have a busy day, old man — what with all these things, and that fellow who is coming down from London with your solicitor.'

'He's not coming,' replied Lavering.

'I thought — .'

'It was fixed for to-day, but as soon as we got back I managed to get through to Cantling, just in time to cancel the appointment.'

'Good idea!' said George. 'Any day will do for him.'

'Or no day,' said Lavering. 'I've changed my mind about Nancrannon.'

Tessa's coffee cup shook so much in her hand that she was compelled to put it back into the saucer.

'You mean — you aren't going to sell it?' she asked.

'That's right.'

'You — you are going to live here?'

'That's possible.'

Tessa passed a hand across her brow, and then stood up.

'At last I'm really — really sleepy,' she said. 'Do you mind if — if — '

'Sleep as long as you like,' replied Lavering. 'I shall be busy for a bit. George, too, looks as if he could do with a little shut-eye.'

'You read men's thoughts,' replied George. 'Waste of a beautiful day, some might say, but I disagree utterly.'

It was late afternoon before any sounds came from the upper part of the house. In the interim, Poltimore came as usual. He had heard what had taken place, and was deeply affected.

'It was Providence all right, Mr. Lavering,' he said. 'Those that sow the wind reap the whirlwind. The Zafferys have been a curse in these parts for generations. They laughed at all that was good and decent. If I had realised that twenty years ago my life would have been different. But when you're young the heart talks louder than the head. But God isn't mocked. In His own time He squares all accounts.'

'Yes, that's true,' replied Lavering.

Then came Inspector Warren, looking tired and a little deflated. He frankly admitted that he was disappointed, for he had hoped to make an arrest and to stage a trial with all the legal trappings and publicity. As matters stood he was unlikely to get any kudos at all. On the contrary he would be blamed for permitting Hazel to escape from the house.

'I've been to the mine with Bollin,' he said, 'and have removed the empty chest. We may be able to get it identified, but I doubt it. Old Zaffery may have stolen it off a wrecked ship, or even committed plain burglary. That part of the mystery may never be solved.'

At this juncture, Lavering handed him the small emerald which he had found in the chest.

'This is not likely to be claimed,' he said. 'You will probably be able to get it back later — as a souvenir. Just now I had word that two bodies had been recovered — dead.'

'Which two?'

'Ezra and Mrs. Zaffery. That leads me to believe that Seth did find booty there. There was nothing of value on the clothing of the two corpses. Seth may have crammed the stuff into his pockets, and the weight may have prevented him from either floating or swimming. Of course, that's just a theory.'

'It sounds reasonable enough.'

'Do you propose to bring any charge against the man Bollin?'

'No.'

'In that case there's little more to be said. There's no doubt at all that the larger skeleton is that of old Zaffery, who was believed to have been drowned at sea. The identity of the woman who was with him may never — '

'That clears up another mystery,' interrupted Lavering. 'She was my mother, who was also believed to have been drowned.'

The Inspector gave a little gasp.

'Why, yes, of course,' he said. 'Do you know that never occurred to me. But have you any means of identifying her?'

Lavering produced the small mascot, and explained its significance. After examining it, the Inspector handed it back gravely.

'Forges the last link,' he said. 'I presume you will make your own arrangements.'

'Yes. I have telephoned the Rector. He is coming over to see me this afternoon.'

The Rector came and Lavering explained the situation. Arrangements were made for a burial service and the interment, and after that Lavering felt that a curtain was slowly being drawn over the past.

28

Another week had passed, and all that remained of Mrs. Lavering lay under six feet of earth behind the little church on the hill.

'That is what she would have wished,' said Lavering to George. 'She loved the sea in all its many moods. Now it can rage and croon by her side through all eternity.'

George nodded. He was a little sad, for now only two days remained of the holiday.

'I seem to have lived a lifetime these past few weeks,' he said. 'Jerry, I'll never forget it.'

'Nor I.'

It was evening, and the scent of flowers was heavy over the garden. Boozer was sprawled at their feet on the terrace, pretending to be asleep. But at times he would cock one eye at Lavering, waiting for a single word which would be the signal for that wild scamper over the cliff. But to-night the word did not come, for Lavering had other things in his mind.

'Where's Tessa?' he asked.

'Beautifying herself. God knows why.'

'You know why, and I know why.'

'Well, why?' asked George.

'Because it makes her feel better. I'll go and find her. I want to ask her advice on something.'

'You shouldn't encourage her. By the way, how's the arm behaving?'

Lavering bent his forearm without so much as a wince, and then laughed, and went into the house. Tessa was coming down the broad staircase, pushing her mass of glorious hair back, and looking radiant.

'If you're coming up, don't pass me on the stairs,' she said. 'It's unlucky.'

'Rubbish!'

But he stayed where he was until Tessa had descended the last step.

'Now you may go up,' she said.

'I don't want to go up. Tessa, some time ago you suggested I should make some changes here — shift the furniture about, or burn it and buy some more. I believe you were right.'

Tessa made a mock curtsey.

'You've got some ideas about it — haven't you?'

'Hundreds.'

'Then will you take over the job? Fling out what you don't like. Tell me what I need to bring a new spirit into the house. Wipe out the past — '

'No, Jerry.'

'Isn't that — ?'

'Some of the past is very lovely. Here and there you ought to be able to recapture it — when you wish. That's different from having it shrieking out at you from every room — every corner. It could be lovely here — the old and the new mingling and harmonising. Bright curtains, better lighting, more colour in the decorations. You know, something has happened here in the past few days. I'm a bit psychic — don't laugh. I know Zillah used to say she was, too, but one can't stay in this house long without feeling that it has a soul. All the brooding which seemed to lay over it has gone. It's as if it

431

had gained something, and was liking it.'

'It has gained something. You!'

'That's no gain. It was a calamity.'

Lavering shook his head and then took her hands in his.

'Tessa, I cabled my chum in Canada this morning. He helped to make that little place of mine, and is as proud of it as I was.'

'Was?'

'Yes — was. I told him the place was his — that I had certain ties here, and could not go back.'

'Jerry! Then you're really going to live here — at Nancrannon?'

'That's for you to decide.'

'Me?'

'You're the tie, Tessa. I could no more live without you than fly. As George would say, 'I've got you under my skin,' and scratching is no use. Don't force me to borrow from the past again, and go on my knees to tell you I love you. You know that as well as you know anything.'

'Yes, I know,' murmured Tessa.

'Then what's the answer?'

Tessa, wet-eyed, opened her arms, and

George, who chose that moment to drift into the house to see if a meal was in the offing, had the mortification of seeing his 'kid-sister' and her host in a situation more reminiscent of the films than of real life. He started to beat a retreat, but was stopped by Lavering.

'Shocked, George?' he asked.

'Disgusted. Well, I warned you, didn't I?'

'You did.'

'No recriminations?'

'On the contrary.'

'Well, that appears to be that. Now, I suppose, we shall be allowed to eat?'

'You're awful,' complained Tessa, linking her arm in Lavering's. 'You've no sense of romance at all.'

'Alas, no,' replied George. 'But I've got an excellent digestion.'